BATTLES LOST AND WON

BATTLES LOST AND WON

Beryl Matthews

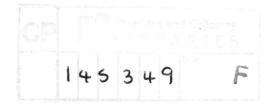
WINDSOR
PARAGON

First published 2011
by Severn House Publishers
This Large Print edition published 2012
by AudioGO Ltd
by arrangement with
Severn House Publishers Ltd

Hardcover   ISBN: 978 1 445 89095 1
Softcover   ISBN: 978 1 445 89096 8

British Library Cataloguing in Publication Data available

Printed and bound in Great Britain by
MPG Books Group Limited

One

Canning Town, London, 1919

The war was over and the men were beginning to come home. Robert Hunter couldn't wait to see his dad again. His mother wasn't strong, and the last year had been hard for her. He had done his best to see she had plenty of rest, and he was taking any job he could so he could buy decent food and help to pay the rent. It wasn't easy though, and he could only get casual work. They struggled even with him doing two jobs a day. But he was strong, just like his dad, and once he was home there would be two of them to look after her. Without the worry she'd be all right again.

'Bob! Bob!' Ruth Cooper from next door tumbled into the scullery where he was preparing a stew for their dinner.

He placed a large hand on top of his little friend's head to stop her jumping up and down. 'What's up?'

'Dad's on his way home! Mum's had a letter saying his ship has arrived in Portsmouth. He'll be back any time now!' Her large hazel eyes were shining with excitement.

'That's terrific, Ruthie.'

'Any news about your dad yet?' she asked.

'No, but he should be back soon.'

'Should be.' Her expression became troubled. 'Hope they're all right. I saw Mr Hall from number eight, and he can't stop shaking, and the man from number twenty-three has lost a leg.'

1

Bob stopped what he was doing. 'I know it's terrible, Ruthie, but you mustn't worry about your dad. He's in the Navy, and hasn't been in the trenches. Mine has, but he's a strong man. They both are. They'll be all right, and anyway, if they'd been hurt we would have heard.'

'Of course.' Her smile was back. 'How's your mum?'

'Better today, but I've made her take a little nap. All the worry about Dad has been hard on her, but that's over now. Once he's home she'll be strong again.'

Ruth nodded. 'Are you still working at the market?'

'Yes, and I've also been able to get some work at the docks in the afternoon. With the men home that won't last long, but I'll take whatever I can get. I'm trying to get a permanent job there, but I don't hold out much hope at the moment.'

'You work too hard, Bob. You're only sixteen, and you never have time to go out with your mates. You ought to be having some fun.'

He laughed. 'You're a fine one to be talking. You take care of your young sister and two brothers, and just about anyone else in the street who needs help!'

'I enjoy helping people,' she protested.

Bob leant back and rested against the large scrubbed kitchen table. 'I know you do, Ruthie, and it's time you thought about what you're going to do. You're fourteen now, intelligent, and have a real nice way with people. Why don't you see if you can train to be a nurse, or something like that?'

She shrugged. 'I can't leave home. Mum needs me. You know she has to do home sewing to help

2

with the food. She's got five of us to feed.'

'I know, but she'll be all right when your dad's home for good. Think about it.'

'I will.'

'Promise?'

'I promise.' She glanced at the clock on the mantle shelf. 'Oh, I must go! The kids will be home from school soon. Bye.'

'That girl's always in a hurry.'

Bob turned and saw his mum standing in the doorway, a smile on her face. He smiled back, relieved to see her looking rested, and with some colour in her cheeks for a change. 'I've been trying to get her to train for nursing, or something like that. She's always looking after people and ought to think about her own future. But she won't do anything about it.'

'Keep on trying, Bob. Daisy's quite capable of managing, and she'll have Steve home soon. I'll have a word with her about Ruth, if you like.'

'Thanks, Mum. I do worry about Ruthie. She's a bright kid and ought to think about doing something useful with her life.' Bob poured her a cup of tea. 'They've heard Steve's ship has docked and he's on his way. When do you think Dad will come home? The war's been over for three months now.'

'There's hundreds—thousands—of troops stuck in France and Germany. They'll get them all back eventually. I expect he'll just turn up one day . . .'

*   *   *

Two days later Ruth came in all excited. 'Dad came home last night, but it was late and I didn't see him until this morning. Mum's ever so happy, but the kids just keep staring at him, because he's been away so long they don't remember him. It's the first time he's ever seen Sally, but she's chatting away.' Ruth grinned. 'You know what she's like, and she's making him smile.'

'I'm glad he's back safely,' Helen said. 'How is he, Ruth?'

'All right, I think.' Ruth chewed her bottom lip. 'He looks awful tired. Mum's told us we mustn't ask him about the war, because he won't want to talk about it.'

'That's right,' Helen agreed. 'They'll talk when they feel like it, but we must leave them to do it in their own time.'

Ruth nodded. 'I'm going to the shops, Mrs Hunter, so is there anything I can get you? There's a nasty wind blowing today and I wouldn't be surprised if it snowed.'

'That's a good idea, Mum.' Bob put another piece of wood on the kitchen stove. 'You stay in the warm, and I'll be home about one o'clock to get you something to eat.'

'Oh, you two,' she laughed. 'I don't need you both running around after me. I'm feeling much better now.'

'The weather's bitter though, Mum. What's the point of going out in it when you don't have to?'

'Write me a list, Mrs Hunter.' Ruth fished a piece of paper out of her pocket, and a short stub of pencil. 'It won't be any trouble to get your shopping along with ours.'

Seeing she was busy writing down what she wanted, Bob grabbed his coat. 'I must be off. Don't want to lose my job at the market.'

He ran all the way, his long legs eating up the distance to the market, where the fruit and vegetables were already being unloaded. He skidded to a halt and pushed his light brown hair out of his eyes.

'Ah, there you are, lad.' The stallholder looked uncomfortable. 'But you needn't have rushed. Ted's back now and I promised to keep his job for him. Sorry, Bob, but I can't afford to employ you as well. You've been a good worker and I'll be sorry to lose you, but I must keep my word. You understand?'

Bob glanced at the man setting up the stall, and he nodded. 'Do you know anyone else who needs a strong hand, Mr Peters?'

'Not at the moment, but I'll keep my ear open and let you know if I hear anything.'

'Thank you for employing me; I've enjoyed working for you.' Bob walked away, bitterly disappointed. He'd known this could happen, of course, with men streaming back looking for work again, but he had hoped he would be able to keep this job.

He hurried towards the docks to see if he could get some extra work there today. They were never going to manage if he didn't earn some money. Dad's army money would stop as soon as he came home, and he had to earn enough to see them through until his dad found a job. Then they'd be all right.

That thought lifted his spirits, and he began to whistle as he strode along. Perhaps he'd be able to continue his education and become a teacher. It was something he had always thought he would like to do. He had loved school and hadn't wanted to leave. Mr Jenkins at school had said he'd make a good teacher, and would easily pass the tests. Yes, he would seriously consider that once things had settled down at home.

*   *   *

As promised, Bob went home at lunchtime. Mum had lost a lot of weight lately and he wanted to make sure she ate something. It had been a depressing morning, but he smiled brightly, not wanting to worry her. Not only had he lost his job at the market, but there hadn't been anything for him at the docks either.

After the meal he banked up the fire, concerned at how low their stock of coal and wood was. The weather was bitter, and it was only the beginning of February. Spring was a way off yet, so he'd have to see what he could do about it.

'I'm off, Mum. You have a nice rest, and stay in the warm.'

'Bob,' she laughed. 'All I've done is rest!'

'I know, but it's done you good, hasn't it?'

'It has, but you mustn't worry so. I'm fine now. I'll get your dad's best suit out and give it a press. He'll need that when he gets back.'

'All right, but you make sure that's all you do today.'

'Go on,' she laughed, 'and stop giving me orders. Ruth got us a nice piece of cod today, so we'll have that for our tea. You'll be home at the usual time?'

'Same as always.' He closed the door behind him, determined to find a job of some kind. He'd do anything.

The first person he saw was the coalman, hunched up on his cart and looking miserable in

6

the cold. 'Hey, Tom, you on your own today? Want some help?'

'Could do with it. Jump on, Bob, and I'll give you a bag of coal if you help with the deliveries.'

Remembering their depleted stock, Bob leapt up, blessing his good fortune. 'Where's your lad today?'

'Got a shocking cold. Little devil hasn't got the strength to hump sacks of coal, so I told him to go back to bed.' Tom pulled the horse to a stop. 'Two sacks here. Coal bunker's round the side.'

They didn't finish the deliveries until six that evening. It was dark, and very cold when Tom stopped outside Bob's house. 'Thanks for your help. Take that last sack as payment. I'd never have managed without you.'

Jumping down, Bob lifted the sack on to his shoulders. 'Are you going to need help tomorrow?'

'I expect so. Come to the depot in the morning. I'm sure we can find a strong lad like you something to do.'

'I'll be there.'

After tipping the precious coal into their bunker, Bob went into the scullery, dirty, but well pleased with his afternoon's work. He might even have a job for tomorrow too with any luck.

When he saw the man sitting at the table with his mother, he had to look at him hard. It was such a long time since he'd seen him, and he wasn't sure.

'Dad?'

'Hello Bob.'

'Oh, it's good to have you home! When did you arrive?'

'Couple of hours ago.'

'What have you been doing?' his mother asked.

'You're filthy.'

'I've been humping coal.' He couldn't stop smiling. His father seemed rather quiet, but that was understandable. It must feel strange being back after all this time, and it would take a while for him to get used to everything again. He sat down and gulped the tea his mother had poured for him. 'They didn't want me at the market or docks because the men are taking their old jobs back.'

'Oh, that's a disappointment for you, Bob, but it's only to be expected.'

'And only right, Mum.' He held his cup out for a refill and smiled at his dad. 'I expect they'll be glad to have you back at the docks, Dad.'

'Give me a chance! I've only just got home.'

Bob was surprised at his sharp tone. He couldn't remember him ever raising his voice before, but put it down to him being unsettled. 'I was only telling you how things are, but of course you'll need a couple of days to sort yourself out again. I expect it all feels odd at the moment.'

'You're right about that.' Alfred Hunter gave a tight smile. 'Get your coat, Helen, and we'll go to the pub with Steve and Daisy.'

'Not on an empty stomach, Alf. We'll have something to eat first. I can make the fish stretch to three meals, and I've got a fresh loaf of bread. Bob, you'd better clean up before we eat.'

'Right.' He went to the washhouse, beat the dust from his clothes and washed his hands and face. That would have to do for the moment. He'd get the tin bath out later and clean up properly.

During the meal they talked about what was going on in the street. Bob and his mother avoided any mention of the war. As soon as the meal was

8

over he washed the dishes, then stood at the front window to watch them walk up the road with Ruth's parents. It was good to see them all together again.

Returning to the scullery he went out the back door and leapt over the fence. After a brief knock on Ruth's door he went in.

'They're going to celebrate tonight,' he said, smiling. 'We won't see them until closing time.'

'Is your dad all right?' Ruth looked concerned. 'I hardly recognized him.'

'I had to look twice, as well, but it's a long time since we've seen him. He's a bit quiet, that's all. He isn't injured or shaking like some of the poor devils.'

'That's good.' Ruth grabbed her little sister as she rushed in and made straight for Bob. 'Sally, you should be in bed.'

'I heard Bob come in,' she protested, struggling free.

He swung her up so she could sit on his lap, and the little girl gave her big sister a smug look. When the two boys also appeared, Ruth threw her hands up in resignation.

'I think everyone's too excited to sleep.'

Bob nodded. 'I think we'd better play a game and tire everyone out. Let's see who can say their two times table the best.'

Amid the howls of protest, Bob and Ruth grinned at each other. The men were home and everything would be all right now. They could put the dreadful war behind them.

Two

Within two weeks Bob knew just how wrong he had been to believe that things would be better now his dad was home. They were worse, and he was worried sick. Dad spent every opening hour at the pub, and after closing time he staggered home to sleep it off. He had been home for a month now and showed no sign of sobering up or looking for a job. Bob was still working for the coal merchant. It was a hard, dirty job, and every penny he brought home seemed to go into the old man's pocket for beer.

Well, he wasn't getting any of this week's money, Bob decided as he walked home after another long day. They needed it for rent. His mother was really having a rough time trying to make ends meet while coping with a drunk—for that is what his dad had become. It was no good denying it any longer. She had improved a lot before he came home, but now she looked ill again.

When he walked into the scullery he stopped in amazement. His mother was ironing a massive pile of clothes, and holding on to the table in an effort to stay on her feet. 'What the hell are you doing?' He took the flat iron from her hand and made her sit down. 'Where did all this come from?'

'I'm taking in some washing. It's the only work I could get, Bob.' She pushed him away from the table. 'Don't get coal dust over everything. I'll have to wash it all over again if you do.'

Bob was so incensed he could hardly speak, but he managed it through clenched teeth. 'I'll finish this when I've cleaned up, then deliver it and tell the people you won't be doing it again.'

'Don't you dare!' She was on her feet again, taking a fresh iron from the stove. 'The rent man's due tomorrow and I'm getting behind with the payments. He won't wait much longer for his money.' She gave her son an imploring look. 'Please don't try to stop me, Bob. I'll do whatever it takes to keep a roof over our heads.'

He felt his eyes filling with moisture, but quickly wiped it away. Their situation was obviously desperate now. 'But you're not strong enough, Mum. All this worry is making you ill again. I got paid today and will see to the overdue rent.'

Helen Hunter hugged her son gratefully. 'You mustn't worry about me all the time. I know I can do this. You work so hard, and I hate taking all your money, but I don't have a choice. I don't know what I'd do without you.'

'Where is he?' he asked, changing the subject before his despair for her spilled over.

'Asleep, at the moment. He can't seem to rest at night.' She gave Bob a weary smile. 'Go and clean up and I'll get us something to eat.'

When he returned he found his father alone in the scullery and going through his mother's bag. 'What are you doing?'

The bleary-eyed man glared at him. 'I need some money for tonight.'

'Well, you are wasting your time. She hasn't got any. You've used it all to drink yourself senseless every day, and you're not getting another farthing out of us!'

'Don't you use that tone with me, lad. I'm your father.'

'Not any more, you're not! You're a pathetic drunk who can't look after his family properly. Mum's been reduced to taking in washing now, and she isn't strong enough. Don't you care?'

'Bob!' His mother came into the room. 'Alf's had a bad time, but he'll pull himself together eventually.'

'When? We'll be in the workhouse by the time he does that. We've made excuses for him long enough, but no more, Mum. Lots of men have suffered, but most of them are back and working again. Dad's all in one piece—not like some other poor devils—'

'Shut up!' his dad shouted. 'You don't know what you're talking about. I need a drink to stop the bloody nightmares, so hand over the money you've got.'

'No! You'll have to go without your booze. I'm going to pay the rent so we don't get thrown out on the street! You might be happy to sleep in the gutter, but we're not!'

'Oh, Bob,' his mother gasped.

'Think you're tough, do you?' Alfred Hunter stood in front of his son. 'Come on then, show me.'

Bob's laugh was without humour. 'Don't tempt me. Haven't you noticed that I'm as tall as you now—and stronger?'

'Stop this at once!' Helen came between them, pushing so they had to step away from each other. Taking a coin out of her apron pocket she held it out to her husband. 'That's all I've got, Alf. Bob's right, the rent must be paid this week or we'll really be in trouble.'

He took the coin, kissed his wife briefly on the cheek, and then turned and walked out of the

12

house.

'You shouldn't give him any money,' Bob told her gently, his anger draining away.

'I'm sorry, Bob. I know just how it must grieve you to see the money wasted in this way, but he needs the drink.'

'It isn't his drinking that worries me so much, Mum. If he wants to ruin his life like that it's up to him, but I can see how his behaviour is making you ill again.'

'You mustn't be concerned for me,' she told him. 'I've got to do what I feel is right, and that's all any of us can do. It's hard, I know, but he needs our support. Try to understand, Bob. He's sick.'

'So are you, Mum. Let me take you to a doctor.'

'There's nothing they can do. I'm just tired, that's all.' She looked up at her son and managed a smile. 'We'll get through this bad patch eventually.'

After they'd finished their meal, Bob made his mother go to bed and he set about finishing the ironing. It wasn't expertly done, but it was clean, and gathering up the piles of washing he went out into the cold again. The meagre amount of money he collected he kept in his pocket to buy food.

On his return he checked that his mother was all right—she was fast asleep—and then he jumped over the fence to see Ruth. His emotions were chaotic, a mixture of anger and despair. He had pinned all of his hopes on his dad's return, believing that would be the end of their troubles, but the man living in their house bore no resemblance to the father he remembered. This stranger had brought back nothing but heartache. He needed to talk to Ruth because she understood people. She seemed to be able to see right inside

13

them and find some good in everyone, but he couldn't fathom people at all.

She greeted him with a smile, but as soon as she saw his face, she frowned. 'You're angry.'

'Bloody furious!' He sat down and told her what had happened. He ran a hand through his hair. 'This can't go on, Ruthie, but I don't know what I can do. We nearly came to blows tonight, and that upsets Mum even more.'

'Fighting with him isn't going to help any of you. I know it's hard, Bob, but you must control your temper.'

He grimaced. 'I know I can erupt easily, and I really am trying, but I don't know which way to turn at the moment.'

She nodded. 'You like to be in control of your emotions, and I can see you're finding that impossible at the moment, but you're doing well in a terrible situation, Bob. Just carry on the way you are, and I'll keep an eye on your mum while you're working.'

'Oh, thanks, Ruthie.' He gave a tight smile. 'It always helps to have a talk with you.'

'That's what friends are for.'

*   *   *

Spring came, then it was June, but nothing had changed. Bob still had his job at the coal depot, and although he hated it, he couldn't leave. They desperately needed the money he was bringing in. He never handed his wages over to his mother now, but made sure he paid the rent personally, and even did the food shopping on his way home from work. That way he knew he could keep a roof over

14

their heads and food on the table. His mother was still taking in washing, and insisting that she was all right. Ruth was helping her through the day, and he spent his evenings ironing and delivering the fresh laundry. The money went into his mother's pocket, but he knew it didn't stay there for long. It ended up at the pub down the road.

It was a wretched way to live and Bob never bothered to speak to the old man now. He had pleaded and begged him to stop drinking, but it had been a wasted effort. The situation was hopeless. His dad was too far gone for help.

Tired and dirty, Bob walked into the scullery and plonked the shopping on the table. Then all the breath left his lungs and he fell to his knees in front of the old armchair that was tucked in beside the stove.

'Mum!' He cradled her head in his large hands, but he knew—he just knew. She was dead.

Lifting her off the chair he carried her upstairs and laid her on the bed. Then, consumed with grief and anger he hurtled down the stairs, bursting into the front room where the old man was sitting senseless, as usual.

Bob dragged him out of the armchair and shook him until he opened his eyes. 'You bastard! She's dead, and it's your fault! You don't care, do you? You've been too bloody drunk to notice how she's been suffering. All you've been worried about is yourself! You're beneath contempt.'

He threw him back on to the armchair and glared at him in disgust. 'I ought to beat some sense into you, but you're not worth it.'

His father reached out a hand to him, but Bob turned away, left the room and somehow made his way next door.

As soon as he walked into the Coopers' scullery, Daisy grabbed his arm. 'What's happened, Bob?'

He stood there swaying with shock, unable to speak.

'Steve! Ruth!' Daisy called, still holding on to Bob. 'Come here, quick!'

The room was immediately full of people, but it seemed to Bob as if everything was happening through a thick fog.

'Sit down, lad.' Firm hands held him upright in a chair. 'Tell us what's happened?'

He gulped. 'Mum . . .'

Daisy caught hold of his hands and said to her husband, 'Go and see, Steve. Ruth, you make some strong tea, and put plenty of sugar in it.'

Bob was on his second cup when Steve returned and spoke quietly to his wife.

She nodded and sat next to the traumatized boy. 'You leave everything to us, Bob, and you can stay here tonight.'

'Thank you, Mrs Cooper.' His mind was beginning to clear, but the pain of loss was awful. 'Sorry I'm so dirty. It's the coal dust . . .'

'Don't you worry about that, lad.' Steve squeezed his shoulder, then said to his wife, 'What are we going to do about Alf, Daisy? He's in a bad way.'

'Does he know what's happened?'

'I think so—'

Bob surged to his feet. 'Don't you bring him near me! I don't know how I stopped myself from giving him a good beating. He was in a drunken stupor while Mum was slumped in the scullery chair— dead! How could he leave her like that? The swine! I'll kill him if I see him again . . . I will!'

'Shush now.' Daisy and Ruth were both trying to make him sit down again, but in a fury he was too big to handle.

Steve finally managed it. 'Your mum was sick, and has been for some time. Even before Alf came back.'

'I know, but that useless man made her worse. She would still be alive today if he'd looked after her like he should. She'd still be alive . . .'

*   *   *

For the first time in her life, Ruth was at a loss. She hated to see her friend suffering like this, and she wanted to help ease his pain. But how could anyone do that? Steve had brought his fresh clothes from the house and Bob was now clean. But he said nothing, and that worried Ruth—and her mother.

The two young boys peeped in the open doorway and whispered, 'Can we come in, Mum?'

'Of course.' Daisy smiled at her sons as they slipped quietly into the room. Steve had explained the situation to them, and they had obviously understood. 'Where's Sally?'

'She's asleep,' they told her.

The youngest, John, was clutching his favourite dog-eared storybook, and he went straight over to Bob, holding it out to him. 'Would you read the story of the dragons for me, please? There's lots of words I don't understand, but I always know them after you've told me.'

Ruth was alarmed and started to get up, but Daisy caught her arm, shaking her head. She sat down again and watched. John loved Bob to read to him, but she didn't think this was the right time.

17

Taking the proffered book, Bob gazed at it for a moment, then reached out and pulled John on to his lap. 'Lots of new words, are there? Have you got the little dictionary I gave you?'

After fishing about in his pocket, John produced an equally tatty little book. 'I've always got it with me.'

'Good boy. Now, do you know what page the story begins on?'

'It's the last story in the book.' John settled down, a look of expectant pleasure on his face.

Eddie grinned at his mum and sister, then went and sat on the floor next to Bob's chair so he could listen as well.

'They're good boys,' Daisy said, quietly.

At first Bob's voice was husky and hesitant, but soon he was speaking normally. Ruth never got tired of listening to him; he spoke well and had a lovely tone to his voice. She often wondered if he could sing, but she had never heard him do so.

Daisy tapped her daughter on the arm, and indicated that they should leave the room now.

'He'll be all right,' she said once they were in the scullery. 'The boys will take his mind off things for a while. I'll wash his clothes out while you make us all some cheese sandwiches, Ruth. I don't suppose any of us feel like eating, but we must have something.'

'He ought to be a teacher, Mum. Although he's in shock after finding his mum like that, he's still got time for the boys and their reading.'

Daisy nodded. 'I doubt he's ever going to get the chance to become a teacher now though.'

'Why not?'

'Because we are considered the poor, Ruth, and people in our station don't get many chances in life

18

to improve ourselves.'

Ruth snorted in disgust. 'I thought the war was supposed to change all that! Isn't this now a land fit for heroes, like they promised? It's not our fault we're so poor. We're not daft, and should all be judged on our abilities, not on where we live, or how poor we are.'

'Ah, that sounds like Bob talking. What a world that would be.' Daisy smiled at her daughter, then turned her attention to her husband as he walked into the scullery. 'How's Alf? Does he know what's happened to Helen?'

'He's a mess, but he knows she's dead. He was just too drunk to do anything about it. He's crying with shame.' Steve sat down and wiped a hand over his eyes. 'Lord knows what's going to happen to both of them now. As sick as she was, Helen held that family together.'

'She knew she was dying,' Daisy told her husband, 'but she so wanted to live long enough to see Alf through his problems. She just didn't have enough strength to hang on any longer.'

'But Bob did everything he could for her, didn't he?' Ruth said.

'He did, darling.' Steve smiled wearily at his caring daughter. 'He's a good lad, but I fear for him now. Unless he can learn to forgive, that anger he's carrying around will drag him down, if he isn't careful.'

'I'll keep an eye on him.' Ruth's expression was grim as she piled sandwiches on a plate. 'He's my friend, and I'll help him.'

'I know you will, and we'll have to watch out for Alf, Daisy.' Steve pinched a sandwich from the plate, and then stood up. 'We'll have to arrange

19

everything, and I'd better start immediately. We can't leave Helen in the house. Did she have any funeral insurance?'

'Yes, she told me her mother had taken out a penny one when she'd been born, and she'd kept it up. The policy's in a biscuit tin at the back of her wardrobe.'

'That's a relief. At least we'll be able to arrange a proper funeral.' He hauled himself up, and left, eating as he went.

Three

The next day Bob went to work as usual, saying nothing about his mother's death. It was too painful to talk about, and the last thing he wanted, or needed, was sympathy. He couldn't handle that at the moment. The Coopers were seeing to all the distressing details, and he was enormously grateful to them. They had always been like a second family to him, but now they were all he had.

Somehow he got through the day, and when he reached home, Ruth was waiting for him.

'The undertakers have been, Bob, and you can stay with us again if you don't want to go into your own house at the moment.'

'Thanks.' He laid a large hand on her shoulder and shook his head. 'You've all been very kind, Ruthie, but I've got to face up to everything. As much as I hate the old man, he's got to get through the funeral. I'll have to sober him up enough to stand at the graveside with some kind of dignity. Mum deserves that.'

'He's very upset,' Ruth told him.

Bob's expression darkened. 'So he should be! I suppose it's asking too much to expect him to have stayed sober today?'

When Ruth just shook her head, he turned away and swore under his breath, then spun back to face her. 'Is he down the pub already?'

'He went as soon as they opened. I'm sorry. We did try to stop him.'

'Dear Lord, Ruthie, you don't have to apologize. There's only one person who can help that man, and that's himself. Until he recognizes what he's doing to himself and those around him, he's never going to change. I did hope that the shock of Mum's death might have brought him to his senses, but it seems not.'

'I know you're right.' Tears shone in her clear blue eyes. 'I do so wish we could help him.'

He looked at his little friend with affection. 'You'd save the whole world if you could, but some people are beyond help. Don't you worry; I'll get him through the funeral. Tell your mum and dad I'll be in to see them later to discuss the arrangements with them.'

'All right. Have you got any food in the house? Mum said you could eat with us if you haven't, and she'll take a dinner in for your dad.'

'Don't worry about that. I did the shopping yesterday and there's plenty there.' His voice broke slightly, and he turned away, hiding his emotions. 'I'll see you later.'

Ruth watched her friend walk into his house, and sadness for him made her shoulders droop. He had taken on the responsibility of the man of the house all through the war, doing any dirty job he could find just to earn some money, and never once had she heard him complain. To have it end this way must be devastating for him.

*   *   *

Bob waited for the old man to come home from the pub, and pushed a strong cup of tea towards him as he slumped at the scullery table.

'Drink that,' he ordered, standing over him with the teapot in his hand. As soon as the cup was empty he refilled it, again and again.

When the pot was empty, Bob put it down and towered over his father, hands on hips. 'The funeral is in six days' time, and this is what we're going to do. I don't care how much you drink for the next five days, but on the day of the funeral you are going to remain sober. I will not have you disgrace Mum by falling down drunk as we lay her to rest. Do you understand?'

Alfred Hunter gazed up at his son with tortured eyes. 'I won't disgrace her or you.'

'Good. Now, I know it won't be easy for you because you've been permanently drunk since you arrived home, but I'll help you through the next week. After that you are on your own.'

'I have tried, really I have . . . I'm sorry, son.'

'It's too late for apologies.' Bob took some coins out of his pocket and put them on the table. 'That should get you through the week, but it's the last I'll be giving you.' Then he left the scullery and made his way upstairs to try and get some sleep. He had done all he could for the moment.

*   *   *

The morning of the funeral dawned bright and warm, and Bob was grateful for the sunshine. If it had been a gloomy day it would have made everything even more upsetting.

Steve walked into the scullery. 'Where is he, Bob?'

'Still in bed, and I was about to drag him out. I don't think he had quite as much to drink last night as he usually does, but I doubt he will be completely sober this morning.'

Steve nodded, his expression grim. 'Come on, lad, I'll give you a hand. We'll manage him between us.'

'Thanks.'

Alfred Hunter was up, washed and dressed without a murmur. With Bob on one side of him and Steve on the other they arrived at the church without mishap.

During the service and at the graveside, Alf pushed aside their restraining hands and stood unaided, tears rolling silently down his cheeks. Bob didn't dare look at him or his anger would rise again, and this was no place for such emotions. He needed to remember his mum with love in his heart. She had been so brave.

Daisy and Ruth had prepared sandwiches, cakes and tea for the neighbours and friends who had attended. Both parents had been only children, so there weren't any close relatives, but it had been a good turnout. Helen had been well liked and quite a few had come to pay their respects.

*   *   *

It had been a simple funeral, but a dignified one, and Bob was immensely grateful to the Coopers. Finally the last person left, and Bob sat at the table, giving a huge sigh of relief. Everything had gone well and the old man had made an effort, talking to people and remaining on his feet.

Steve Cooper gathered his family together. 'Time to go. Bob will want to be on his own now.'

Bob gave him a grateful look. 'Where is he?'

'Asleep in the armchair,' Daisy told him. 'I should leave him there, Bob, he's exhausted. And so are you. Try and get some rest.'

He nodded wearily. 'I'll try. Thank you for all your help. You've been wonderful.'

Steve gripped his shoulder for a moment, and then herded his family out of the door.

When he was finally alone, Bob rested his head in his hands and cried for the first time that day. After a while he dried his eyes and put the kettle on to make a strong cup of tea, feeling better now he'd let his sorrow come out. He'd been bottling it up ever since his mum had died.

Holding a fresh cup of tea between his hands he took a deep breath. All he had been able to think about was getting through the funeral, but now that was over it was time to make some decisions.

After draining the cup he stood up and went to the front room. The man asleep in the armchair seemed like a stranger to him, and he felt pity when he remembered the vital man who had once been his dad. But pity wasn't going to do either of them any good. He knew the only way he was going to find peace again was to forgive the worry and sadness this man had caused his mother. But at the moment he couldn't do that. Perhaps one day, but

24

not now.

'I'm sorry, Mum,' he said quietly. 'I've done all I can for him. It's now time for me to move on.'

Four

Robert Hunter closed the door of the house he had called home, and fighting back the crippling sadness that threatened to tear him apart, he walked up the street. He'd loved his dad, but the man who had returned from the war had changed beyond recognition. Now Bob only felt contempt for the man who had caused his gentle mother so much pain.

'Bob!'

Ignoring the call he kept going, his step never faltering. He had made up his mind and no one was going to turn him back. The decision had been hard because it meant leaving everything he was familiar with, and that included good friends and neighbours . . .

'Where are you going?' Ruth caught his arm, looking anxiously at the bundle he had tied with string and slung over his shoulder.

He shook off the restraining hand, being sharper than he should, but it was the only way he was going to hold on to his composure. He had been desperately hoping no one would see him so that he could slip away unnoticed. 'I'm leaving,' he said simply.

Tears filled Ruth's eyes. 'You don't need to do that. Mum said you could come and live with us if you'd rather not live in the same house as your dad.'

'Don't be daft!' he snapped. 'You haven't got enough room for me. Your house is full and she has quite enough people to look after as it is.'

'We'd make room,' she pleaded. 'And you'd still be close enough to keep an eye on your dad. He needs you, Bob.'

'No!' He felt rotten when he saw her face crumple. She didn't deserve to be spoken to like this. Hell, he sounded just like his old man, and that was something he must never do. 'Your mum's a kind woman, Ruth. You thank her for me, but I can't stay. I've got to try and make something of myself.' Bob's mouth set in a grim line as he looked at the row of squalid houses. 'I'm not going to end up like my old man who can't face the world sober.'

'He's a troubled man—'

'That's no excuse. So are lots of other people.' Bob's voice came out in a snarl. 'Mum would still be alive today if he'd stayed away from the drink and found a job. She was dreadfully ill, and he didn't even notice. He can take care of himself now!'

'We all know how bad things have been.' Ruth touched his arm in sympathy. 'But you've got friends here who will help and support you. If you leave you'll be on your own. Where will you go? What will you do?'

'I'll be all right.' He straightened up, trying to appear confident, his grey eyes hooded to hide his emotions. 'I'm strong and can do any kind of heavy work. I'll move around, picking up jobs where I can.'

'Have you got any money?' Ruth delved into her pocket and held out two pennies.

'No, Ruth.' He backed away. 'I've got enough. I

can't take your money.'

'I want you to have it.' She stepped forward and thrust the coins into his large hand. 'You can pay me back when you're rich and famous.'

He smiled then. 'All right, Ruthie. You'll get it back with interest, and that's a promise.'

'And you make sure you bring it yourself.'

'I will.' Bob looked at his little friend with affection. He knew she had been doing jobs for neighbours so she could earn enough to buy herself a badly needed winter coat, but she was the kind of girl who always put other people first. 'You're a fine girl, Ruth, and with your dark hair and hazel eyes, you'll be real pretty when you've grown a bit.'

She tipped her head to one side and made an attempt at a smile. 'Well then, you'd better come back to find out, hadn't you?'

On impulse he bent and kissed her cheek, slipping the coins back into her pocket without her noticing. 'You take care of yourself, little Ruthie, and don't settle for this kind of life. You deserve better.' He straightened up, turned and strode away, not daring to look back.

*   *   *

'Where's Bob off to?' Ruth's mother asked when she went back into the house.

'He's left, Mum.'

Daisy Cooper stopped chopping the carrots and shook her head. 'I was afraid of that. Did he say where he's going?'

Ruth shook her head, near to tears. 'I told him he could come and live with us, but he wouldn't hear of it. He said you had quite enough to do

27

looking after us lot.'

'He's always been a considerate boy, but if he really couldn't stand living in that house any longer, we'd have made room for him.' Daisy went back to chopping the vegetables for a nourishing soup. A few dumplings and a chunk of bread and it would fill her family up nicely. 'But I don't like to think of him all alone now. And God knows what's going to happen to Alf. If he doesn't sort himself out he's going to end up in the workhouse. That man is a real mess, but in his own way he loves his boy.'

'Well it's a pity he forgot how to show it.' Ruth's voice wavered, still upset at losing her friend. 'Bob tried so hard to help both his mum and his dad, and he might have stayed if he'd thought his dad cared.'

'I know, but things are not always what they seem.' Daisy reached out and pulled her daughter close, smiling down at her. 'Life gets hard at times, Ruthie, trying to keep a roof over our heads and food on the table. We don't always show how much we love each other.'

Suddenly three children erupted into the scullery, yelling and fighting.

'Stop that!' Ruth grabbed the youngest and pulled her out of harm's way. Sally was only three and no match for her boisterous brothers, Eddie aged ten, and John aged eight.

'He pushed me!' John glared at his brother. 'He made me fall over and tear my trousers. Look.'

'I did not! You tripped.'

'That's enough!' Daisy silenced her squabbling children.

John's bottom lip trembled as he fingered the hole on the leg of his trousers. 'I'm sorry, Mum.'

Bending down, Daisy inspected the damage, and

then ruffled her little son's dark hair. 'That's all right, John, accidents happen. Your sister will patch it for you, won't you, Ruth? You know how clever she is with a needle.'

'Of course. Take them off, John, and I'll do it now.' Ruth smiled at her sensitive brother. 'You won't even be able to see where the hole was when I've finished.'

The worry cleared from his little face. 'Oh, thanks, Ruthie. Eddie, can I borrow your other trousers till mine are fixed?'

'All right. They'll be a bit big, but we can tie a piece of string around to keep them up. Come on.'

Friends again, the boys left together and scampered up the narrow stairs.

Ruth returned to the subject of the friend she adored. 'Bob said I should get out of here when I'm older. He doesn't believe we should live like this.'

'Bob's a dreamer, Ruthie; you shouldn't take too much notice of what he says. We were born poor. That's our lot in life and there's no way we can change that. You need a good education to get anywhere, and there's no hope of that around here.'

'But we aren't daft, and Bob's ever so clever.' Ruth's eyes shone with admiration. 'He'll make something of himself. You'll see.'

'I hope he finds the kind of future he's looking for.' Daisy gave a sad smile. 'The problem with that boy is he thinks too much. He's also too clever for his own good.'

Ruth didn't see how anyone could be 'too clever for their own good', but she said nothing.

*   *   *

29

Around five o'clock they were all sitting at the scullery table having their tea of bread and jam when the door burst open and Alf Hunter tumbled in.

'Look at this!' he shouted, holding up a sheet of paper. 'That bloody kid's left me. What's he want to go and do a daft thing like that for? Where's he gone?'

'Stop shouting, Alf.' Daisy pushed the distraught man into a chair. 'And watch your language in front of the kids.'

'Sorry, Daisy.' Alf wiped a shaking hand over his eyes. 'Where's he gone? He's only a kid. Why's he done this?'

Daisy looked at her neighbour and saw that he was more or less sober for a change. It was time he faced the truth. 'He's sixteen years old, Alf, and quite capable of looking after himself. We don't know where he's gone, but the why is obvious. He blames you for Helen's death, and believes she could have lived longer if you'd stayed off the drink.'

A muffled groan came from Alf. 'I'm not much of a man, am I, Daisy? Helen died too young, and I've driven my son away.'

Ruth had poured Alf a cup of tea and placed it in front of him. 'Drink that, Mr Hunter.'

'You've got to pull yourself together, Alf,' Daisy said, watching as he gulped down the hot liquid. 'You're only forty, and if you'd get that drink out of you, all your strength would come back. Steve said there's work to be found at the docks if you aren't too fussy what you do.'

'Won't bring my boy back, though, will it?'

'No. What's done is done. We can't change that.'

30

Daisy sat beside Alf and gripped his hand. 'Bob's looking for a better future, and you can do the same. Take this chance to change your life, then when he comes back he'll find the father he'd loved when he was a little boy.'

Alf glanced up, a glimmer of hope in his eyes. 'Do you think he'll come back, Daisy?'

'Of course he will. Now, why don't you show him you can change?'

'Can ... can I have another cup of tea, please?' He raised his head, and for the first time since his return from the war, Alf Hunter had a glint of determination in his eyes.

Ruth poured another cup for him. 'Would you like a slice of bread and jam, Mr Hunter? We've got enough.'

'I'd like that. Thank you.'

'Bob will be all right,' Ruth told him as she cut a thick slice of bread for him. 'He's ever so clever. He was top of the school all the time.'

'Yes. He's got brains, and he certainly didn't get them from me.'

'Don't put yourself down, Alf,' Daisy scolded. 'You ain't so daft. It's only the drink fuddling your mind.'

After putting a scraping of jam on the bread, Ruth handed it to Bob's dad. 'I gave him a bit of money I'd saved up, and he promised to return it, so he will come back. He always keeps his promise.'

'He'll do that for you.' Alf reached out and patted Ruth's hand. 'He's always said you're the nicest kid around here.'

As Alf heaved himself unsteadily out of the chair, Daisy said, 'If there's anything we can do for you, Alf, you just let us know.'

'That's good of you, girl, but you've got enough to cope with without being burdened with a drunk. I shortened my Helen's life and drove my son away. I'm going to make sure I don't hurt any more people.'

Daisy caught his arm in alarm. 'Now don't you go doing anything stupid!'

Alf gave a wry smile. 'Oh, I'm not thinking of doing away with myself. I don't deserve such a merciful end. Don't you fret, Daisy.' Alf straightened up to his full height of just over six feet, remorse etching deep lines on his face. 'I've got to sort myself out so I can show my son I can face life with courage, just like him.'

When the scullery door had closed behind Alf, Ruth looked enquiringly at her mother. 'Do you think he can sober up, Mum?'

'Only the Lord knows.'

'What made him like that?'

'The war. He was in the trenches in France and watched all his friends die. Helen said he had terrible nightmares when he came back, and he started to drink so he could sleep. The trouble was he couldn't stop.' Daisy sat beside her daughter. 'The men saw terrible things during that war and their mental scars might never heal completely.'

'Dad was all right though, wasn't he?' Ruth's inquisitive mind wouldn't let the subject drop. Her mother had warned her not to ask the men anything about the war, so she knew very little. 'He wasn't in France, was he?'

'No, he was in the Navy. There was a big battle at a place called Jutland, and he was there. His ship was sunk and lots of the men died, but by some miracle he survived.'

'Oh!' Ruth's mouth opened in surprise. 'He's never said anything about it.'

'And I don't think he ever will. None of the men ever talk about their experiences in the war. It's too hard for them, and that's why I told you kids not to go asking questions.'

'I never have.'

'I know.' Daisy smiled at her daughter. 'We must keep an eye on Alf, and pray he can keep off the drink at last.'

*   *   *

When Ruth undressed to get ready for bed she found the money Bob had put back in her pocket. 'Oh, Bob, why didn't you take it?' She was upset that he'd refused her help. 'You're going to need a bit of extra money, because I know you can't have much. I wanted you to have it!'

Five

Time lost all meaning as Alfred Hunter began his struggle. He tossed through the night, moaning in pain as his body craved alcohol, incapable of doing anything but curl up on the bed in distress. At one point he must have tumbled down the stairs because he found himself frantically searching every inch of the small house looking for a drink.

With a cry of anguish he sunk to his knees and wept for the wreck he had become. No wonder his son had left him. Out of the corner of his eye he saw a movement, and when he turned his head he saw a multicoloured snake climbing up the wall. When it grinned at him he screamed at it to go away. Somehow he found the strength to stand, and holding on to the table for support with one hand, he shook his fist at the ridiculous apparition. 'You can bloody well disappear. I'm not ever going touch another drop of drink!'

His fist slammed on the wall. 'This ends now!'

'All right, Alf.' Strong hands helped him into a chair. 'Put the kettle on, Daisy. Ruth, go and get the iodine and a bandage. He's split his knuckles.'

Alf looked up at the man giving quiet orders. 'The bloody thing grinned at me, Steve. I'm not having that. I've got to beat this. My wife died and my boy's left me. I need to know he's all right. It's a tough world out there; he shouldn't be alone. I don't care how hard it is, I'm staying off the booze!'

'You hold on to that thought because you're going to need it. You've got some rough days ahead of you, mate.'

The tears still ran down Alf's ravaged face as he gulped the hot tea from the cup Daisy held up to his mouth. When that was empty it was refilled, and while he drank that, Ruth saw to his damaged hand.

*　　　　*　　　　*

The next few days were just a blur, but Alf was aware of Steve and his family taking care of him. In a lucid moment he recognized just how much he owed them because the withdrawal from drink was so dreadful. He knew he would never make it without their support. Somehow he would repay them for their kindness.

Church bells woke him up early one morning,

34

and he opened his eyes cautiously. There was nothing crawling up the walls, and he had actually slept all night. Afraid to move in case the torment returned, he closed his eyes and concentrated on the church bells. It was a lovely sound, soothing ... Sunday. It must be Sunday. He could picture families making their way to the service. How long had it been since he'd done anything as normal as that? Too long.

He opened his eyes again and the room was bathed in sunshine. Taking a deep breath he eased himself upright and turned so he was sitting on the edge of the bed. There was only a slight dizziness, so gritting his teeth he stood up and made his way down the stairs. It was slow going, but he made it to the scullery without falling down. He sat at the table waiting for the trembling to ease before he moved again. Running his hand over his face he felt several days' growth of beard. He must clean himself up.

It was nearly an hour before he felt able to haul himself upright again. He wasn't capable of getting out the tin bath and filling it with hot water, so a wash would have to do, but that would be a start.

The task took some time, but Alf never wavered in his determination to make himself presentable.

When Daisy and Ruth came in they found Alf sitting at the scullery table, clean, shaved, wearing his Sunday suit, and drinking a cup of tea he'd made himself.

'Oh, Alf,' Daisy said, her face alight with pleasure. 'You look wonderful. Go and get your dad, Ruthie.'

Steve came at a run, bursting through the scullery door with his kids right behind him. He took in the scene and smiled. 'Well done, Alf.'

'I couldn't have done it without you.' He gazed at the Cooper family crowded around the table. 'I'm in your debt, every one of you.'

'You don't owe us anything.' Steve pulled up a chair and sat down. 'Your own determination has pulled you through this far, but you know it isn't the end, don't you?'

Alf nodded, his mouth turned down in disgust. 'Every day will be a struggle. I must never touch a drop of drink again. No matter how tempted I am I'll keep off the booze, because I couldn't go through this hell again.'

'Good.' Steve slapped Alf gently on the shoulder. 'But if things ever get too bad you come to me and I'll help you.'

'Thanks, mate, it'll be a comfort to know you're there if I need you. Now, is there any news of my boy?'

'Sorry, Alf.' Daisy shook her head. 'We've asked around and someone said they thought they'd seen him going into the railway station, but they weren't sure. No one else has seen him.'

'He's left London then.' Alf's expression was grim. 'But where would he go, Ruth? You know him better than most.'

'I don't know, Mr Hunter. All he said was that he would move around getting work where he could.'

'We'll keep on asking. Someone might see him. Dear Lord, I hope he's all right.' Alf slapped his hand on the table in anger and hauled himself upright. 'He could be in all sorts of trouble while his drunken father struggles to come to his senses. I'll never be able to forgive myself for this. I'm a weak fool, and good for nothing. But that's going to change from now on.'

'Where are you going?' Daisy asked as Alf headed for the door.

'I'm going to church.'

'Mr Hunter,' Ruth called.

'Yes?'

'If Bob knew how bravely you're fighting to get well again he would be proud of you.'

'I don't think that boy's got any respect left for me, and I don't blame him.' Unable to say anything else he walked out of the door in an effort to hide his anguish.

The church was empty now, and the peace and quiet was just what he needed. Finding a pew at the back of the church he sat down and rested his head in his hands. He'd never been much of a churchgoer, but he remembered praying in the trenches—they all did. They reached out in the desperate hope that someone cared about their plight. The carnage and suffering had blighted many a life, including his, but he was alive, and it was time he started to live like a proper man again. The war was past, and that's where he should leave it. Taking a deep, shuddering breath, he let the soothing atmosphere of the empty church settle his jangling nerves.

After spending about an hour in solitude he'd cleared his mind and began to think clearly. And one thing he knew for certain was that the next few weeks were not going to be easy, but if he wanted to regain his self-respect, it had to be done. He would succeed for his wife who had died too young, and for his son. They might never know how much he still loved them, but that wouldn't stop him trying to rebuild his life.

He lifted his head, stood up and walked out of the church, feeling more in control. He was going to put his life to rights and earn back his dignity. If Bob did return one day he would show him a father he could respect.

Six

There was a little warmth in the sun and Bob let his thoughts relive the last few months.

He had left home without knowing where he would go, or what he would do. A train had been due as soon as he'd reached the station and he'd bought a ticket, not caring where it was going. It was daft, he knew, and he should have had some kind of plan, but he just hadn't been able to think straight. The only thing on his mind was to get as far away as he could.

When the train stopped at Maidstone in Kent, he'd got off, and for a few weeks had moved around picking up jobs where he could. At a place called Hunton he'd been taken on at Pearson's Farm. It had been a hard winter living in a barn, and he didn't even want to think about Christmas. He had pictured himself sitting round a blazing fire with his mum and the Coopers, and that memory had been so painful he had been relieved when 1920 had arrived. It was spring now and the farmer had paid him off. He wasn't sorry.

With his meagre pay in his pocket he picked up his belongings and began to walk to the nearest village. He deserved a comfortable bed for the night.

The house with the sign in the window saying 'rooms to let' was pristine. Bob glanced down at his filthy clothes and grimaced. The lady in the village shop had recommended this place to him, but after months of digging ditches and sleeping in barns, he had his doubts about going in. He had cleaned up as best as he could, but he needed a bath and somewhere to wash his clothes. There was enough money in his pocket for one night, so he really hoped the landlady wouldn't turn him away.

He glanced at the house again. Well, there was only one way to find out, he thought, as he lifted his head and walked up to the door. It opened before he could knock and he was confronted with a diminutive woman of around sixty, he guessed, and she was smiling up at him.

'Took you a while to make up your mind, lad. Want somewhere to stay?'

'Er, yes please, if you'll take me. I can pay. Mrs Johnson in the shop said you were reasonable.'

'Of course I am. Come on in. I'm Mrs Trent.'

Before stepping into the immaculate front room he removed his boots and held them in his hand. 'Sorry I'm in such a mess, Mrs Trent, but I've been roughing it for a while.'

'I know, lad. You're Bob Hunter, and you've been ditching for Farmer Pearson. I doubt the old skinflint gave you a decent meal either.'

He was astonished that she knew his name, and showed it. 'Actually, his wife fed me quite well. But how did you know who I was?'

'Don't look so surprised. The whole village knows about you. You're that quiet boy from London who works at any dirty job with never a complaint.' Her laugh was infectious. 'You come with me and I'll find you some clean clothes. My late husband was a tall man so his clobber should fit you.'

She was very agile for her age and Bob had to take the stairs two at a time to keep up with her. He waited politely outside the room as she bustled around taking garments out of drawers and the wardrobe, holding each one up to him to see if they would fit. Finally satisfied she urged him towards another door on the landing.

'Now, you go and have a nice bath. There's a towel and soap waiting for you. When you've finished put on the clean clothes and come downstairs again. I'll have a nice dinner waiting for you.'

Giving him another brilliant smile she pushed him through the door, and then bustled away.

By now Bob was quite bemused. She had acted as if she'd been expecting him, but it was a small village and perhaps the lady in the shop had sent a message to say she had told him to come here. He took a deep breath. Whatever had happened, he wasn't about to do anything but enjoy his good luck. When he finally glanced around him he gasped. This was a proper bathroom with taps and hot water from a device over the bath. After two weeks of working in dirt and sleeping in a barn, this was heavenly. He sang softly to himself as he ran the water and undressed.

After wallowing in the bath until the water was almost cold, Bob dried himself and then put on the clean clothes Mrs Trent had given him. They were just a little on the small side for him, but it was wonderful to have something decent to wear.

When he went downstairs, the landlady gave

him a thorough inspection. 'That's better. You're a handsome boy now you're not covered in dirt. Leave the clothes outside your door tonight and I'll let them out a bit. They should fit you perfectly then.'

'Oh, Mrs Trent, you don't need to go to all that trouble. Once my own clothes are washed—'

She held up her hand to stop him. 'Now, don't you worry about anything. I used to be a dressmaker, so it won't take me long to make the alterations. Dinner's ready. Come and meet my other tenant.'

Sensing it would be useless to argue, Bob followed her into a small dining room. The dark furniture shone with years of dedicated polishing, and he breathed in the clean smell with pleasure. How his mother would have loved this house. She might have lived longer if things hadn't been so harsh for her. This was how people should be living, and not in the squalor of the slums.

'Bob, this is Jim,' the landlady said.

'Pleased to meet you.' Bob shook hands with a man in his late twenties, or even a little older than that. He was of average height, with brown hair and blue eyes that shone with good humour. He liked him on sight.

'Sit down,' Mrs Trent urged. 'You two can get to know each other after you've eaten. I'm sure you're both starving.'

It was the best steak and kidney pie Bob had ever tasted. Mrs Trent had evaded any mention of her charges for such luxury, but by now he didn't care if the night's lodging took every penny he'd earned. It was worth it!

'Off you go to the front room and I'll bring you a

nice pot of tea.' The landlady was busy clearing the table, smiling approval at the empty plates.

The front room had the same lovely smell of polish and Bob sighed with pleasure as he settled in a large comfortable armchair.

'How long are you staying?' Jim asked.

'I don't think I can afford more than one night of this luxury, but I was desperate for a chance to clean up and sleep in a decent bed for a change. The job I had at Pearson's Farm didn't pay much and I'll have to move on tomorrow and find another job.'

'Hmm.' Jim studied the tall boy in front of him. 'Know anything about horses?'

'Not a thing.'

'Would you mind being a stable boy?'

Bob sat forward eagerly. 'I'll do anything. Do you know of a job going?'

'I work at the big house about ten minutes' walk from here. I'm head groom and one of my lads has just left, so I can put in a word for you with the master, if you like?'

'Would you? I'd be grateful. I'm a hard worker and wouldn't let you down.' Bob was on his feet and shaking Jim's hand.

Laughing, Jim waved him back into his chair. 'I'll have a word with Captain Russell in the morning. You come to the house at ten. The captain will want to meet you before he agrees to take you on.'

'Of course.' Bob sat down again just as their landlady came in with their tea and a large fruitcake.

Bob was already thinking about the interview and knew he had to look presentable. 'Mrs Trent, could I possibly borrow these clothes for tomorrow? Jim is going to arrange an interview for me with his boss. They need a stable boy, and if I'm lucky, I might get the job.'

'The clothes are yours now, Bob. You don't have to return them.'

'But ...' He was immediately worried. 'I can't afford to pay for them.'

'It's been my pleasure to give them to you, dear boy. I don't want to take your hard-earned money for them. They were only sitting upstairs doing nothing.' She poured the tea and cut them both a large slice of cake. 'I'll leave that here so you can help yourselves. Oh, yes,' she turned to Bob. 'Did I hear you say you couldn't stay more than one night?'

'That's right, Mrs Trent. As much as I would like to, I'm afraid it just isn't possible.'

'Anything is possible if you set your mind to it. Once you get that job you'll be able to be my permanent guest, like Jim here.' She smiled happily at both of them. 'I'll love having two such fine young men to look after. Now, don't you worry, Bob, it will all work out.'

As she left the room, Bob sat down again and closed his eyes for a moment to gain control of his emotions. He still felt uneasy about leaving his father to cope on his own, but some kind guiding hand had led him to this, and he was grateful for the kindness being shown him.

'Don't get your hopes up too much, Bob,' Jim said quietly. 'I will recommend you, but it will be the captain's decision. I can't guarantee anything, you understand?'

Bob opened his eyes and smiled. 'I know, but it's a chance, and I thank you for that.'

'You're obviously a Londoner, so what brings you to Kent?'

'Work is hard to come by where I lived, so I thought there might be more chance in another part of the country.' Bob pulled a face. 'And this was as far as my money would take me.'

'Which part of London are you from?'

'Oh, around the docks, and there's too many men chasing too few jobs. There wasn't anything to keep me there, so I left.'

'No family?'

Bob took a bite of the cake and shook his head, changing the subject. 'Mrs Trent's a good cook, isn't she?'

Jim took the hint, dropped the subject, and helped himself to another cup of tea. He talked about his work at the stables until it was time to retire.

As soon as Bob settled in the clean, comfortable bed, exhaustion sent him into a deep sleep almost at once.

*   *   *

The next morning Bob was at the imposing house well before the appointed time. The place was huge, and the land appeared to stretch as far as the eye could see and beyond. This wasn't a titled family, but they were obviously very wealthy.

A butler showed him to a room downstairs and told him he would be called when Captain Russell was ready to see him.

Unable to relax he prowled the room, inspecting every picture and piece of furniture, marvelling at the fine workmanship of every item. There had to be a fortune in this one room, he decided, jumping as a voice spoke right behind him. The man moved without making a sound.

'The master will see you now. Follow me.'

Bob did as ordered, and waited while the butler tapped on a door, opened it and walked in. He followed only a couple of steps inside the room and stopped in astonishment. The room was full of books, from floor to ceiling, and scattered around were small tables and dark red leather chairs. It was the most beautiful room Bob had ever seen in his life, but there was something that made him recoil.

When the butler announced him, he turned his attention to the man he was here to see. Sitting behind a large desk was a distinguished man with dark hair greying slightly at the temples. In front of him was a glass with some amber liquid in it, and there was no mistaking the strong smell of alcohol. It was something Bob was well acquainted with and was instantly on his guard.

'Thank you, Green.' Captain Russell turned his attention to Bob. 'What is your name?'

'Robert Hunter, sir.'

The captain drained his glass and held it out to Bob. 'Pour me another whisky. The decanters are on the table by the window.'

'No, sir!' Bob didn't move, knowing that he had just ruined any chance he had of getting this job. The disappointment was crushing, but he would never lift a finger to help any man drink, especially at this time in the morning.

'What did you say?' The captain's eyes narrowed as he stood up, swaying slightly.

'I said I wouldn't get you another drink, sir. I mean no disrespect, but I won't help you drink yourself senseless. It's only ten o'clock, and I'd say you've had enough already.'

'Oh, you would, would you?'

'Yes, sir.' Bob didn't think there was much use minding his words. He'd wanted this job so much, but it was gone now, so he might as well have his say. 'I've seen the despair drunkenness brings to a family. While you are drowning your senses in drink, those who love you suffer. You don't need to do this. You have a beautiful home, and I expect there's a family who care for you. Do you want to lose their love and respect? Because that is what will happen. Believe me, I know!'

When the captain just stared at his empty glass and said nothing, Bob turned and made to leave the room.

'Where are you going?'

He turned back. 'Leaving. You won't employ me now.'

'Don't you want this job?'

'Very much.'

'Then sit down. I haven't dismissed you yet.'

There was no doubt he was a man used to being obeyed, and having nothing to lose by staying, Bob sat on the edge of the nearest chair.

The captain studied Bob carefully for some uncomfortable minutes, and then said, 'You owe me an explanation. I want to know how you come to know about men who drink too much.'

'That's my business, sir.' Bob started to get up again, but was waved back into his seat.

'You have insulted me in my own home, young man, and you will tell me why.'

'All right!' Furious that this softly spoken man had brought the pain and anguish he felt to the surface again, the words poured out. It had been bottled up inside him, and now released, he told the captain of every bitter struggle and argument as he'd watched his mother's health deteriorate with such tragic results.

There was silence in the room when he stopped talking, and wracked with emotion he stood up and turned his back, regretting his outburst. He'd told this man far too much. What had happened was nothing to do with him or anyone else.

'So you left your father alone.'

Bob spun back. 'I tried! I begged, pleaded and reasoned with him, but it was useless. He wouldn't listen.'

'So you ran away.'

That stung! 'Yes, I ran away. What else could I do? And I'd be obliged if you would keep this to yourself, sir. It's my business and that's the way I want to keep it.'

Captain Russell made no comment, but picked up a bell from his desk and rang it. When the butler arrived, he said, 'Have Mr Hunter taken round to the stables. Jim's expecting him. And ask Cook to bring me a tray of tea and some toast, please.'

'At once, sir.'

Bob followed the butler without looking back at the man behind the desk. He couldn't believe he'd been given the job after the way he'd spoken to the captain.

As he closed the door behind him he heard the sound of breaking glass.

Seven

The stables were large, housing twelve fine-looking horses. They were nothing like the hacks he'd seen at home pulling the rag-and-bone carts, and he fell in love with them immediately. He was put to work mucking out the stables, and after digging ditches for months this was sheer pleasure. He threw himself into the work with enthusiasm. The men and boys working there were a lively bunch, and Bob soon found himself laughing again—something he hadn't done for some time. He had been able to stay with Mrs Trent and, much to his relief, he hadn't seen the captain again. Ten days after the interview he still cringed with embarrassment. Captain Russell had as good as called him a coward for leaving his father, and he had the uncomfortable feeling that he might be right.

Putting such vexing thoughts out of his mind, he settled in to his work. Four of the horses were racing stock and Bob was proud that he was now allowed to saddle them up ready for their daily workout. He loved seeing them in full gallop, and wished he could be a jockey—but of course, he was far too big.

One beautiful morning while he was busy helping get the horses ready he felt a tug on his trouser leg, and a childish voice asking, 'Are you the cheeky sod who told my daddy not to drink?'

Startled, he looked down at a small girl gazing at him with a pair of bright blue eyes. Her hair was in blonde pigtails.

'Lillian!' Captain Russell strode up to them.

48

'You know you mustn't swear!'

'But that's what you said, Daddy. I heard you.'

'You mustn't repeat what you hear.' He stooped down in front of his daughter. 'And little girls don't swear.'

'Why?'

'It isn't ladylike.'

She looked thoughtful. 'If the new baby's a boy will he be able to swear?'

'Not until he's a man.' Her father pushed a strand of escaping hair away from her face. 'Now, apologize to Robert.'

Bob had been watching father and daughter with amusement, while closely studying the captain. He was sure he was sober and there wasn't the slightest smell of alcohol on him.

The little girl tugged at his trouser leg again to gain his attention. 'You didn't mind what I said to you, did you?'

'Lillian!'

She pulled a face, never taking her eyes off Bob. 'Daddy always calls me Lillian when he's cross with me, but you can call me Lilly, like everyone else.'

'Thank you, Lilly. And you can call me Bob.'

She turned and grinned at her father. 'I like him. He's ever so tall, isn't he?'

'Yes, darling,' her father sighed. 'Now, what did I ask you to do?'

'Um . . . Oh yes.' She tugged at Bob again. 'Bend down. I'm getting a stiff neck looking up at you.'

Stifling a laugh, Bob stooped down to her level.

Lilly became serious as she whispered in his ear, 'Daddy smashed his glass in the fireplace and he hasn't had a drink since. Mummy said that's very good.'

'It certainly is.'

'Lillian, stop whispering and let me hear you apologize.'

'I'm sorry I said a naughty word to you,' she said clearly.

'I accept your apology, Lilly, but you must remember what your father told you. You'll shock all the ladies if you're not careful.'

There was a clatter of horses as two grooms arrived with a large black stallion and a small white pony, already saddled.

Lilly's father lifted her on to the pony, and then mounted his own horse. He turned to Bob. 'Can you ride?'

'No, sir.'

'Jim, teach Bob to ride, and put him on Midnight.'

The head groom couldn't hide his surprise. 'Perhaps something more docile would be better, sir? Midnight is rather fractious for a beginner.'

There was a gleam of devilment in Captain Russell's eyes. 'Then they should suit each other very well. And he's the only animal strong enough to take someone of his size.'

Bob watched father and daughter as they left the yard, returning Lilly's wave.

'You've made a conquest with the daughter, but I'm not sure about the father.' Jim shook his head. 'It's good to see the master more like his old self, but I can't put you on Midnight. That animal will have the time of his life unseating you.'

'You haven't got a choice, Jim. That man has decided to get his own back on me.'

'So it seems.' Jim studied the tall boy in front of him carefully. 'Just what did happen at your interview?'

'We had words.' Bob shrugged and changed the subject. 'How old is the girl?'

'She's just turned seven, and another one is due soon. That's why we haven't seen much of his wife lately. She's had a worrying time since the captain returned. He was in quite a state, but it looks as if he's over that now. Thank goodness. He's a fine man, and his wife is a gracious lady.' Jim grinned. 'We're all hoping the baby will be a boy this time.'

'That would be good.' Bob rubbed his hands together in anticipation. 'When do I get my first lesson? I wouldn't like to deprive Midnight, or the master, of their fun.'

*   *   *

'Did you enjoy your ride?' Emma held out her hand to her husband.

'Very much.' Benjamin Russell kissed his wife's cheek. 'Lilly is quite an accomplished rider already. How are you feeling, my dear?'

'I'm fine. The doctor said all is well and the baby should be born within the next month.' She gave her husband a relieved smile. 'You are looking much better, Ben.'

He nodded and sat down. 'That young lad made me see what I was doing to myself—and you. I'm sorry, my dear.'

'You were troubled, but I knew you were strong enough to come through it.'

'Maybe I would have eventually come to my senses, but young Robert Hunter gave me quite a lecture on the evils of drink.' Ben gave a grimace. 'When I saw the pain in those stormy grey eyes as he told me about his father, it almost tore me apart. Poor little devil.'

'Not so little,' Emma remarked.

'True, and that's why I've told Jim to teach him to ride—on Midnight.'

'You haven't! Oh, Ben, that's wicked of you. That animal enjoys being hard to manage.'

They were both laughing at the thought, and Ben sat back, relaxed and happy for the first time since the war. 'He's the tallest animal in the stables, and that boy tops six feet already. He'll cope with Midnight.'

'I just hope you're right.' Emma gave him a speculative look. 'You have faith in him?'

'I do, but I'm also concerned about him.' Ben was suddenly serious. 'He's full of anger, and although he would deny it, I believe he's also feeling guilty about leaving his father. There was such anguish in his voice when he said, "What else could I do?"'

'It sounds as if he's as much a casualty of the war as those of you who fought in it.'

'You're quite right. So many men have returned damaged, mentally and physically, and it's their families who are bearing the burden as their loved ones try to adjust.' Ben stood up and began to pace the room. 'I was too lost in my own nightmare to realize that there are hundreds—thousands—of men suffering the aftermath of the war like Bob's father. I would like to do something to help. But what?'

'It's an enormous problem, darling, and there is little one man can do on his own.'

'You're right, of course, but if I could give support to a few ...' Ben sat down again, deep in

52

thought for a while, and then he rang the bell. When the butler arrived, he said, 'Ask Jim to come and see me, Green.'

'At once, sir.'

Jim arrived within ten minutes, flustered, but with a grin on his face.

'How are the riding lessons going?' Ben asked, immediately guessing what was causing his groom so much amusement.

Jim shook his head, still smiling. 'You had to see it to believe it, sir. Midnight had him off twice and then galloped around the field kicking his legs in delight. Bob dusted himself down, stalked over to the animal, and stood right in front of him with his hands on his hips. Then he said, "All right, you've had your fun, but now it's time to get something straight. As far as you are concerned I'm the boss! I know I'm inexperienced, but you're going to have to let me stay on you long enough to learn how to ride. Is that clear?"'

'And what did Midnight say?' Ben kept a straight face with difficulty. He could just imagine the scene as the large animal and tall boy faced each other.

'Well sir, you'll never believe it, but after that he behaved himself. That boy's got a way with animals.'

'So it seems. Do you know where his home in London is?'

'Not exactly. I did ask him once but all he said was that he lived near the docks. He obviously didn't want to talk about it, so I dropped the subject.'

'Has he ever mentioned his family?'

Jim shook his head. 'He doesn't talk about himself. I got the impression that he doesn't want

53

anything to do with his past. But he's a good, honest boy, sir, I'm sure of that, or I wouldn't have recommended him to you.'

Ben nodded. 'Thank you, Jim. Keep up with the lessons.'

'Yes, sir.'

When the head groom had left, Emma said, 'If you're thinking of tracking down the boy's father, then you'll have an almost impossible task. The London docks cover a large area.'

'And it's densely populated. But his father was in the Army, and I might be able to trace him that way. I think I'll pay a visit to General Hampton. He might be able to help.'

'And what do you intend to do if you manage to find him?'

'That depends on what I find.'

Emma looked concerned. 'Robert Hunter won't thank you for interfering in his life, Ben.'

'Then we'll have to keep this to ourselves. Excuse me while I go and change for lunch, my dear.'

After Ben had left the room, Lilly came rushing in. 'We had a lovely ride today, Mummy. Daddy's happy again, isn't he?'

'Yes, sweetheart.' Emma smoothed her daughter's hair into place. It never would stay where it should. 'He's going to be all right now.'

'Is that because he isn't drinking now?'

'Yes, and now your daddy will be able to go riding with you often.'

'Oh, goody! I'll go and see how Bob's getting on with his riding lessons.' Giving a giggle she tore out of the room.

Emma laid her head back and sighed with relief. It had been a worrying time, but it looked as if

54

her husband had come through his troubles. The trauma was still there under the surface, but at last he was coming to terms with it, and was in control again. She could relax and await the birth of their child.

Eight

Everything seemed so bright and clear. Alfred Hunter took a deep breath and savoured the smells, noise and general bustle of the docks. Such ordinary, everyday sounds were like the sweetest music to him. He had been living in a fog, trying not to remember the terrible things he'd seen and done during the war, but no amount of drink had been able to chase the images away. They were still there, and he now knew that it was something he would have to learn to live with. His friend Steve was managing to do that, and he'd had his ship blown out from under him at Jutland. It must have been terrible to see his shipmates dying in the sea.

But that was all over now, and he had to pull his life together. He owed it to Helen, who had understood and sacrificed what little strength she had left to support him in his misery. It had taken his son to bring him to his senses. How he wished Bob were here to see the change in him . . .

'Hello, Alf.' The man in charge of the hiring nodded as Alf reached the front of the queue of men looking for work at the docks. 'Good to see you. But I can't give you your old job as charge hand back, I'm afraid.'

'I'll do anything, Fred. I've still got plenty of muscle, and I'm not fussy.'

'Right.' Fred consulted his papers. 'You can join Harry Jones' team. They're about to unload that ship just docking. The job is permanent.'

'Thanks.' Alf took off, elated. There were loads of men looking for work and he had only expected temporary employment, but it was good to know he wouldn't have to queue every day to see what was going.

As he approached the group of men waiting to start on the ship as soon as she was docked, one turned round and smiled with pleasure.

'Alf!' The man rushed towards him. 'It's good to see you. I tried to find you after they patched me up, but it was bloody chaos out there, and I didn't know your surname.'

They clasped hands. 'Pete! I didn't know if you had survived. It's wonderful to see you looking so fit.'

'Thanks to you!' Pete led Alf over to the other men. 'Hey, meet the man who saved my life in France. I was injured and he came out of the trenches, picked me up and carried me back. Damn bullets whizzing all around us, but he just kept running with me on his shoulders. That was what I would call courage.'

As the men gathered around, Alf gave an embarrassed smile. 'More like stupidity.'

They all laughed, and Alf was immediately accepted as one of the crew. It was a wonderful feeling. These men were hailing him as a hero for saving Pete, but he knew that what his son had done for him was real courage. When the boy had walked away from him, it had given him the jolt he'd needed. But he was still only a kid, and he was desperately sad that his drinking had driven him away from everything and everyone he knew. Some day he hoped to show him that his sacrifice had not been in vain.

The hard physical labour through the day helped him to control the urge to drink, and he did the work of two men, never stopping. By the end of the day he was so tired that the chances of sleeping that night were good.

'I owe you a drink, Alf,' Pete said as he came over to him. 'The Red Lion will be open now.'

Alf was so tempted to accept, but he knew that if he did he would soon be back to his old ways. He had found out the hard way that he wasn't the kind of man who could have a couple of drinks and leave it at that. He decided to be honest. 'Thanks, but I can't. I've been drinking ever since I arrived back, and have only just managed to sober up. If I have only one drink I'll be back to it again, and I'm not going to put myself through that agony again.'

'That bad, was it?'

Alf nodded. 'I started drinking to stop the nightmares even before I got back, but it got out of control. I don't dare go near a pub again.'

Pete nodded, understanding. 'How about us going across the road to the cafe? They serve a hearty pie and mash. The tea's good and strong as well.'

'Just what I need. I'm starving.'

After a filling meal, Alf made his way home, crossing the road every time he had to pass a pub. He was scared even to get a smell of beer. As he crossed from one side of the street to the other he couldn't help a wry smile. He had never realized there were so many pubs in this area. It had felt good sitting in the cafe talking to Pete. They hadn't mentioned the war, of course, and he'd enjoyed relaxing over a meal.

'Mr Hunter!' Ruth was running toward him, all smiles. 'There's someone waiting in our house to see you. A real toff, he is, but he's got good news.'

'What's he want with me?' he asked, looking down at her animated face.

'You'll see.'

The Coopers had put the man in the front room, and the children were entertaining him. As soon as Alf saw his bearing he knew he was an officer. 'You wanted to see me, sir?'

'I wasn't sure if I had the right Hunter, but after talking with your friends, it seems that I have found you at last. My name is Russell—'

'Rank, sir?' Alf asked. He wanted to make sure he addressed this man in the right way.

'Captain.'

Alf nodded. 'What can I do for you, Captain Russell?'

'I have news of your son, Robert.'

'Sit down.' Daisy came into the room and ushered the children out. 'I'll make you a pot of tea.'

When they were settled, the captain began to tell him about his first meeting with Bob, and when he'd finished, Alf was nodding his head, pride showing in his eyes. 'That's my boy! Thank God he's all right! I thank you, Captain, for bringing me this good news.' He hesitated. 'I don't suppose he would see me?'

'He doesn't know I'm here, Mr Hunter, and he's still carrying a lot of hurt around with him. He's settling in well, though, so perhaps in time . . .'

'Of course.' Alf couldn't hide his disappointment; he was desperate to make things right between them, but it would have to wait. 'At least I know he's doing all right.'

'You have a courageous son, Mr Hunter.' A smile crossed Captain Russell's face. 'He wanted the job on my estate very much, but he didn't hesitate to tell me that I shouldn't drink so much, even though he was sure I would throw him out.'

'But you didn't.'

'No, and I haven't touched a drop of alcohol since that first meeting with your son. To have this young boy telling me not to drink was a shock,' he told them. 'It was the expression of pain in his eyes that got to me.'

'You had more sense than me, sir. He felt he had done all he could for me and had to leave. That brought me to my senses. It isn't easy. Each day is a struggle, but I've got a job now, and I'm not going to throw that away by taking another drink.'

'Neither am I.'

There was a tap on the door and Ruth looked in. 'Mum said would you like some more tea, and a piece of cake? She's just taken it out of the oven.'

'That would be excellent. And perhaps you would all join us?' Captain Russell suggested.

Ruth smiled. 'Thank you, sir.'

'The Coopers are a good family,' the captain remarked.

'The best neighbours a man could have. I wouldn't have got through the sobering-up without them. Ruth and my boy have been friends since they were born. She adores him, and has always defended him when he's been in trouble.' Alf pursed his lips. 'And that was quite often. He's always been quick to anger, and outspoken, Captain, and some people don't like that, but he has a good heart.'

The door opened and the entire Cooper family came in, all carrying something for their tea.

John made straight for the captain again. 'Dad just told us Bob's with you. Will you tell him to come back because I've got a new storybook and it's ever so hard to read. Dad reads it to me, but he's not as good as Bob.'

Everyone laughed.

'Oh, thanks, John,' Steve said, a broad smile on his face.

'Bob's always wanted to be a teacher,' Ruth told the captain as she handed him a piece of freshly baked fruitcake.

'Really? I didn't know that. And what do you want to do?'

'Er ... well, I help with the children, but Bob thinks I ought to be a nurse.'

'And what do you think about that idea?'

She became thoughtful for a moment, and then her smile lit up the room. 'Well, Bob's usually right, but I'm not sure.'

'How old are you?'

'Fourteen, sir, but I'll soon be fifteen.'

'Ah, you are a little young for training at the moment, but you should seriously think about what you want to do.'

Ruth sighed. 'Mum said it's hard for us to get decent jobs because we live in the slums, and people think we're not worth employing. But we're not daft, sir. Bob said we are as good as anyone else, and quite capable of doing something with our lives, if we only get the chance.'

'He's quite right.' He found himself intrigued by this young girl.

'He's special, and very clever. What's he doing at your place?'

'Working with horses, and he's learning to ride.'

'Have you got a horse big enough for him?' young Eddie exclaimed.

'Just one.' Captain Russell told them about Midnight, and had them all roaring with laughter.

Alf slapped his knee with delight. 'Oh, this news has made me feel like a new man.'

They talked until the teapot was empty, and only crumbs of the cake left.

On his way out, Captain Russell stopped and asked Alf, 'Is there anything I can do for you?'

'You've already given me news of my son, and that's all I needed. Just look after him for me.'

'It will be my pleasure.' The captain turned to Steve Cooper. 'May I have a word with you outside?'

Steve nodded and followed him out.

'Do you agree with the idea of your daughter training to become a nurse when she's old enough?'

'She's ideally suited to the profession, but as she said, she's not sure that's what she wants to do.'

'Hmm.' The captain looked thoughtful. 'I'd like to help her. Would you object if I tried to find her a suitable position somewhere? But it would almost certainly mean she would have to leave home.'

'We only want what's best for our children, Captain Russell, and we'd be grateful if you could do something for her. She hasn't got much chance around here.'

He nodded. 'Leave it with me and I'll see what I

can do. No promises, though.'

'Understood. It was good of you to come and let us know Bob's all right. It will help his father.'

'I wish his son could see him now, but I fear that if he ever finds out I've been here he will never forgive me. If there is anything I can ever do for Mr Hunter will you let me know?'

'He's doing well now. But thanks. We keep an eye on him.'

'Of course.' The captain watched as a man walked by on crutches, and then he looked at Steve. 'There's still so much suffering from that bloody war. It makes a man feel helpless. What on earth can those of us who escaped relatively unscathed do?'

'If we can help just one man—one family—then we are doing something,' Steve said quietly.

'You're right, of course. It's been a pleasure meeting you and your family, Mr Cooper.' Captain Russell shook hands with him, and then walked up the road.

'What did he want to talk to you about?' Daisy asked as soon as her husband came in the scullery.

'He was asking about Ruth.' Steve smiled at his daughter. 'He said he'd try to get you a good position somewhere. It would be worth considering, Ruthie, because he's a wealthy man with good connections. He said he'd try—no promises though.'

Ruth smiled and nodded. 'I expect he'll forget all about it when he gets home, but I like him, he's a real gent.'

'I pegged him for an officer as soon as I saw him,' Alf said. 'Bob's done well to get in with him. It's taken a load off my mind, I can tell you.'

They all agreed with that, and the kettle went on again to make a celebratory cup of tea.

Nine

'Are you and Midnight friends yet?'

Bob glanced round, and then winked at Lilly who was standing next to her father. 'We tolerate each other.'

'Good enough. Saddle him up and come with us this morning.'

After standing the broom against the stable wall and dusting off his hands, Bob gave a soft whistle. Midnight answered and stamped his feet impatiently. 'He gets excited when he thinks he might have a chance to throw me off.'

Captain Russell's laugh was infectious. 'Better not keep him waiting then. Sounds as if he's about to break down the door.'

'Sir.' Bob strode over to the stall and disappeared inside.

'Does he need any help?' the captain asked Jim.

'No, they'll fight and struggle with each other, but Bob usually wins.'

'Usually?' he asked as a commotion broke out in the stall. 'I'd put my money on Midnight.'

Jim grinned and nodded. 'I think that animal actually likes him, but can't resist trying to make things difficult for him. No wonder we got that animal at a reasonable price; no one else wanted him.'

'Pack it up!' Bob's voice rose above the racket. 'We're going for a ride whether you like it or not.

63

It's no good you complaining.'

Then there was another sound, and Lilly tipped her head to one side, listening. 'What's he doing?' she asked.

'He's singing to Midnight,' Jim told her. 'The daft animal loves it.'

The commotion stopped, and Bob soon appeared leading the horse towards them.

'Good heavens!' The captain was smiling with amusement. 'That's some trick. I've never seen Midnight look that docile.'

'Oh, he'll revert back as soon as I try to ride him.' Bob rubbed the horse's nose. 'Won't you? You crafty beast.'

Midnight lowered his head and gave Bob a hefty shove.

'Better start singing again,' Jim laughed. 'I think he only plays up so you will serenade him.'

The other two horses were waiting in the yard, and the girl tugged at Bob's hand. 'Sing to my pony. She'd like it too.'

'I'd better not while Midnight is here. He might get jealous.'

Lilly pulled a face as she studied the large animal. 'That wouldn't be good.'

'It certainly wouldn't.' He lifted the little girl into the saddle, and then, after a bit of a tussle, managed to get astride Midnight.

As soon as Bob had gained some kind of control over the horse, they set off at a gentle canter. This was the first time Bob had seen the extent of the estate, and couldn't believe that one family could own so much land. There were fields with cows and sheep grazing, pigs, chickens, ducks, and more fields with all manner of crops growing. And that wasn't all—there were orchards, strawberry fields and rows of soft fruits too. 'This is a glorious place,' he said in awe, when they stopped for a moment.

'It's been in my family for generations,' the captain told him. 'And I love every acre of it.'

Bob nodded. 'You are blessed, Captain Russell.'

'I agree, but for a while after I came home I forgot that.' He turned and smiled at Bob. 'But then came along some cheeky sod and reminded me how lucky I was.'

*   *   *

Over the next couple of weeks this early morning ride around the estate became a regular thing, and Bob loved every moment of it. Then one morning, instead of the captain and his daughter arriving at the stables, the butler appeared, looking unusually flustered.

'Bob, the master wants you at the house immediately.' And then Green turned and hurried back.

In a couple of long strides Bob caught him up. 'Is anything wrong?'

'The mistress has gone into labour. Lillian's nanny is busy with Mrs Russell and her tutor is not here today. You know how inquisitive she is, and they don't want her getting in the way.'

The captain met him at the door. 'Keep Lilly busy with her lessons today, will you? She's already in the schoolroom at the top of the stairs—second door on the right. Show him, Green.'

The room was bright, with books lining one wall and more shelves piled with enough paper and pencils for a whole class of pupils. A magnificent

65

globe of the world was next to a single desk, and the girl sitting there was spinning it with one finger.

When Lilly saw him she smiled. 'Daddy said you would be my teacher today because everyone else is busy. I'm having a baby brother.'

'It might be a sister,' Bob said as he walked over to where a blackboard was standing on an easel.

'No.' She shook her head. 'I don't want a sister, and nanny said Daddy needs a son, so it's got to be a boy.'

'We shall have to wait and see. Now, show me what you have been working on.' He wasn't sure how this would go, but he'd do his best to find something to interest Lilly. He didn't think it would be too difficult for she had a lively mind.

She held out an exercise book, looking at him expectantly. 'I like writing, but I'm not very good at sums. I can draw and I love learning about all the old Kings and Queens.'

'You like history?'

She nodded, slipped off her seat and went over to the bookshelf. 'I've got some picture books. Would you like to see them?'

'Yes, bring them over and we'll spend the first hour on history.' This was Bob's favourite subject and would be a good way to start.

The morning flew by. Not only was Lilly a bright child, but she continually bombarded him with questions. Her reading was good for one so young, and he realized she must have an excellent tutor. Although he had never met him, Bob hoped one day to have a talk with him. It was a challenge keeping a lively child's mind off what was happening, but he felt he was doing a reasonably good job. Perhaps he should see if he could become a teacher after all. He knew he was reaching for the impossible because he had only received an elementary education at school, but it didn't hurt to have something to reach for. One teacher had encouraged him by taking the trouble to give him homework on subjects not covered in class. Not many teachers working in the slum areas bothered very much with the children, and he would always be grateful to that man. School would have become boring for him otherwise, because he was always way ahead of the other children. The extra work kept his mind stimulated.

They took a break when lunch was brought up to them, and they were just about to resume lessons when the captain entered the schoolroom.

Lilly rushed up to her father. 'Is my brother here yet?'

'Yes, darling.' The captain swung his daughter up, smiling broadly. 'Your mother and the baby are resting now, but they are both well, and it is a boy.'

She grinned at Bob as her father put her down again. 'I told you, didn't I?'

'You did. Congratulations, sir.'

'Thank you, Bob, we are both delighted. Now, Lilly, have you been a good girl and studied your lessons?'

'Yes, Daddy. We've had a lovely time. Bob knows ever such a lot of things. He's the best teacher I've ever had—just like you said he would be.'

Bob frowned. He hadn't questioned why he had been called upon to teach Lilly, because someone had to keep the girl occupied and they had always got on well together, but now it did seem strange that a stable boy had been given the task. 'How did you know I could do this, sir?' he asked quietly.

'Your daddy told him,' Lilly burst out, gazing up at her father. 'Can I see Mummy and the baby now?'

The little girl's excited chatter faded into the background. 'Has he been here, sir?' Bob asked.

'No. I told him I didn't think it would be a good idea for you to meet yet.'

'You tracked him down?' Bob didn't want to believe that, but when he looked in the captain's eyes he saw the truth—and it hurt. He had liked and respected this man, but he had no right to interfere in this way. He should at least have told him what he'd wanted to do! Without a word, Bob walked out of the room, down the stairs, and out of the house. And he kept on walking.

*　　　　*　　　　*

'Green!' Ben shouted at the top of his voice, and the butler arrived out of breath. 'Look after Lillian for me.' Then he was running down the stairs, intent on catching Bob.

He was nearly at Mrs Trent's lodging house before he saw the boy, and called for him to stop.

Bob turned to face him, his expression thunderous. 'I only told you about my family so you would see the damage excessive drinking could do. You had no right to do this without telling me. I trusted you to keep what I'd told you to yourself, and you've broken that trust.'

'You asked, but if you remember, I never agreed. But trust—that's the important thing to you, is it?'

'Yes. I believed that when Dad came home he would take care of Mum. I'd done my best during

68

the war, but I was only a kid, and he was big and strong. The man I remembered never came back.'

'We were all changed,' Ben told him quietly.

'I soon realized that, Captain, but I couldn't trust him to stay sober long enough to get a job so we could pay the rent. When Mum died I felt he had betrayed both of us.'

'It must have been devastating for a young boy, but I'm not going to apologize. I met some very kind people who care deeply for you. They had a right to know you are safe.'

'And you thought you had the right to tell them?'

'Someone had to. You haven't even sent a note to the Coopers to let them know you are safe. You're father is sober and working, but he's had a rough time, and has been worried about you. Don't you care?'

'I'm glad he's managed to pull himself together, but as far as I'm concerned, it's too late. Goodbye, Captain Russell. Take good care of your lovely family.'

'Where the hell do you think you are going?'

'I really don't know.' Bob turned and walked towards the house where Mrs Trent was standing at the door.

The captain tried one last plea. 'Lilly will miss you. She will be upset.'

Bob's long stride faltered for a moment, then lengthened again. He didn't look back.

'Dammit, Bob, you don't have to do this!' But his plea went unanswered as he followed him into the house.

'All right,' he called to the boy, taking the stairs three at a time. 'I should have asked your permission before going to see your father, but you helped me and I wanted to do something for your family in return.'

A door closed upstairs with a thud and Ben sighed. 'That daughter of mine has big ears, Mrs Trent, and she remembers everything we say. What's he going to do? Go back to digging ditches?'

'What's happened, Captain Russell?'

He told her and she nodded her understanding. 'That boy is in a mess. He clearly loved his mother very much, and watching her suffer has damaged him.'

Ben's expression was grim. 'I don't want him to go, but I can't stop him.'

'No, you can't, Captain. He's got to work this out for himself.'

Bob came down the stairs with his bundle of clothes over his shoulder, and the captain stepped up to him. 'I know you feel you can't stay now, but if you ever want to come back there will always be a place here for you. And for God's sake come to me if you are ever in any trouble or need a helping hand.'

'And your room will be waiting for you,' Mrs Trent told him.

He kissed her lightly on the cheek, and then walked out of the door and up the road towards the station.

Ten

There was a nip in the air and Bob shoved his hands in his pockets as he walked beside the Thames. For the last couple of weeks he had been moving

70

restlessly from place to place doing a variety of jobs ranging from errand boy to farm labourer, and anything else he could get. On the whole he had done quite well, and always had enough for a proper bed at night. He had been determined that there would be no more sleeping in barns, but the summer was almost over and he didn't fancy wandering around the country during the winter months. It was time to find something more permanent for a while.

He stopped to watch some swans gliding along and a smile touched his lips. Richmond upon Thames seemed a nice place, so perhaps he could find something here. He badly needed time to sort out his confused thoughts. He had been happy with the Russells ... No, not happy, he hadn't been happy since his mum died, but he'd been content— yes that was it. Why had Captain Russell interfered and brought all the pain to the surface again? He'd worked hard, never causing any trouble, and that should have been enough for him.

The light was fading and this stirred him into action. He must find somewhere to sleep tonight. At least this time he had carefully saved money in his pocket, but after seeing the large houses along the river he decided to walk up the hill and find something more modest. At the top the view was lovely and he told himself he must come here again when there was enough light to see clearly. There was a road to his left with a few small shops, so he headed for those. The butcher's shop was preparing to close.

'Could you tell me if there is anywhere around here I could find lodgings for the night?' he asked the man.

'You could try Mrs Summers; she takes in lodgers. You want Forest Road, number twenty-eight. It's the first turning on the left.'

'Thanks. And I'll have one of your pies, please.'

'Finest steak and kidney pies you can get,' the butcher told him proudly. 'And all ready to eat.'

Bob paid him and munched as he looked for the house. He soon found it and was lucky: she had a spare room, and had even given him sandwiches and tea when he'd arrived.

The lady of the house—Pat, he'd been told to call her—served a hearty breakfast, and after eating everything put in front of him, he asked, 'Is there any chance of work in this area? I'm not fussy what I do.'

Pat studied him for a moment, then said, 'Well, you're a strong boy and they could probably do with you at Grove House. You can walk there from here.'

She gave him instructions and he set off, hopeful of finding something to do. It was another lovely day and Bob whistled as he walked along. He quite liked this place and really hoped he could stay for a while.

He soon found the large house, but when he stepped inside, he stopped dead, frowning as he caught sight of a nurse pushing someone in a wheelchair. Was this a hospital?

'Can I help you?'

The quiet voice behind him made him spin around to face the woman who had spoken. She had the most serene expression on her face, and for some reason it tugged at his heart. 'I was told there might be a job going here.'

'We could certainly use someone with your

build and strength, but it will depend upon your temperament. What is your name?'

'Robert Hunter.' What on earth did she mean by that?

'I'm Sister Headley. Come into my office, Robert, and we'll have a talk.'

'Everyone calls me Bob, Sister.' He waited for her to sit before doing so himself, then he remained silent, not asking any questions. For some odd reason he was relaxed and almost at peace, and he felt that somehow this woman's inner tranquillity was touching him. How strange.

'This is a special place, Bob,' she began. 'We care for men who were badly injured in the war, and our aim is to help them to become as independent as possible. You could be a big help to us, but it is not a job everyone can do.'

Bob was shocked, and knew he should walk out of here, but somehow he couldn't.

'We would be happy to employ you for a trial period of two weeks, but if at any time you want to leave, you can do so. Would you like me to show you around the house?'

'Please.' He stood up and allowed her to walk out of the room first, then he followed, wondering what on earth he was still doing here.

By the end of the tour Bob was numb. The men they were caring for here were very seriously injured, and when he considered the kind of life they had ahead of them he wanted to cry. But he didn't. He talked and smiled and even gave a hand with lifting when it was needed.

Back in the office, Sister said, 'I believe you would fit in here, Bob, and we would be pleased to have you.'

73

He took a deep breath. He could do a few days, and could walk away if he wanted to. 'I'll give it a try, Sister, but I'm not making any promises.'

'That is understood. All I ask is that you come to me at once if you have any problems coping.'

Bob nodded. 'I'll do my best.'

'I know you will.' She smiled and shook his hand. 'We'll see you tomorrow morning at nine o'clock then?'

'I'll be here.' As Bob walked out of the door he wondered if he'd lost his mind.

Eleven

It had been several weeks since that nice captain had visited them with the wonderful news that Bob was safe. Ruth was saving every penny she could earn doing odd jobs for people. She never took money from the old or sick, but anything else she was given was put in a purse, and when she had enough she would visit Bob. It would be so good to see him again, and she couldn't wait to find out what he looked like riding a horse. She would tease him about that. She missed him so much . . .

'Ruth!' her dad called up the stairs. 'Come here, please.'

Hurrying to the scullery she saw him with a letter in his hand. That was exciting because they didn't get many letters. 'What's up?' she asked, sitting down and waiting expectantly.

'We've had a letter from Captain Russell,' Daisy said. 'You explain, Steve.'

'The captain and his wife have had another

baby—a boy this time.'

'That's nice for them.' Ruth smiled, never taking her eyes off the letter. 'Is Bob all right?'

'I expect so. He doesn't mention him.' Steve turned to face his daughter. 'Before I tell you what he's said in his letter, I want you to know that we have discussed this, and both agree that you must be free to decide for yourself.'

Now Ruth was getting rather worried as she looked from one to the other. 'Decide what?'

'They now have two children and the captain's mother is coming to stay with them because she is suffering from rheumatism. They need someone to help with the lady and the children. The captain is offering you the job.'

Ruth gasped. She knew her dad had talked about this with the captain, but she had never expected anything to come of it. People often made promises they had no intention of keeping, and she hadn't been able to see why this rich man should bother with them. He had done them the kindness of bringing news about Bob, and they certainly didn't expect anything more from him.

'You will live in the house and have your own room.' When his daughter didn't answer, Steve took hold of her hand. 'You've been a good girl looking after your mum and the kids while I was away, but you're old enough to go out to work now, Ruth, and this is a good chance for you to get away from here.'

'But . . . but . . .' She gave her mother a worried look. 'How will you manage without me?'

'You mustn't worry about us, Ruthie. Now your Dad's home and working regular, we'll be fine,' Daisy told her. 'We only want what's best for you.'

75

'Captain Russell said you could go there and see if you like it, and if at any time you're not happy, you can return home at once.'

'Oh.' Ruth chewed her bottom lip as she thought about this. It was comforting to know she needn't stay if she didn't like it there. And it would mean she'd see Bob again, and have two children and an elderly woman to look after. She'd like that, and it would be exciting to live in a fine house. But still . . .

'Put the kettle on, Daisy,' Steve told his wife. 'Let's have a nice cup of tea while our daughter considers her future. You know, the captain must have told Bob he'd been here or he wouldn't be offering Ruth a job at the house.'

'He must have,' his wife agreed.

After reading the letter through twice, Ruth put it down and drew in a deep breath. 'I would be silly not to give it a try, and Bob will be there to help me settle in. I'll be sad to leave you, but I'll go.'

'Good girl!' Steve sat back, a satisfied expression on his face. 'Chances like this don't come along often in life, and you're right to go and see what the job is like. I'll write straight away and let him know you're coming in a week's time.'

*　　　*　　　*

The day of Ruth's departure came all too soon, and there were tears as she boarded the train.

'There will be someone at Maidstone to meet you,' Steve assured her, 'so you'll be all right.'

The train started with a jolt, making her sit down suddenly, but she peered out of the window until her family had disappeared in the distance.

76

Although she was full of fears and doubts, the journey was exciting, and she watched with fascination as London gave way to beautiful open countryside.

When she arrived at her destination, she jumped from the train, eagerly looking for the familiar tall figure of her friend Bob.

'Miss Cooper?'

Ruth spun round to face the young boy who had spoken. 'Yes.'

'Oh, good.' He smiled shyly and politely took her bag from her. 'The captain sent me to collect you. I've got a horse and buggy outside. My name's Tim, Miss Cooper.'

She walked beside him, disappointed it wasn't Bob, but relieved someone was here for her. 'Call me Ruth, please.'

My goodness, Ruth thought as she climbed into the buggy. What an adventure this was turning out to be.

They trotted along and she listened to Tim talking about the estate and the horses he obviously loved. But when they swept through large iron gates and the house came into view, she was stunned. It was a palace!

'Nice, isn't it?'

'It's the most beautiful place I've ever seen— apart from Buckingham Palace, of course. Am I really going to live there?'

'You're here to help the family so you'll have a room in the main house. The captain's strict, but fair, and the mistress is a quiet lady, but kind. You'll like it, I'm sure.'

Tim went to the rear of the house and stopped. He helped Ruth down and grabbed her bag before she could pick it up herself. Then he opened the door. 'Mrs Perkins!'

'I'm coming, Tim. You don't have to shout.' A stout woman came towards them, looking quite severe, until she smiled at Ruth, then her expression softened. 'Welcome, young lady, the mistress will be pleased to see you. She has her hands full with the new baby, and her mother-in-law has just moved in as well. Come with me and I'll show you to your room, and then you can meet the family.'

Before following the housekeeper, Ruth whispered to Tim, 'Would you tell Bob Hunter that I've arrived, please.'

'Bob?' Tim frowned. 'He don't work here now.'

There wasn't time to ask questions, but Ruth couldn't believe that. Tim was obviously mistaken. Nevertheless, she felt her heart sink. Suppose it was true? The kind of mood Bob had been in when he'd left home meant he was liable to do anything; even something as daft as leaving this lovely place. But one of the reasons she had taken this job was because they would be together again. They were friends, and always had been.

So lost in confusion, Ruth had to trot to catch up with the housekeeper. She was surprisingly agile for a large woman, and she climbed the stairs to the top of the house without even getting out of breath.

Mrs Perkins opened a door. 'This is your room, Ruth, and the bathroom is at the end of the landing. Leave your bag and I'll take you to meet the mistress, and then we can see about getting you something to eat.' She smiled. 'I expect you're hungry after your journey.'

'Thank you, Mrs Perkins.' Not even taking time

to look around, Ruth tossed her bag beside the bed and went down the long winding stairs again.

Mrs Perkins knocked on a door leading from the impressive entrance hall, and she ushered Ruth inside. 'Miss Cooper has arrived, madam.'

'Oh, splendid. Welcome, my dear, did you have a good journey?'

'Yes, thank you, madam. This is the first time I've been out of London, and it was very interesting. I've never seen so much green grass before. The London parks are beautiful, of course, but nothing like this. There's so much space . . .'

The captain smiled kindly. 'We will have pleasure showing you the estate. Lillian, our daughter, will enjoy taking you to see everything.'

Ruth smiled back, feeling more at ease. She had liked the captain when she'd met him at her home, and his wife was softly spoken and seemed quite nice. Casting a quick glance at the other occupants of the comfortable room, she saw only one, an elderly lady who was studying her intently. Her nerves came flooding back.

'Come here, child, and let me have a proper look at you. My eyes are not what they used to be.'

The woman sitting in a large armchair beckoned her over, and Ruth didn't care for the tone of the command. She summed her up immediately. This was a person who expected to be obeyed without question. All nervousness vanished as she stepped forward. 'I am not a child, madam. I am fifteen.'

'Really, that old?' Her expression didn't change, but her mouth twitched at the corners. 'I apologize for my mistake. How do you like to be addressed?'

'My name is Ruth, if you please, madam.'

'Very well, Ruth, my son has told me you will be helping with the children.'

She nodded. 'And I will be pleased to help you as well, madam. I believe that is also to be a part of my job.'

'And what experience have you had?'

'I've looked after my brothers and sister since they were born, and I did what I could for the elderly and sick in our street.'

There was a smothered laugh, and the captain cleared his throat. 'I believe Ruth has answered all your questions, Mother.'

At that moment the door burst open and a little girl rushed in, followed by a nurse carrying the baby.

'This is our daughter, Lillian, but nearly everyone calls her Lilly, and the baby is our son, Robert Benjamin.'

As soon as she heard the name, Ruth smiled with pleasure and gazed at the child. 'He's beautiful.'

'He cries a lot!'

'Babies do that, Lilly. It's their way of letting us know they need something,' she said, turning her attention to the girl.

'Hmm. Can you ride?'

'Ride what?'

'A horse!' Lilly turned to her father. 'I don't suppose she can. Jim can teach her though, can't he, Daddy?'

'We'll see about that later. But first we must let Ruth settle in. She must be tired and hungry after her journey. Why don't you show her to the kitchen where Cook has a meal waiting for her? And then you can help her unpack.'

'Can I show Ruth the horses, after that?' Lilly's

face shone with excitement.

'Only if she isn't too tired.'

Before Lilly could tow her out of the room, Ruth faced the captain. She just had to know. 'Is it true that Bob isn't here any more, sir?'

'Yes, I'm sorry to say it is.'

Her disappointment was crushing and she couldn't hide her feelings. 'But why did he leave?'

'He found out I had visited his father, and he was very angry. I tried to stop him, but he wouldn't listen.'

'Oh, the fool!' For the first time in her life Ruth was furious with him. 'He's got to learn not to run every time something happens he doesn't like. Do you know where he's gone?'

'No, I'm sorry, Ruth. I don't think even he knew where he was going. He just walked away.'

'It was my fault.' Lilly looked up at her with an imploring look in her eyes, and slipped her hand in Ruth's. 'I didn't know it was a secret. You won't go away as well, will you?'

'No, of course I won't.' She squeezed the girl's hand and managed a smile. 'It was very kind of your daddy to come and see us, and Bob should have known that. But he's confused, angry and lost. He needs to find himself.'

Lilly looked puzzled. 'But he knows where he is.'

'No he doesn't, darling. On the outside he's big and tough, but inside he's all at sea, as my dad says.'

'I liked him,' Lilly sighed. 'And I cried when I knew he'd gone away, and it was my fault.'

'You mustn't blame yourself. Bob's good and kind, but he needs to pull himself together.'

Lilly giggled. 'You do say some funny things.'

'I'm full of odd sayings.' Ruth rubbed her tummy.

81

'Now, show me where the food is. I'm starving.'

'Cook's made you a huge apple pie.' Lilly tugged her towards the door, her upset forgotten.

Twelve

'Surprising confidence for one so young.'

'I agree, Mother, but they have to grow up quickly where Ruth comes from, or they don't survive,' Ben said. 'She's also very perceptive, don't you think?'

His mother gave a quick laugh. 'She summed me up very quickly. This house must seem like a palace to her, but she wasn't intimidated by the grandeur. She spoke her mind, and I liked that. She also handled Lillian very well. I think she will do very nicely, Benjamin.'

'What do you think, my dear?' he asked his wife.

'She appears to be good with children and the elderly . . .'

That remark caused laughter from her husband and mother-in-law.

'I was impressed, and she will be a great asset, I'm sure. But will she stay, Ben? She was expecting to find Bob here, and is obviously very disappointed.'

'That's something only time will tell. If she misses her family too much, she won't stay long.'

'I think you are underestimating the girl, Benjamin,' his mother pointed out. 'Her friend, Bob, is trying to run from his problems, but she isn't a fool, and knows this is a good opportunity for her. She'll stick it out no matter how homesick she is.'

'You sound very sure, Mother.'

'I am.'

Ben shrugged. 'Remember that I saw her first in her own environment, surrounded by her family. She's a bright child and I was impressed when I met her, but she appeared to be quite content helping her family. There is a lack of ambition and drive to improve her lot in life, but living like they do could make them apathetic, drifting along from day to day.'

Emma nodded. 'That could be true. She's certainly bright, and Bob has a fine brain. It's a tragedy that they are being deprived of reaching their full potential just because of their background.'

'I know, my dear, and that's why I've brought her here, in the hope that it will open her eyes to other possibilities. And the shame of it all is that their fathers fought in the war. They were promised a land fit for heroes, and all they've got for their suffering is the same daily struggle to exist. These men have returned to poverty, with mental scars, and no one seems to care!' Ben's expression was grim.

*   *   *

'A piece of apple pie, Ruth?' The cook removed her empty dinner plate, smiling in approval.

'I'm not sure I can manage another mouthful, Mrs Barker. That was absolutely delicious.'

'You must have the pie!' Lilly was horrified. 'The apples come from our orchards and Cook's famous for her apple pies.'

'Oh well, just a small piece, please.'

Ruth picked up her spoon and tasted the pie. 'Oh my, that's the best pie I've ever tasted. How do you get your pastry so crumbly, Mrs Barker?'

'That's my secret.' She winked at the girls and walked away to let them finish eating.

As soon as the plates were empty, Lilly was on her feet, tugging impatiently at Ruth's hand. 'Come on, I'll show you the horses now, and Jim can pick out one for you to ride.'

A young man saw them coming and walked over to them. 'You must be Ruth. Welcome to the Russell Estate. I'm Jim.'

Lilly was bouncing with excitement. 'Ruth can't ride, so we've got to teach her. What horse can she have?'

Ruth gazed with apprehension at the sleek animals in the paddock. 'Not one of those, I hope!'

'No, we'll find you a nice gentle one.' Jim laughed at her expression. 'Come to the stables and see what you think of Cherry.'

When they entered the stable block, Jim gave Ruth a carrot, and then they approached a horse looking over the stall. 'This is her. Say hello to Ruth, Cherry. She's brought you a treat.'

Ruth was eyed with interest, and although she was hesitant about approaching the animal, she just had to admire her. She was a deep copper colour, and had a gentle look in her eyes, but she held back. She had never been this close to a horse before.

'She won't hurt you.' Jim guided her forward. 'Hold out your hand and she'll take the carrot from you.'

Taking a deep breath, Ruth held out the carrot, trying to keep her hand steady. Cherry gave a snort of pleasure and the carrot was gone, making Ruth laugh with relief. 'I hardly felt her take it.'

'You'll soon be friends. We'll start the lessons when you're settled in.'

'Tomorrow,' Lilly announced. 'Can we see Midnight now, Jim? Where is he?'

'In the far paddock, but you are not to go near him. He isn't in a very good mood since Bob left.'

Ruth was led to a paddock with only one horse cropping at the lush grass. When they approached the fence he lifted his head, studied them for a moment, and then continued eating.

'He's beautiful.' Ruth had never seen such a fine animal, and she could just imagine Bob riding him. They must have made a handsome pair. That thought made her so sad for a moment, but then her anger surfaced. How could he have walked away from here? The Russells had obviously liked him. For an intelligent boy he was being very stupid!

As they walked back to the house, Ruth knew she would have the unpleasant task of writing to her dad to let him know Bob was no longer here. He would know the best way to tell Mr Hunter. It was going to be a bitter blow to him, and as much as she loved Bob, it was hard to forgive him for causing them all this worry.

*   *   *

That night in her comfortable room, the letter was written, and although this was the most beautiful place she had ever seen, she felt terribly sad. There was no escaping the fact that she was missing everyone already. If Bob had been here it would

85

have been easier. Now she felt so alone, and a little frightened. She had never had a room to herself, and everything was so strange, so she buried her head in the pillow and had a little weep.

* * *

'What is it?' Daisy frowned when she heard her husband cursing under his breath as he read the recently delivered letter. 'Is Ruth all right?'

'She's all right, but Bob's disappeared again, and Ruth is asking me to break the news to Alf.'

'But I thought he was happy with the Russells. Does Ruth say why he left?'

'It seems he found out that the captain had been here and he didn't like it. I credited the lad with more sense than that.' Steve handed the letter to Daisy. 'Ruth must have been terribly disappointed when she found out he wasn't there. I'm sure that one of the reasons she agreed to take the job was because she thought Bob was there. You know they've never been apart before and she must miss him very much.'

'Hmm.' Daisy read the letter, then put it back in the envelope. 'From the tone of her letter it's obvious that she's angry at him, and I've never heard her say a word against him before. Oh, darling, Alf's going to take this hard. He's been so much happier since the captain's visit.'

'I know, but he must be told.' Steve stood up. 'Better get it over with.'

Alf was sitting at the table in the scullery writing in a notebook when Steve arrived. He closed the book and smiled. 'Hello Steve.'

'You look busy. Are you writing your memoirs?'

86

he joked, trying to delay telling his friend the unpleasant news.

'Something like that.' Alf fingered the book, looking slightly embarrassed. 'From the moment I joined the army I kept a sort of diary. It helped me to keep things straight in my head when I was in the trenches, and I've just kept it up. Except for the times when I was too drunk to even think,' he admitted.

'Have you still got all of the diaries?' Steve was immediately interested, and when Alf nodded, he asked, 'Would you let me see them?'

'Some of it isn't pleasant. Might stir up nasty memories for you.'

'I'd still like to read them.'

Still looking very doubtful, Alf took a deep breath, and then opened a large drawer in the table. It was crammed full of notebooks, odd pieces of paper and even old cigarette packets torn open. Every piece was covered in writing.

'My God!' Steve exclaimed as Alf began to lay them all out on the table.

'Bit of a mess, I'm afraid. I had to write on anything I could find, but it's all dated.'

Steve didn't speak, he was too busy trying to sort the pile of papers into some sort of order, and read at the same time.

Eventually he stopped what he was doing, and exclaimed, 'Bloody hell, Alf, you've got a record of exactly what it was like from the ordinary soldier's point of view. As far as I can see you've described the fear, pain, tragedy and even the lighter moments. Will you let me take this and put it in the right order?'

'What do you want to do that for?'

'The new Imperial War Museum is asking for things like this.'

'Oh, the place at the Crystal Palace?'

'Yes, and this is just the sort of thing they're looking for.'

Alf shrugged. 'Can't think why they would want my scribbling, but we could give it a try, if that's what you want to do.'

'Thanks, Alf.' Steve began to gather up the writings, knowing he couldn't delay any longer, so he pitched straight in. 'We had a letter from Ruth today, and I've got some bad news. Bob found out that the captain had been here, and he was angry about it. He's left the Russells, Alf, and they don't know where he is. I'm sorry.'

'You've got nothing to be sorry about, Steve. I'm the one who messed up that kid!' Alf shook his head, clearly upset. 'The damned fool! He's just like I was when I arrived home—not thinking straight. Well, I sorted myself out, and he's got to do the same.'

'He will, Alf.' Steve was relieved to see he wasn't going to fall apart at the news. 'Ruth's really angry with him, and when she sees him he'll get the sharp end of her tongue, no matter how big he is.'

Alf gave a wry smile. 'That should knock some sense into his thick skull. Your little girl's a gentle soul, until she's roused.'

'True,' Steve laughed. 'Daisy's made a huge steamed bacon roll for supper. Fancy helping us eat it?'

'Sounds smashing, and thanks, I'll be glad of a bit of company.'

Both men walked out, loaded with all the pieces of paper and notebooks.

Thirteen

It was two o'clock in the morning and Steve was still working on the writings. He couldn't leave it alone because he now knew that this was something special. Alf had written from the heart, and his descriptions were so graphic that Steve could have been there. Parts were heart-rending, others funny, but through it all the horrors of the trenches came to life.

'Aren't you coming to bed?' Daisy asked quietly.

Steve glanced at the clock and ran a hand through his tousled hair. 'Good heavens, is that the time?'

Sitting next to her husband, Daisy looked at the assortment of papers strewn across the table. 'This is going to take time to sort out, darling; you can't do it in one night.'

'I know. Alf's used any old piece of paper he could find, but at least they are all dated.' Steve sat back and rubbed his tired eyes. 'I want to get this done as quickly as possible. This is an extraordinary record. If only more men had thought to do this, then the true accounts of the war wouldn't be lost. The sheer scale of human sacrifice mustn't be forgotten, Daisy. Alf has not only set down his own feelings and experiences, but those of the men around him.'

She listened, her heart beating, for this was the first time Steve had talked about the war. This wasn't unusual because none of the men ever mentioned it. She knew her husband's experiences were very different in the Navy, but he was talking, and she took that as a good sign. She wasn't sure it was a good idea to bottle everything up inside, and when she had mentioned this, Steve had only shaken his head and said that he didn't want to rake up all the memories again.

'If you like what Alf has done, why don't you write about your time in the Navy? The war wasn't only fought in the trenches. The sailors and airmen should have their stories told as well.'

'I know you're right.' Steve gave a tight smile. 'Come on; let's get some sleep. I'll leave all this in our bedroom so the kids can't get their hands on it. It's not the sort of thing they should read until they are much older.'

*   *   *

It took nearly a week of working every evening before Steve had the diaries in a condition fit to show someone at the Imperial War Museum. It had been a harrowing task because it meant he'd had to read everything, and he had chain-smoked all the time, but Daisy hadn't said anything, leaving him to cope with the work in his own way.

After fitting the last scraps of paper in place, Steve rested his head in his hands. 'Thank heaven's that's done!'

Daisy placed a cup of tea in front of him, and pointed to the pile her husband had discarded. 'What are those?'

'Alf's diaries since he returned home. They are too personal, but they must be kept safe. I hope that one day Bob will read all of this and understand just what his dad went through. Perhaps it will help him to forgive.'

90

'Let's hope so. I wonder where he is now?'

'To be honest, Daisy, after reading this, I don't care.' Steve stood up. 'The lad has chosen to run away from his problems. I call that desertion.'

'Oh, that's harsh, darling. After Alf joined the army, Bob took over the role of man of the house. Helen was ill and he cared for her, working two jobs so she had enough money without worrying where the next meal was coming from. He had convinced himself that it was only the war making her ill, and that everything would be all right when his dad came home. When it wasn't he couldn't handle it. He's only young, Steve.'

'A whole generation of young boys died in the war, and I'm in no mood to be charitable at the moment. Bob has the chance to grow up—many had that taken from them.' Steve grimaced. 'Sorry, Daisy.'

She stood on tiptoe and kissed his cheek. 'No need to apologize. I know you like Bob really, but reading about Alf's war has clouded your mind. You'll soon get over it.'

He laughed then. 'Of course I like the boy, but if he walked in here now I'd tan his hide.'

'And I'll help you.' Alf was standing inside the back door. 'The two of us together might be able to handle him.'

'Go on, the pair of you,' Daisy chided. 'If he appeared now you would both cry with relief and happiness.'

'Maybe after we'd given him a good hiding first,' Steve admitted. 'Let's hope he's stopped growing or we'll have to enlist Ruth's help as well!'

When both men laughed, Daisy was relieved. This last week had been tense, but now the job was done she could see the grim expression fading from Steve's face. And although Alf knew about Bob leaving the Russell estate, he was taking it well this time.

'We're off to the Crystal Palace, Daisy.' Steve kissed her on the cheek. 'Just wait till they get a look at this.'

'They'll tell us to put it on the bonfire where it belongs,' Alf snorted. 'I don't know why I'm going along with this daft scheme of Steve's. Who on earth is going to want to read my scribbling?'

A bus arrived as soon as they reached the stop at the end of the road, and they went upstairs so they could smoke.

Alf lit a cigarette and took a deep drag, blowing the smoke towards the roof of the bus. 'This is a waste of time. They're not going to be interested. I'm sure a lot of it doesn't even make sense.'

'Have you ever read these through yourself?'

Alf shook his head. 'I lived it; I don't want to read about it. I only wrote it all down to keep my sanity.'

'Well, you can take my word for it, the museum will want it.' Steve turned to face his friend. 'And it's very well written.'

After a while Steve stood up. 'This is our stop.'

Alf hesitated at the door of the museum, so Steve took hold of his friend's arm and pulled him inside. 'You're not going to make me go in on my own, are you? This is your work and they'll probably want to talk to you. We're going to do this together.'

There was a man sitting by a table, and Steve went straight over to him. 'I've got something the museum will be interested in.'

'Oh?' The man looked up expectantly. 'May I see it, please?'

Steve placed the writings in front of him and watched as he started to read.

After only a few minutes the man was on his feet and gathering the papers together. 'Please wait here.' Then he disappeared through another door.

'Told you,' Steve said smugly.

'He's just trying to find a polite way to get rid of us.'

'We'll see.'

It was nearly an hour before the door opened again and a man of around forty came towards them.

'Officer,' Alf muttered. 'I can spot them a mile off.'

'Who is Mr Hunter?'

'That's me, sir.' Alf stood up. 'And this is Mr Cooper. He took the trouble to put my writings into some sort of order.'

'My name's Stanton,' he smiled, shaking hands with them. 'I'm delighted to meet you both. Would you come into my office, please?'

When they were seated, Stanton wasted no time. 'I would like your permission to keep your diaries so I can read them properly. I'll take good care of them, Mr Hunter.'

Alf nodded. 'That's all right by me, sir.'

'No need to call me sir. I'm retired now.' He turned his attention to Steve. 'Were you in the Army, Mr Cooper?'

'No, the Navy.'

'Really?' Stanton leant forward. 'Do you have diaries as well?'

'Never thought about it, but after reading Alf's I

wish I had done the same.'

'Indeed. Would you consider writing one now? We'd be very interested.'

'Oh, I don't think so.' Steve grimaced. 'I've been trying to forget it.'

'I understand. Now, if you would come and see me next week, I'll let you know how we can use this material.'

*   *   *

He hadn't believed the Imperial War Museum would be interested in his account of war in the trenches, but when the time came to go and see them again, Alf had to admit that he was quite excited. If they thought his diaries were good enough to do something with, then that would give him great satisfaction. It would also help to restore his belief in himself, and that was something he badly needed.

Stanton met them as soon as they walked in. 'Come into my office. I have good news for you. Your memoirs have caused quite a stir, Mr Hunter.'

'Told you!' Steve murmured in Alf's ear.

On his desk was a neat manuscript, and he slid it across to Alf. 'What do you think of that?'

The two men studied the top few pages, and then looked at each other in amazement.

'Those are only proofs,' Stanton explained, 'and we'd like you to look through them carefully and let us know if you want to change anything.' He stood up. 'I'll leave you to it and have tea sent in for you.'

'Crikey!' Alf muttered when they were alone. 'What's going on, Steve?'

'Looks like they're going to make it into a book.'

'Never!'

Steve grinned. 'We'd better get on with the checking.'

For the next two hours they worked, totally absorbed in the task, and didn't notice when the tea arrived.

'I can't believe this is my writing,' Alf said when they had finished.

'It is, and all they've changed, as far as I can see, is the layout.' Steve sat back and took a deep breath. 'I knew it was good, mate, but put into print like this it's brilliant.'

'That's our opinion as well,' Stanton said, coming back into the office. 'Are there any changes you would like to make?'

Alf shook his head, hardly able to believe this was happening to him. 'No, it looks all right. What are you going to do with it?'

'A friend of mine, Charles Davis, is gathering together as many first-hand accounts of the war as he can, and he would like to put this into book form for us. It will be easier for anyone to read then. Only a few copies at first, and you will be given a couple, of course. Do we have your permission to go ahead with this?'

'Yes, of course, and thank you.'

'No, we must thank you for being courageous enough to bring this to us. There is just one more thing. We would like to keep the original for a while. We are working on a trench warfare display, and your records are just what we need. As I've said before—we will take good care of them for you.'

'That's all right.' Alf smiled. 'I'm glad you've found them of use.'

'This museum is important to us, and we are all

very excited to have received your material. As I've said, only a few copies will be printed at first, but Mr Davis has asked if you would consider writing a few more pages to explain your first few months after the war.'

'Ah . . . I've got something, but I'm not sure if it's any good. I was drunk most of the time,' Alf admitted.

'It's a bit disjointed and I didn't include that because I felt it was too personal,' Steve said. 'But we could soon sort it out, Alf, if that's what you want to do.'

Seeing Alf was doubtful, Stanton said, 'Let me explain. As a new publisher my friend would like the option to print copies for sale, should the demand arise some time in the future. That would be a fitting end to the story.' Stanton placed an official-looking document in front of Alf. 'Charles will, of course, pay you for the right.'

'How much?'

'Twenty-five pounds immediately, with the possibility of more later.'

Alf stubbed out his cigarette in the ashtray. 'Make it fifty and I'll do it.'

'Thirty.'

'Forty.'

Stanton nodded and smiled, altered the amount on the document and gave it back to Alf. 'Sign at the bottom of the page, Mr Hunter, and we have a deal.'

Alf read every word before putting his signature on it. 'Can't be too careful,' he told Steve.

Stanton took back the document and nodded in approval. 'You will be hearing from Mr Davis in due course, and please feel free to come here any time. The advice of both of you would be invaluable to us, and if you have any badges, medals, uniforms or anything you may have brought home with you as souvenirs, we would love to have them.'

'I'll sort through my kitbag,' Alf said. 'I haven't opened it since I got home. What about you, Steve?'

'I'll see what I can find.'

'Thank you.' Stanton stood up and shook hands with them, and then they left.

Once outside they grinned at each other, and Steve said, 'Well done, you handled that like an expert.'

'What a turn up.' Alf shook his head in disbelief. 'I was so sure no one would be interested, and certainly not prepared to pay good money for the diaries. Thanks for getting my mess into order. I'm sure it made all the difference.'

'Think nothing of it, mate, I'm delighted it's turned out so well. Let's get home and tell Daisy, and we must both write to Ruth. She will be excited about this.'

*　　　*　　　*

The two men worked well into the night, and through the following week, until they were satisfied with the last piece.

'That's it.' Steve finally sat back and gulped down the tea his wife had kept supplying.

'Thank the Lord!' Alf picked up his cup with shaking hands. 'That was damned hard.'

'I know, but you managed it well. We'll take it to Stanton tomorrow, then all you've got to do is wait for the money and the book.'

Fourteen

They met Charles Davis at the museum this time, and after reading the extra pages, he nodded. 'This is just what is needed, Mr Hunter. It couldn't have been easy for you, but this could be a help to others who are still suffering.'

'There are plenty,' Alf said, his expression grim. 'Even if some look quite all right on the outside, they could still be a mess inside. I know I was. We're told that the memories and nightmares would fade eventually, but none of us will ever be able to forget.'

'No, we won't.'

Both men looked intently at Charles Davies, and it was only then they realized that he had remained seated the whole time.

'What were you in?' Steve asked.

'I was in the Navy, like you, Mr Cooper, and lost a leg when my ship was blown up. I'll walk again when I get my artificial leg. It is because of my experiences that I'm helping with the War Museum, and trying to get my hands on as many written accounts as possible. The sacrifices made by so many must be preserved for future generations. Now, I assume you would like to be paid in cash, Mr Hunter?'

'To tell you the truth, Mr Davis, I'm feeling a bit awkward about taking money from you. You're trying to do something worthwhile here, and it don't seem right for me to be paid.'

'I insist you take the money,' Charles Davis declared. 'I am a reasonably wealthy man, and I'm sure you can do with a bit of extra cash.'

'Well, it would be welcome, but . . .'

Charles Davis held up his hand. 'You deserve to be paid, and I insist you take the money.'

The money was handed over and Alf slipped it into his pocket without another word.

With the business finished, they spent the next hour looking at the exhibits already completed, and others being prepared. The museum hadn't been open long, but they had many plans for the future, and plenty of enthusiasm for the project. It made a big impression on the two men and they talked about it all the way home.

As soon as they were back in Daisy's scullery, Alf found himself surrounded by the Cooper family wanting to know all the details of their visit to the Crystal Palace.

'What are you going to do with the money?' Daisy asked. 'You could put it in a bank.'

'No.' Alf shook his head. 'Steve did all the work so I want you to have half.'

'Certainly not!' Steve was adamant. 'I won't take a penny from you. All I did was put it in some kind of order.'

'Steve's right,' Daisy agreed. 'You do something with it.'

It would be useless to argue with them, as Alf knew only too well. 'All right, but at least let me treat you all to fish and chips tonight.'

The children whooped with delight, and Daisy and Steve agreed, laughing.

*   *   *

Alf didn't sleep much that night; he was too excited.

He'd never had so much money in his life, and he was determined to put it to good use. Since he'd been back at work he'd lived simply, managing to save quite a bit of his wages, and added to what he had been given made a tidy sum. How he wished Helen could share in this bounty. He sighed deeply with regret. He couldn't do anything for his wife now, but he could try to secure a decent future for his son. His mind wouldn't rest while he went over all the possibilities, and it was the early hours of the morning before he had decided what to do.

He kept his plans to himself, and the next Saturday afternoon he made his way to Wandsworth. He was going to see if he could buy a small house, but he wanted it to be well away from the docks. There were plenty for sale, he noted as he walked the streets. Stopping outside one small terraced house, he examined it carefully. The outside was in a state of neglect, but he'd guessed this was probably the best he could afford. Still, with a bit of work it would be quite nice, and the street wasn't too rough.

'You interested?'

Alf spun round to face the man who had spoken to him. He was of average height, around fifty, and wearing a suit that had seen better days, but it was well pressed and clean.

'I might be. Are you the owner?'

'No, I'm selling it for the owner, Mr Hughes, who is old now and has gone to live with his son. My name's Carter.' He shook hands with Alf. 'Want to have a look around?'

The front door stuck a bit, but it was in surprisingly good condition inside. All it needed was a thorough clean and a coat of paint, and he could do that easily, but he kept these thoughts to himself. 'Needs a lot doing to it.'

After a great deal of bartering, Alf bought the house for a price that would leave him enough money to do the necessary work. Carter was clearly delighted, and Alf guessed that he had been trying to sell this house for some time, and that was why he had been able to knock down the price quite a bit.

'When are you thinking of moving in?'

'I'm not going to live here myself, but once I've done the house up I'll rent it out. The rent will be reasonable, and I'd like an ex-soldier and his family to live here. Do you know anyone?'

'I could easily find you a suitable tenant, and I would be happy to collect the rent for you, sir.'

It amused Alf to be called sir, but this man seemed almost desperate for work. 'Were you in the forces?'

'Army, and I was wounded so bad I can't do heavy work no more.'

Alf nodded. 'I'll want to see prospective tenants first, and I'll pay you to collect the rent for me, but there will be no pressing for payment should they fall behind. Is that clear?'

'Perfectly, sir, and I might have just the right family for you. The man lost an arm in the war and is desperate for somewhere to live. He has a wife and two young children. He has a job delivering and selling newspapers, but times are hard for them.'

'Ask him to meet me here tomorrow evening at eight o'clock.'

'Yes, sir.'

Alf smiled all the way home. He couldn't wait to tell Steve and Daisy that he'd bought a house!

'You're going to live in Wandsworth?' Daisy asked, astonished at Alf's news.

'No,' he laughed, still buoyant from his day's work. It was unheard of for the likes of them to own property. 'I can't move away from the docks while I'm working there. I'm going to rent it out after I've done a bit of work on it. You told me to do something with the money, Daisy, and I have.'

'And buying a house is sensible,' Steve said, smiling with delight for his friend. 'I'd be happy to give you a hand doing it up.'

'Thanks, Steve; another pair of hands will make all the difference. There isn't any hard graft; it just needs a good clean and a lick of paint. This money has given me an unexpected chance to prove to myself and my son that I can amount to something.'

'You will, Alf. Now, when can we see the house?' Daisy asked eagerly.

'I've got to go there tomorrow evening to meet a family who might be interested in renting. You can all come then, if you like.'

'I can't wait!' Daisy smiled at her husband. 'Isn't this exciting? Alf's going to be a landlord!'

The next evening when they arrived at the house, the children rushed through the back door, shouting, 'You've got a garden!'

'Be careful!' Daisy called. 'You don't know what's under all that undergrowth. That's going to take some clearing, Alf.'

'I know.' Alf watched the children dodging

in and out of the overgrown vegetation, a smile on his face. All they had where they lived was a small backyard, so a garden was a novelty to the youngsters. 'This whole project will be a challenge, and that's what I need. Each day is still a struggle, and this will give some purpose to my life. I've won a couple of battles, but there's plenty ahead.'

The prospective tenants arrived and the Coopers all went into the garden and started to clear some of the weeds. Screams of delight could be heard.

Standing in front of Alf was a tall man, and he immediately recognized the haunted look in his eyes. So many men had the same expression and he didn't ask questions about what he did in the war. The wife was a pretty woman, with blonde hair and blue eyes, and she stood close to her husband. The two children were five and seven, Alf guessed, and they were peering out the window at the Cooper children. 'Why don't you go out there and help them while I talk to your mum and dad?'

'Oh, can we?' the eldest asked his dad, fidgeting with eagerness.

'Of course, off you go.'

They were through the back door almost before the words were out of his mouth, and they all smiled at each other.

'Right.' Alf indicated that they should all sit down. 'My name's Hunter, and you are?'

'Mr and Mrs Selby.'

'I've just bought this house, Mrs Selby. It's in a mess at the moment, but I'm going to do it up before anyone moves in. I understand you are looking for somewhere to live.'

'Yes, we are. The rooms we're living in at the moment are cramped, the area is rough, and it's no place to bring up children. I've got a job, and the pay is low, but I'm lucky to have anything. Fortunately I'm right-handed so there is still a lot I can do.'

Alf nodded, knowing how hard it must be for him with his left arm missing. 'I won't charge you more than you can afford, but before we go into that have a look round and see if you think the house might be all right for you. It has three bedrooms. Two of them are small, but they would be suitable for the children.'

Mrs Selby now had a hopeful look in her eyes, and Alf had already decided that he would like them to rent the house. The money didn't matter to him; this was an investment for his son's future.

Alf left the Selbys to explore on their own, and when they came back to the kitchen, he said, 'What do you think?'

'It would be perfect for us, Mr Hunter.' Mr Selby sat down. 'But can we afford it?'

'Could you manage two shillings a week?'

They gasped. 'We could, but Mr Hunter, it's worth much more than that!'

'If you and your family want it then that's all I'm asking. And if you should fall on hard times and can't pay, you must come to me and we'll sort something out. I will not throw you out, and that's a promise. You look after the place, keep the garden tidy, and do your best to pay the rent, and then I'll be happy. Is it a deal?'

'It's a deal!' Mr Selby stood up and shook Alf's hand, a smile of relief on his face. 'You are being very generous, Mr Hunter, and we are grateful.'

'It's my way of helping. I had terrible problems when I arrived home and my family suffered.

My wife died and my son walked out on me, so I understand what many ex-soldiers are going through. I've come through it,' he smiled wryly, 'so there's hope for others to do the same. Now, shall we go into the garden and tell your children the good news?'

There was much excitement, and Daisy had brought everything with her to make tea, so they eventually all sat around the kitchen table, talking and laughing, while all the children played together in the garden.

By the time they returned home that evening, Alf was well satisfied. Plans had been made for the work, and Mrs Selby had suggested certain colour paints. Steve had promised to help, and even Derek Selby was going to come round after work and do a bit of painting.

For the first time since he had returned home, Alf slept soundly, free of nightmares.

*   *   *

Sitting cross-legged on her bed Ruth opened the bulky envelope. Much to her delight it contained a separate letter from everyone—even Sally had put in a little drawing of a house. Of course, it didn't look anything like their house, but it brought a tear to her eyes. She missed them all so much. It was lovely here, but she was lonely, which was ridiculous because she was with people all day. But they weren't family or friends. If only Bob still worked here then she wouldn't be quite so lonely. She sighed, still cross with him for running away again.

The first letter she opened was from Eddie and he gave her all the news about the neighbours they were helping; John said he missed her and asked when she was coming home. That brought a lump to her throat and she moved on quickly to her dad's letter. He told her all about their visits to the Imperial War Museum, and the astounding news that Mr Hunter had bought a house in Wandsworth with the money from his diaries. And one more piece of lovely news was that her dad had been promoted, and now worked in the main office at the docks, with an increase in pay.

'Oh, my goodness,' she gasped, absolutely thrilled with all the news. 'Where are you, Bob? You ought to see what's going on at home!' But in her heart she knew he wouldn't be going home any time soon. He had walked away twice from everyone who cared for him, and she suspected that he didn't want to be close to anyone in case he was hurt again. She understood, but that didn't make it right. 'We all need someone, Bob, and one day you'll find that out.'

The last letter was from her mum and had her laughing as she read about the scrapes her brothers and sister kept getting into.

Carefully putting the letters back in the envelope, Ruth began writing. Each one would get a separate reply, and she would send a special one to Mr Hunter to congratulate him.

Glancing at the small clock on top of the chest of drawers, Ruth tumbled off the bed. It was time to help the senior Mrs Russell to get ready for her afternoon nap. She still had a sharp mind, but her condition was painful and drained her strength. This often made her short-tempered, and she was very good at giving orders. Ruth smiled to herself as she hurried along the passage. The letters would have to wait until this evening when she was free. Her mind was still on the good news from her family when she collided with someone.

'Watch where you're going!'

'Oh, I'm so sorry.' Ruth looked into the face of a furious maid. She had seen her a few times, but hadn't spoken to her yet. 'Betty, isn't it? I'm Ruth.'

'I know who you are! You're that common bitch the master found in the slums.'

Ruth was stunned by the girl's rudeness.

'I've worked here for five years,' the maid continued, 'and I should have been given the job you've got.'

'Perhaps the Russells didn't consider you suitable.' Ruth had never been spoken to like this before, and she wasn't going to ignore it.

'And you think you bloody well are?'

'Well, at least my language is better.' Ruth wanted to keep walking, but the girl had blocked the way.

'Think you're so clever, don't you?' Betty sneered. 'But you won't last long.'

'We shall see. Now, will you move out of my way, and I'm sure you have work to do.'

The maid stepped aside and as Ruth walked away she heard her mutter, 'Bloody slum bitch!'

That hurt. There had been a nasty tone to the girl's voice, and Ruth was under no illusion that the maid hated her for taking the job she wanted. She had only been here for three weeks and had begun to think that she might get over her doubts about living away from her family, but after that nasty incident she was sorry she had taken the job. Whenever she'd had problems in the past she'd only had to go to Bob, and he had always put things right for her. But she would have to deal with this on her own, and the best thing she could do was to keep out of the maid's way.

When she reached the door of the elderly Mrs Russell's rooms, Ruth stopped for a moment, took a couple of deep breaths to calm herself, then knocked on the door.

'Come.'

Putting on a bright smile she went in. 'Good afternoon, madam. How are you feeling today?'

'Reasonable. I'll sit up and read today, so help me off with my shoes and pile up the pillows for me.'

Bending down, Ruth began to remove the shoes. Madam didn't seem quite so sharp today, and that was a blessing after the encounter she had just had.

'How are your riding lessons going?'

'Not very well, madam. Cherry is a docile animal, but I'm not happy in the saddle.' Ruth had difficulty keeping the disappointment out of her voice.

'Not everyone likes riding, so don't do it if you'd rather not.'

'I'll give it a bit longer. I might get used to it.'

'Hmm.' Madam cupped Ruth's chin and made her look up. 'You are not your usual bright self today. Has someone upset you?'

'No, it's just that I've had a letter today and it's made me a bit homesick.' There was no way she was going to tell anyone about what the maid had said—it would probably get her dismissed, and Ruth wouldn't want to do that, even if the girl had been nasty to her. They were only words and couldn't hurt her unless she allowed them to.

Fifteen

Over the next three weeks Ruth settled into the routine of the household, and was content. She hadn't seen the maid often, and much to her relief there hadn't been any further unpleasantness. Pete had called a halt to her riding lessons, saying that it wasn't right to force someone to ride when they obviously didn't enjoy it. Lilly had accepted this and she was grateful for their understanding. Now, when Lilly wanted to go somewhere on the estate, one of the stable lads took them in the buggy. So apart from still missing her family, she was happy enough, and had decided to stay. It was such a beautiful place; she loved the open fields and the sound of birds singing in the morning. After the noise and grime of London, this really was wonderful.

She had just received a message that she was needed in Mrs Russell's private rooms, and she walked there humming softly to herself. She knocked on the door and looked in. Mrs Russell was there with her mother-in-law. 'You sent for me, madam?'

'Come in, Ruth.' Emma looked distracted as she turned to her mother-in-law and pointed to the pile of gowns strewn across the bed. 'But there isn't time to get a new gown made. What am I going to do? Everything is too tight around the bodice and waist.'

Waiting patiently to be told what she was to do, Ruth studied the beautiful creations, and one in particular caught her attention. It was made of silk in a glorious shade of sapphire blue. Mrs Russell would look stunning in that, she thought, as it was almost the same colour as her eyes. She itched to reach out and touch it, but didn't dare.

'The regimental dinner is tomorrow evening, and I cannot understand why we have been given such short notice. I shall have to go in one of the pregnancy dresses and will feel very dowdy!'

'The navy one is presentable, and people will understand.'

Mrs Russell's expression was so crestfallen Ruth couldn't keep quiet any longer. 'I am quite good at sewing. Perhaps one of the dresses could be altered.'

Both ladies turned and studied her, as if they had forgotten she was there, and then the elderly lady said, 'It might be worth a try, Emma.'

'Do you really think you could do the alterations, Ruth?'

'As long as there is enough material in the dress.' She reached out and picked up the sapphire one, quickly looking inside to inspect the seams. 'I might be able to do something with this.'

'Oh, would you try? That is my husband's favourite and I would so like to wear it.'

Ruth held it out. 'Would you try it on for me, please? Do you have a workbox?'

'Yes, there is one over by the window. It should hold everything you need.'

By the time Ruth had found a tape measure, marking chalk and pins, Mrs Russell had the dress on, but was unable to fasten it. She set about measuring and marking. Finally she stood back. 'It only needs letting out a little, and there is plenty of material, so I'm sure I can make the necessary alterations.'

'I would be most obliged if you could. You are relieved of all other duties today, and you may work in my sitting room.'

'I'll start at once.' Ruth picked up the workbox and waited while Mrs Russell removed the gown, then she carried everything she would need into the other room and shut the door.

*   *   *

The elderly lady glanced at the clock. 'The child has been in there for over three hours. Have you sent in refreshments, Emma?'

'Yes, Mother, but I cannot believe she is capable of the skilled work necessary to make the gown wearable. I had to let her try because she seemed so positive.'

After nearly another hour there was a light knock on their door, and Ruth came in with the dress. 'I'm sorry it took me so long, but the material is very fine and I had to be careful not to damage it. I have already pressed it, so would you try it on for me, please?'

Emma went into the dressing room and almost at once called for her mother-in-law to help with the fastenings. She gasped when she looked at her reflection in the long mirror, turning round and round to inspect the gown from every angle. 'Remarkable!'

When the two ladies came out of the dressing room, Ruth's face lit up with pleasure. 'You look beautiful. I knew that was the one you should wear.'

'It's a perfect fit, Ruth, and any professional would be proud of the stitching. Where did you learn to do such fine work?'

111

'My mum worked for a dressmaker before she was married and she taught me. Keeping a little sister and two lively brothers in clothes has given me plenty of practice. Of course, I've never worked on expensive material before, so I had to be extra careful.'

'You've done an excellent job, and I thank you very much, Ruth.'

'Glad I could help, madam. I've left the sitting room and workbox tidy. Do you need me for anything else, as I promised to go with Lilly to say goodnight to the horses?'

Both women laughed, and Emma shook her head. 'My daughter is mad about animals. Of course you must go.'

Ruth grinned, then turned and left the room, happy she had been able to help.

Emma kept the gown on and went to the library where her husband was working. 'Look at this, darling! I won't have to attend your regimental dinner in one of my dowdy dresses. Ruth has altered this one for me, and it fits perfectly. Her stitching is so fine it is impossible to see where she has made the alteration. Who would have thought she had such talent?'

'Indeed, she is a surprising girl.' He came over and kissed her cheek. 'You look beautiful, my dear.'

'I do believe I shall even enjoy your stuffy old gathering now.'

Ben laughed. 'And I shall be proud to have such a lovely woman on my arm. We must also think of a way to reward Ruth. I'll give it some thought while I'm away on business next week.'

*   *   *

There was a strange air about the house. Ruth had been out in the buggy with Lilly all afternoon and was curious to know what was going on, but every time she asked someone they just shook their heads and turned away.

The butler saw her and came up to her at once. 'Ah, there you are. The mistress wants to see you in the library, Ruth.'

'Oh, right.' Her concern faded as she made her way to the library. There was probably a last-minute function being arranged for when the captain returned, and there might be another dress to alter. The last one had been a challenge, but she had really enjoyed doing it, and would love to work on such beautiful materials again.

She knocked on the door and went in when told to. Mrs Russell was sitting behind the captain's desk and her mother-in-law next to her. They both looked very serious and the older lady was clearly furious about something.

'You sent for me, madam?'

'Something very unpleasant has happened and we would like an explanation.'

Ruth frowned at her tone. 'About what, madam?'

The senior Mrs Russell stood up and moved towards Ruth. 'When you were working in the private sitting room did you notice one of my brooches on the table by the fireplace?'

'I didn't see it. I went straight to the window where the light was better and stayed there.' Ruth was now very concerned. She didn't like the sound of this at all. 'Have you misplaced the brooch?'

'No, we've found it.'

'Oh, that's good.' Ruth smiled. 'Where was it?'

'In your room, hidden under your pillow.'

The two women in front of Ruth went out of focus as her head swam in disbelief. 'But how did it get there?'

'Enough of this!' The captain's mother turned to her daughter-in-law. 'This child doesn't even have the decency to own up!' She faced Ruth again. 'It was there because you put it there.'

The accusation hit her with tremendous force and she staggered towards the desk so she could grip on to it and steady herself. 'No! No! Someone must have put it in my room.'

'Who would do such a thing—and why? You'll have to come up with a better story than that before I believe you! You saw the brooch and couldn't resist it. That's the truth, isn't it?'

By now Ruth could hardly stand upright, and when she tried to speak, the words wouldn't come, so she just shook her head.

'You need to convince us that you are innocent of this crime,' the captain's wife said. 'If you didn't take it, then tell us who you believe might have put it in your room.'

This was a nightmare and Ruth fought back the tears. How could this be happening to her? She had never stolen anything in her life, and never would. She couldn't tell them about the maid, Betty, because she had no proof the girl hated her enough to do this terrible thing to her.

'Speak,' the captain's mother demanded. 'Your silence only confirms your guilt.'

'I'm not a thief,' Ruth managed to whisper.

'All the evidence says otherwise.' She sat next to her daughter-in-law again. 'Emma, we don't need to pursue this any further. We should call in the police.'

'I'd rather not do that. It would be better to wait for Benjamin and he will settle this matter in the right way.'

'Don't be foolish, Emma! You are responsible for the running of this household, and it is up to you to deal with this now! You cannot have a thief in the house. The girl must be sent away at once.'

The captain's wife sighed deeply and then looked up at Ruth. 'You will leave this house immediately and forfeit any pay due to you. I shall, of course, give you enough money for your train fare home.' She placed some coins on the desk.

Ruth had to get out of here—she would be sick any moment. Gathering up the money for her fare, she turned and ran out of the room. She just made it to the bathroom, and when she staggered out the butler was waiting for her and caught her arm.

'Steady.' He helped her back to her room and stood just inside the door while she began to gather together her few belongings.

'Will you wait outside, please?'

'I've been told to stay with you and see you off the premises.'

Tears were streaming down her face and she was shaking badly. 'I need to change out of the clothes they gave me. I'll leave with only the things I brought with me. I'm not a thief! I didn't take the brooch. I never saw it when I was in the sitting room. How can they believe I would do such a terrible thing? If you don't trust me you can search my bag before I leave.'

Without a word, Green left and shut the door behind him.

It didn't take her more than five minutes. The fact that the captain's mother had wanted to call the police terrified her, and all she could think about was getting out of here. Opening the door she thrust her bag at the butler. 'You'd better check this.'

'That won't be necessary.'

'I demand that you search my bag. I will not risk being accused of taking anything else from this house.'

He opened the bag, quickly looked inside, and then handed it back, shaking his head sadly. 'I don't like what is happening here, but I have to follow orders. Do you understand?'

She nodded and wiped away the tears that were clouding her vision. 'You have a member of your staff who can't be trusted, but it isn't me, and you would be wise to find out who it is.'

'Will you tell me who you think it is?'

'No, because I have no proof, and I will not be the cause of another person being accused of a crime they haven't committed.' Without another word she began to make her way down the servants' stairs, holding on tightly to stop herself from falling. Her legs didn't seem to belong to her.

The butler escorted her to the gate and Ruth walked away without looking back. It was a long way to the station, and she hoped she could make it. If her legs gave out she would have to sit beside the road until she felt strong enough to carry on walking, but she wouldn't allow her weakness to show until she was well away from the house.

As she gritted her teeth and put one foot in front of the other, she cried for Bob. This would never have happened if he'd been here. He would have

116

sorted it out, as he had always done when she'd had any problems. But he wasn't here; she was on her own and so frightened.

The sound of a horse coming up behind her made her heart race in panic, and she began to run. They'd sent the police after her! She would be put in prison . . .

'Ruth! Please stop.' The buggy kept pace with her.

Recognizing the voice, she looked up, gasping for breath, and her terror plain to see. She stopped and stood there trembling.

Jim cursed under his breath. 'I've just heard about this and came to give you a lift to the station. It's more than two miles, and they should never have left you to walk this far. It's a bloody shame the captain is away; he would never have allowed this to happen. Let me see you to the train. You're in no fit state to look after yourself at the moment.'

She doubled over to catch her breath, and Jim was immediately holding her up. 'Easy, Ruth, I'll take you to a kind woman, Mrs Trent, who will put you up for the night, and then you can go home tomorrow when you're feeling stronger.'

'No, no, I must get home now! I didn't do it, Jim,' she sobbed as she tried to get into the buggy. 'I'm so frightened.'

'Of course you didn't.' Jim lifted her into the seat. 'Let's get you home to your family.'

*   *   *

The journey home seemed endless, and it was getting dark as she walked in the back door of their house. She cried out with relief as she reached the

117

safety of her home and family.

'Ruth!' Steve rushed to catch his daughter before she collapsed, and lifted her to a chair.

Daisy was also there, pushing the hair away from her ravaged face. 'Dear God, what's happened?'

A glass of water was put in her trembling hand. 'Tell us what's happened, sweetheart.'

After taking a couple of gulps of water, she stammered, 'They turned me out. They said I was a thief. I'm not ... I'm not. I didn't take the brooch. They'll send the police after me ... I'll go to prison ...'

'Oh, no you won't!' Steve swore furiously. 'I'll sort this out, Ruthie. Only a fool would believe you'd steal from anyone.'

'Don't you worry, darling. You're home now and we won't let anything happen to you. Dad will clear this up. Do you feel up to telling us exactly what happened, or would you prefer to leave it until the morning?'

Ruth caught her breath and began to talk, and by the time she had finished, Steve and Daisy were grim-faced with anger. They were not going to have anyone call their gentle daughter a thief!

Sixteen

'Is she asleep?'

Daisy sat next to her husband at the scullery table and reached for the teapot. 'Yes, at last. She cried so much Sally woke up. She rushed across the room and clambered into Ruth's bed, snuggling up to her, and that quietened her down until she fell asleep. I'm so angry, Steve! Those women have treated her cruelly, and I don't care if they are upper class, they should be ashamed of themselves. We can't leave it like this, darling.'

'I don't intend to. I'm going to Kent tomorrow to see that our daughter's name is cleared. And I'm not leaving there until the real culprit is found!'

'Do you think the maid Ruth mentioned is the one who took the brooch?'

'It seems likely, and I shall demand she be questioned, along with the rest of the staff. Ruth should have told them about her, but you know our daughter, she would never harm anyone if she could avoid it. I know how she feels, but her reputation is at stake, Daisy, and I'll do whatever it takes to put this right.'

* * *

The next morning Steve sent a message to say he would have to take the day off because of a family crisis, and then he caught an early train to Kent.

The house was just as Ruth had described it, but he didn't care how impressive it was, he was here to sort out this mess. No one was going to accuse his daughter of being dishonest. It had torn him apart to see her so frightened.

Steve banged on the front door, and the man he guessed was the butler immediately opened it. 'I've come to see Captain Russell, or his wife if he isn't here.'

'The captain is still away, and Mrs Russell isn't seeing visitors.'

'This isn't a social call. I'm Ruth's father and I'm not leaving here until someone talks to me!'

Green stood aside. 'Come in, Mr Cooper. I'll tell Mrs Russell you are here.'

He waited in the hallway for ten frustrating minutes before the butler returned.

'Mrs Russell will see you, Mr Cooper.' He hesitated, and then said quietly, 'How is Ruth, sir?'

'Devastated! I'm not usually a violent man, but the treatment of my gentle daughter has been disgraceful. She is the kindest girl you could ever meet, always caring about other people, and she most certainly would not steal anything! I will not leave this house until the true culprit has been found.'

The butler nodded. 'Follow me, please.'

He was shown to a comfortable sitting room where two women were waiting for him. Steve knew the older woman was the captain's mother, and the younger one his wife, who was pale and clearly ill at ease. He also noted that the butler had remained in the room.

The older woman spoke first. 'We deeply regret that Ruth had to be dismissed—'

'*Regret?*' Steve had promised himself that he would contain his anger, but this haughty attitude was too much. 'Is that all you can say? When Ruth told you she hadn't stolen the brooch, you didn't even bother to find out who might have put it in her room. You threw her out! How dare you? I demand this be cleared up at once!'

'What is going on here?' At that moment the captain strode into the room and went straight to his wife's side. 'Why are you here shouting at my wife and mother, Mr Cooper?'

'They accused Ruth of stealing, and they threw her out without bothering to look into the matter

120

properly. My *innocent* daughter is terrified the police are going to come and put her in prison. No one treats my child like that! I don't care who the bloody hell they are!'

The captain's expression darkened as he faced his wife and mother. 'Is this true?'

'One of my brooches was missing,' his mother said. 'I had left it in Emma's private sitting room, and the girl had been working in there. When I went in there to collect it later, I couldn't find it. A search was made and it was found in the girl's room. We dismissed her at once without pay. You cannot have a thief in the house, Benjamin.'

'My daughter is not a thief!'

Alarmed by Steve's angry tone, the butler stepped forward and caught his arm. He shook it off. 'Don't you dare touch me!'

'Let's all calm down,' the captain ordered.

'I'll calm down when we find out who put that damned brooch in my daughter's room.'

'And how are we to do that?' the captain's mother asked. 'All your daughter would say was that she didn't take it. She made no attempt to defend herself.'

'She couldn't speak because she was terrified!' Steve fought to rein in his anger. 'Let me tell you something about my daughter. She sees the best in people, no matter their faults, and she will go out of her way to help anyone. If you had taken the trouble to ask the rest of the staff you would have found out that there is someone here who has been nasty to Ruth, accusing her of taking the job she should have had. It is possible she would do something like this to get her out of the way, but Ruth would not tell you who it was, even to save herself. To hurt anyone is not a part of my daughter's character, and she certainly would not take anything belonging to someone else. We may be poor, but we have brought our children up to be honest. You judged too quickly and acted too harshly!'

The captain was now clearly furious. 'Who is this girl?'

'I believe you have a maid by the name of Betty.'

'But she has been with us for five years.' Mrs Russell was shaking her head. 'And she does not clean my private sitting room.'

'Nevertheless, we must look into this.' The captain signalled to the butler. 'Summon all the servants at once, Green.'

The butler left the room and the captain's mother said, 'Benjamin, Ruth was the only one who could have taken the jewel.'

Emma was now looking very distressed. 'You could be wrong, Mother. The sitting room is never locked and anyone could have gone in there. At first I believed it was Ruth, but after seeing how shocked she was I began to have doubts. I was so upset that this should have happened in our house, and when you were so certain she had taken your brooch and told me to dismiss her, I did so without question. I was wrong.' She looked up at her husband. 'I'm sorry, my dear, I acted without proper thought.'

Ben spun round to face his mother. 'You are a guest in this house, Mother, and have no right to have staff dismissed. I make the decisions here, and when I'm away Emma is in charge. You appear to have forgotten that.'

'I agree that Emma was reluctant, but in this

case I overruled her. It was my brooch, Benjamin, the last present your father ever gave me, and I considered I had every right to take immediate action.'

'You did not! In a matter as serious as this you should have waited for me to return! There is no telling what harm you have done to Ruth.'

'You are talking as if the girl is innocent.'

'She is innocent until proven guilty, Mother. You pronounced her guilty without proof.'

Steve watched the captain handle his strong-willed mother, and approved. He guessed that he would deal with her very firmly in private, but for the moment he was happy about the way this was going.

The butler returned. 'The staff will all be here within five minutes, sir.'

'Thank you, Green.'

No one said anything else as the servants began to file into the room, and from what he'd seen so far, Steve was sure that the captain was a man who would handle this crisis fairly. It was a blessing he had arrived home at this time because dealing with the captain's mother would have been difficult, to say the least.

Ben came and stood next to Steve, showing that he was included in this discussion. Together they faced the servants. 'You all know that Ruth was dismissed for stealing. There is considerable doubt that she was the culprit. Do any of you have an opinion about this matter?'

'I'm certain she didn't do it, sir.' Jim stepped forward. 'When I caught her up to give her a lift to the station—'

'She was walking?' Ben cut Jim off sharply.

'Yes, sir, and she was in such a distressed state she could hardly stand. I wanted to take her to Mrs Trent's for the night to recover, but she insisted on going home at once. I put her on the train myself.'

'This is disgraceful!' Ben glared at his mother, but said nothing else.

'Who is that?' Steve asked quietly.

'Jim, my head groom.'

Steve nodded. 'Thank you, Jim. I'm grateful that someone had the decency to look after my daughter.'

'She's a nice girl, Mr Cooper, and I can't believe she would steal anything. Begging your pardon, Captain Russell, but I can't help how I feel, and I'm glad you're now trying to find out the truth.'

'I understand, and I would like all of you to feel you can speak freely.' Ben's glance rested on everyone in turn. 'If Ruth didn't take the brooch, then someone else must have done, and I intend to find out exactly what happened here.'

There was an uncomfortable shuffling as the servants all looked at each other.

'Cook, the housekeeper and the stable staff may all leave.' There was a pause while those servants left the room, then the captain continued. 'That leaves the housemaids, who have easy access to the entire house. Do you have anything to tell me?'

'I never took the ruby brooch!' one of them blurted out.

Emma joined her husband, speaking softly. 'Mother has many brooches, and we never said which one it was.'

He nodded and dismissed the other two maids, leaving only one. 'Only the thief would have known it was a ruby brooch, Betty. Why did you do it?'

Seeing she had given herself away, she became defensive. 'I didn't want it for myself; I just wanted that girl out of the way. I should have had that job. After five years as a maid I deserved it.'

Steve drew in a breath of relief. Ruth's name had been cleared, and that was what he had come here for. It was up to the captain to deal with this mess now.

'You are quite wrong. The fact that you were prepared to hurt an innocent girl shows your character to be flawed.' The captain turned to Steve. 'You have our sincere apologies, Mr Cooper. You may decide what happens to this girl.'

This was the last thing he wanted, but there was no backing away from it now the captain had placed it firmly in his lap. He nodded and stepped towards Betty. 'In my view what you did is unforgivable . . .'

The girl started to shake with fear. 'Please sir, I'm sorry. Don't set the police on me. I need this job . . . my mum's not well . . . please,' she begged. 'I'll never do anything like this again. I promise. I was jealous . . .'

'Nothing you say can excuse your actions. You have caused my daughter great distress and I cannot forgive you for that. However, Ruth is of a gentler nature and she would not wish you to lose your job.'

'Thank you, sir,' she whispered as tears trickled down her face. 'I'm ever so sorry for what I've done. I should have owned up when Ruth was sent away, but I was too frightened.'

'I'm glad you understand that, but of course, it is not up to me to say if you can keep your job or not. Captain and Mrs Russell are your employers, and the final decision is up to them, but you will write a letter of apology to Ruth, and I will take it with me.'

When the maid nodded agreement, Steve joined the captain again. 'Thank you for the way you have handled this. My daughter's name has been cleared, and that is all that concerns me. How you deal with your staff is your business.'

Before speaking Captain Russell gave a slight inclination of his head. 'Because Mr Cooper's daughter has so generously said she doesn't want you to lose your job, you can stay—with the following conditions. You are no longer allowed in the main house. You must help in the servants' quarters only, and do what work the housekeeper gives you. Is that understood?'

'Yes, sir, thank you, sir.'

Ben called the butler over. 'Take Betty downstairs and wait until she has written the letter of apology, then bring it to Mr Cooper.'

When the butler and maid had left the room, Ben turned his attention to his wife and mother. 'You also owe Mr Cooper and Ruth an apology.'

They did so, appearing upset and contrite about the way they had dealt with the theft. They both said they would write letters of apology to Ruth.

'And I will also pay what is owed her,' Emma said.

'Now that is settled, will you stay and lunch with us?' the captain asked Steve.

'No, thank you, Captain Russell. As soon as I have the letter from the maid and Ruth's money, I'll leave.'

'Please lunch with us, and then, with your permission, my wife and I would like to come with you. A very great wrong has been done to your daughter, and I do not consider letters good enough. Please allow us to apologize in person.'

'I'm not sure about that. She was close to collapse when she arrived home, and very frightened.'

'All the more reason for us to reassure her that the culprit has been found and she now has nothing to fear. At least give us the chance to put her mind at rest.'

Steve pictured his terrified daughter and nodded. 'Very well.'

* * *

Voices could be heard in the scullery, so Steve took the Russells straight there. When they walked in, Ruth took one look at the couple with her dad, and shot to her feet. Seeing their big sister's alarm, Eddie, John and little Sally clustered protectively around her.

'You leave our Ruthie alone!' John declared, standing right in front of her. 'What did you bring them here for, Dad?'

'It's all right, sweetheart.' Steve moved the kids out of the way and took hold of his daughter's hands, smiling reassuringly. 'The maid has admitted that she did put the brooch in your room, and the captain and his wife have come to apologize.'

Mrs Russell spoke first. 'We were wrong to dismiss you without looking into the matter thoroughly. Our treatment of you was harsh and we offer our sincere apologies. I am so sorry, Ruth. Would you please consider coming back with us?'

'No, I can't do that. I would be terrified in case

something else went missing because I don't feel you would ever really trust me again.'

'That isn't so, Ruth,' Captain Russell said. 'We know you were not responsible for the missing brooch, and that you would never do such a thing. Please reconsider.'

'No, sir.' Ruth shook her head firmly.

'I suppose it was too much to hope that you would forgive us and come back.'

'You weren't there, sir, so there's no need for me to forgive you. Mrs Russell did what she thought was right at the time, but it hurt me badly. I expect I could forgive you in time, but I would never work for you again.'

'No, I don't suppose you could.' Mrs Russell was visibly upset. 'I am ashamed.'

'What will happen to the maid?' Ruth asked.

'She will be kept on, but under strict supervision.' The captain handed Ruth an envelope. 'That is the money we owe you. Would you write to us now and again to let us know how you are getting on?'

'Er ... yes, if you want me to.' She thought it was a strange request in the circumstances, but she would do as he asked.

'Thank you. Now we will take our leave, and again, please accept our sincere apologies.'

Steve saw them to the door, and then returned to his family. 'Do you know, I feel sorry for that man. He has a mess to sort out at home, but as soon as he found out what had happened, he acted quickly and with honour.'

'And that's all we can ask of anyone.' Daisy put the kettle on the stove. 'I don't know about you, but I need a strong cup of tea.'

Seventeen

Later that evening Steve noticed that the envelope the captain had given Ruth was still on the dresser, untouched.

'Aren't you going to open that?' Steve asked his daughter as she helped to lay the table for tea.

'It won't be much. I wasn't there for very long.' But to please him, Ruth slit open the envelope and looked inside, gave an exclamation of disgust, and then threw it down on to the table. 'Don't they think I have been insulted enough?'

Seeing Ruth's furious expression, Steve picked it up and took out the letter, frowning as he read. 'What's this about a gown you altered?'

'Mrs Russell was going to a regimental dinner with her husband and none of her gowns fitted her after the birth of her son. I let one out, that's all. Why?'

'Captain Russell says the enclosed money is payment for your excellent work.'

'Five pounds! That's more than you earn in a week.'

'It would have cost her more if she'd had to have a new gown made, sweetheart. I expect it was an expensive gown.'

'Hmm, it was the most beautiful silk, and a challenge to work on.'

'And was she pleased when she was able to wear it?' Steve asked.

Ruth nodded. 'She looked lovely, and the captain was pleased because he said it was his favourite gown.'

'Then you must accept the money.' Daisy took it from her husband and pressed it into her daughter's hand. 'Don't be too proud to take payment for a job well done. And don't go spending it on the kids or us. You buy yourself something nice with it.'

*   *   *

'Thank goodness that's over.' Emma placed a hand over her eyes. 'In future I will always give someone the benefit of the doubt. You know, darling, sometimes when you're hiring and firing staff for a large household, it's easy to forget that these are people with hopes and fears, just like us. Your mother is our guest, and I was upset to discover something of hers had been stolen while she was in this house. But that is no excuse for allowing her to overrule me so easily. I liked the girl and should have been suspicious when the jewel was found so quickly. If she really had stolen it then she would have done a better job of hiding it. I was so upset at the time that I didn't see that.'

'It's easy to see that now the truth is known. Mother was pressing you to take immediate action, and you bowed to her wishes. She always ruled her household with a fist of iron, dismissing staff for the slightest misdemeanour, but things have changed, Emma. I fought beside men of all ranks and stations in life. It didn't matter where they came from; they were fighting and dying with courage. It brought home to me that the class divide is unimportant. Everyone has the right to a decent life, and I had hoped that things would change once the war was over, but all anyone appears to be doing is talking about improvements.'

'It will come, darling, but it takes time, and education is a vital step to help the poor improve their lot. Young Bob knew that, and had the desire to do something about it by becoming a teacher himself.'

Ben sighed. 'If only he had stayed I would have helped him. Dear God, Emma, if I was still a drinking man I'd have a stiff brandy now.' When he saw his wife's expression he grimaced. 'Don't worry; I'm not going to. It's obvious that we can't change the world tonight, but we do have to put our own house in order. Do you know where Mother is?'

'I haven't seen her since we arrived back. I'll send Green to find her.'

*　　　*　　　*

'I've ordered tea,' the captain's mother announced as she entered the sitting room. 'How did your trip to London go?'

'Upsetting,' Emma said.

'I don't know why you went. We made an honest mistake and letters would have been enough.'

The tea trolley arrived and Ben waited until they were on their own before speaking. 'Mother, I will not have you interfering in the running of this household. All this unpleasantness could have been avoided if you had let Emma wait for me to return.'

'Benjamin, I have been used to doing things my way. It is kind of you and Emma to have me here, but I am going out of my mind with nothing to do. My body may be creaking, but my mind is still sharp.'

'There is no denying that, and we need to find a solution. What do you think about setting up your own small household in the Gatehouse? You could have your own servants to look after you, and you would have your independence to live as you please. But you would still be close enough for us to keep an eye on you.'

His mother looked startled for a moment, and then broke into a huge smile. 'That is a splendid idea, but is it habitable, Benjamin, because it hasn't been used for some time?'

'I will have it put into good order for you.' Ben was relieved his mother seemed so pleased with the idea. 'You may choose the wallpaper and furniture.'

'That is wonderful, and very generous of you both. I shall enjoy overseeing the refurbishment.'

Ben doubted that the workers would, but he said nothing, and wondered why he hadn't thought of this before. He loved his mother, but the two of them under one roof would never work.

Emma joined in the enthusiasm, also relieved that this was going so well. 'Mother, there are some good pieces of furniture in the attic storage rooms. There might be something there you would like.'

'Splendid. We shall sort through them tomorrow.' She looked intently at her son. 'You will employ the workers quickly, Benjamin?'

'It will be my first task tomorrow, and you should be able to move in within a couple of weeks.'

'The sooner I'm out of your way the better for all of us.' She patted her daughter-in-law's hand and stood up. 'May I ask Green to accompany me to the Gatehouse before dinner? I should like to have a look at it before it's too dark.'

'Of course.' Ben rang for the butler, and when they had left he sat back and closed his eyes for a moment.

'Are you all right, darling?'

He turned his head to look at his wife. 'I'm suddenly tired, and feeling unsettled. This has not been a pleasant day, Emma.'

'I agree, but we have put things right with Ruth, and Mother is happy about moving to the Gatehouse. Not a pleasant day, as you say, but not a wasted one either.'

*   *   *

Three days later Ben opened a letter from Ruth. It was short, thanking them for the money, and saying that she thought it was kind of them to come in person to see her.

He replied at once, but his letter was long and chatty, telling her about the horses, his children and what was happening on the estate. He also asked questions about her brothers and sister, hoping this would prompt her to write again. He really wanted to stay in touch with the Coopers and Bob's father, but after the way Ruth had been treated by them, he knew they would be reluctant to keep in contact. If Ruth wrote again, then he would try to keep the correspondence going, but if she didn't reply then he would have to leave it at that.

Ever since Bob had arrived here and urged him to stop drinking, he had felt a strong connection to all of them. That was why he had taken the trouble to find Alfred Hunter, and offered Ruth a position with them. His good intentions had ended in disaster and he hoped to be able to make amends one day.

Eighteen

'I'm going to a birthday party!'

Ruth put down the mending she was doing and smiled at her little sister. 'That's very exciting. Where is it?'

'At Mr Hunter's new house. Mrs Selby's giving it for Alice. She'll be five. Eddie and John are coming as well.'

'Oh, Alice must be Mrs Selby's youngest girl then.'

'My best frock doesn't fit me any more,' Sally sighed. 'I've grown a lot while you've been away. Could you make it bigger for me?'

'I've already let it out twice, and there isn't enough material to do it again.'

'Oh.' She looked down at the one she was wearing and pulled a face. 'I'll have to go in this one, I suppose.'

'I tell you what, Sally, let's go to the market and get some material to make you a new frock.'

'Will you?' Sally threw herself at Ruth, hugging her fiercely. 'You're the best sister I could have. We're so glad you're back. Don't go away again, please.'

'I never will.'

'Can we come as well?' John asked, and Eddie jumped up in anticipation too.

'Of course, let's go right now.'

Daisy was upstairs making the beds, so Ruth called out, 'Mum, we're all going to the market, do you want anything?'

'You can bring me back a loaf and some

potatoes,' she answered, looking down the narrow stairs at her excited children.

They went straight to the haberdashery stall. It was always piled high with materials of all colours, ribbons and all things needed for sewing. Ruth loved the stall and knew the owner well.

Mrs Law smiled. 'Hello, Ruth, what can I do for you today?'

Sally didn't give her sister a chance to answer. 'Ruth's going to make me a party frock in pink.'

Mrs Law winked at Ruth, then said to the little girl, 'I'm sure we can find you just the colour. What about this? It's a nice bright pink and will go with your dark hair very well.'

'Ooh, that's pretty.' She glanced up at her sister and whispered, 'Will that cost too much?'

Ruth examined the deep pink material, liking the small self-coloured roses all over it. The cloth was light and would hang well, she decided. 'This would make a nice frock, but have a look at everything, Sally, and see if there is anything else you like.'

'All right.' Sally walked round and round looking at every bale of material, then came back to the first one Ruth was still holding. 'I like this the best, but if we can't afford it I'll find a cheaper one.'

'We can afford it, sweetie.' Ruth bought enough to make the frock and found some ribbon of almost the same shade.

The boys were getting fidgety, not at all interested in girls' things, so with the purchases made, they set off to have a good look round the market. Taking hold of Sally's hand to keep her safe in the crowds, they examined the goods on every stall. She had just bought the things her mum wanted when the boys raced over to another stall, shouting with pleasure.

Still holding on to Sally's hand, Ruth followed to find her brothers looking at some wooden toys. They were very well made. The seller was about the same age as her dad, so he had probably fought in the war as well. She had great sympathy for all the men, as work was hard to find, and many were struggling to make a living.

She smiled. 'Did you make these yourself?'

'Yes, Miss.'

'Look at this, Ruthie.' Eddie held up a bright red tram.

'Well, I've bought Sally something so you can have that. John, you choose something as well.'

He pounced on a blue train. 'Can I have this one?'

'Of course.' She paid for the toys, and they continued their walk. While they were going from stall to stall an idea began to form in her mind. 'I want to go back to the material stall, boys,' she called, 'and then we must go home.'

Still clutching their precious toys they followed their sister obediently.

'We're back again, Mrs Law. I was wondering if you have any odd pieces and end of the rolls you can sell me?'

'I get plenty of those. See if there's anything you can use in the box under the stall.'

Ruth was delighted to see the box overflowing with all kinds of materials, some very small and others of a decent size. 'How much do you want for the lot?'

'Sixpence and they're yours, Ruth.'

'Thank you, Mrs Law.' Ruth paid her.

'What you going to do with all that?' Eddie asked as they made their way home.

'I'm going to make things with it.'

'What things?' John wanted to know.

'Not sure yet; I'll decide when I've had a good look at the materials.'

*   *   *

It didn't take Ruth long to make Sally's frock, and she was very pleased with it. Her little sister would look a picture wearing it. She had decorated the sleeves and neck with the ribbon, and put small frills in layers all down the skirt. 'There, that's finished,' she told Sally, 'now try it on for me, sweetie.'

Sally twirled and preened in front of the mirror, beaming with delight at the pretty creation. She put her arms around her big sister's neck and sniffed on her shoulder, quite overcome at having such a beautiful frock. 'Thank you, Ruthie.'

Lifting her down, Ruth laughed. 'Let's see you smile then.'

'Girls are daft,' Eddie said, disgusted. 'All this fuss just because she's got a new frock.'

'You two can't go to the party looking like tramps either.' Ruth had been back to the market without them knowing and now produced her purchases. 'You've both got new trousers and shirts. Go and put them on so I can see if they fit.'

She was so used to making and mending clothes for all the kids that she didn't have any trouble getting the right sizes for them. The boys were obviously pleased to have new clothes instead of hand-me-downs, but of course, they wouldn't show it like their sister. John did give her a quick peck on the cheek though. Eddie just stuck his hands in his pockets and said they fitted all right. Ruth took their reactions to mean they were happy with the new clothes.

'Ruth, what did we tell you?' Her mum was standing in the doorway shaking her head. 'We told you not to spend your money on us.'

'I wanted the kids to look nice for the party, and I've got plenty left. And there's just one more thing.' She hurried out of the room and returned holding her hands behind her back. 'You can't go to a birthday party without taking a present.'

She held out a doll she had made from scraps of material. The face was neatly embroidered on and she was dressed in pretty lemon-coloured clothes.

'Oh, it's beautiful!' Sally cried, reaching out to take hold of the doll. 'Alice will love it.'

'Here's some paper for you to wrap it nicely.' Ruth still had one arm behind her back, and the boys were trying to see what she was holding. She laughed and held out another doll to her sister. 'And this one is for you.'

The little girl gasped in delight, took the doll and examined it in wonder. 'Look, look, Mum, it's got my frock on.'

'I had some material left over.' Ruth smiled at Sally's happy face. 'I'm glad you like it.'

'Oh, I do.' Her little sister hugged her. 'I'm so lucky to have a clever sister.'

'Yes, you are clever, Ruth.' Daisy picked up one of the dolls. 'These are lovely and beautifully made.'

'They have turned out well.' Ruth was pleased with their reaction, and this strengthened her determination to go ahead with her plans, but she

138

said nothing. She wanted to talk to her dad first.

$$* \qquad * \qquad *$$

The next afternoon Daisy had taken the kids off to the party and Ruth had the place to herself. She had spread the pieces of material over the floor in the front room and was busy with the scissors when her dad walked in.

'What are you up to, Ruth? Didn't you want to go to the party?'

'I'm too busy.' She smiled up at him. During the war he had been away so long that he had seemed like a stranger when he'd arrived home, but since then they had become close, and she went to him with any problems. She loved him dearly. 'How's the Imperial War Museum coming along?'

'Fine. They've got a huge amount of material now.' He sat on the floor next to her. 'Are you going to tell me what you're up to?'

'I've got an idea, Dad, but I want to know what you think.' She took some small garments out of a bag and handed them to him. 'You've seen the dolls I made, but what do you think of these?'

'Baby clothes?' He frowned and she laughed at his expression.

'They're not for me—or mum.'

'That's a relief.' He made a show of mopping his brow, and she hit him on the arm, still laughing.

'Stop messing about. This is serious.'

He grinned and began to examine the garments. 'They're beautifully made, Ruth, so what do you intend to do with them?'

'I thought I'd make quite a few things, and see if I could sell them at the market.'

139

'Hmm. The dolls could be popular, especially near Christmas. Do you want to set up a stall?'

She shook her head. 'Not until I know if the things will sell. I'm hoping to persuade Mrs Law to let me have a corner of her stall, for a fee, of course.'

'That's a sensible way to start, and these are so good I don't think you will have trouble selling them.'

'Oh, good. Now all I want is for you to price them for me. You are officially my partner now.'

'If we're going into business together then I'd better draw up a contract,' he joked. 'How much are you going to pay me?'

They were both laughing like a couple of fools now, and Ruth struggled to be serious again. 'I appoint you the boss, and I'm the fingers. Honestly, Dad, I really want to do this, but I need your help. I'm never going into service again so I've got to find some way to earn a living. I can't rely on you forever.'

'I know how you feel, sweetheart, and of course I'll help you. Let's take everything you've made into the scullery, and we'll work out how much you should charge.'

*   *   *

By the time another week had passed, Ruth had used every scrap of material she had. As soon as she had enough things to sell she went with her dad to see Mrs Law at the market. If she didn't agree to let her put them on her stall, then they would have to think again.

'Hello, Mrs Law,' she said, feeling very nervous.

140

'This is my dad.'

'Pleased to meet you, Mr Cooper.' They shook hands. 'I've got another box of scraps, if you want them, Ruth?'

'Er . . .' She glanced imploringly at her dad.

'My daughter has a proposition for you, Mrs Law.' He handed over a bag of garments and stuffed toys. 'What do you think of these?'

The stallholder took each item out and looked at it carefully. 'Did you make these, Ruth?'

'Yes, I'm quite good with a needle.'

'You're more than good, young lady. What is your proposal?' She looked at Steve for the answer.

'We would like to put these on your stall to see if they would sell. We'll give you a penny from every sale to pay for the use of your stall.'

When she didn't answer, Steve said, 'I think that's fair, don't you?'

Mrs Law nodded. 'But for that you will need to do the selling yourself, Ruth. I have my own business to take care of.'

'I'll do that.' Ruth's insides were churning with excitement.

'Do we have a deal?' Steve asked.

'We do.' Mrs Law shook hands with both of them. 'Let's clear a part of the stall right now and set these out.'

Steve stayed as well, and within an hour every toy had been sold, and four items of baby clothing. Ruth couldn't stop smiling, and the stallholder was also very pleased. It had brought more customers to her stall and also increased her own sales.

'I'll take that box of pieces you have,' Ruth said, 'and a couple of longer lengths.'

'Choose what you want.' Mrs Law smiled at

Ruth and Steve. 'Looks like you two are going to be busy.'

* * *

Steve took the bag of materials with him, leaving his daughter working happily on the stall. He had been very worried about her, and was relieved she had found something to become involved in. With her talent this was probably the best thing she could do. She could work from home and still earn some money.

'How did it go?' Daisy asked anxiously when he walked in.

'Things are selling well.' He smiled and put the bag on the table. 'So she's had to buy more material.'

'Oh, that's wonderful!'

He nodded. 'We've both been worried about her after that nasty incident with the Russells, but she's used her head, and her talent for sewing. I think she will be able to put the past behind her now. She's positively brimming with enthusiasm.'

'It tore me apart to see her in such a state, but let's hope it has made her stronger.'

There was a knock on the back door and Alf looked in. 'Ah, good, you're back. Want to have a look around the museum to see how they are getting on?'

'Come in, Alf. I've been sorting out some things they might like. Your book should be ready by now, shouldn't it?'

'That's what I'm hoping. Can't wait to see it.'

In only a few minutes they were on their way, and Steve told Alf all about Ruth's little business venture.

'You don't need to worry about your clever girl,' Alf told him. 'She'll do all right for herself, you just wait and see. I only wish I could feel as confident about my boy. He's out there alone, and goodness knows what he's up to. I only hope he doesn't fall in with the wrong people.'

'It's not a good feeling, I know, Alf, but you can be sure no one's going to take advantage of him. He's too big!'

'Taller than me when he left,' Alf agreed. 'And I'm six feet two.'

Stanton greeted them as soon as they walked through the museum door. 'Your book has just arrived, Mr Hunter.' He handed over three copies.

Alf stared at the photo of the trenches on the cover. 'Will you look at this, Steve?'

'Mr Davis has done a terrific job with it,' Steve said, admiring the book.

'That's for you.' Alf handed one copy to Steve. 'One for me, and one I'll keep for Bob, in the hope that he will read it one day.'

Nineteen

Ruth smiled with pride as she set out her own stall. Spring of 1922 was turning out to be beautiful and exciting. Over the last two years her sales had steadily increased, and her dad had told her that she was ready to start up on her own. She had enjoyed working with Mrs Law, but he was right. Her reputation as a dressmaker was growing and more people were coming to her to make clothes for their older children. To be honest, she had found all this rather frightening and was glad she had such a caring family to give her support and encouragement. Eddie and John had even made a smart notice in bright blue to go on her stall, stating 'Dressmaker'.

'Hello, Ruthie, there's a dance at the church hall tonight. Want to come?'

'No, thanks, Dougie, I'm too busy.'

'Oh come on, you've gotta have a bit of fun. You can't work all the time. I'll let you pay the entrance fee.'

She laughed in exasperation. Now she was seventeen the boys were beginning to flock around her, and she found it a nuisance. Especially as they all thought she had money. She worked hard for only a little profit, but at least she was contributing to the family expenses. 'I enjoy working. You ought to try it sometime.'

'You know I can't get work around here.'

'Then try somewhere else. London's a big place.'

'I know what you're doing,' he sneered, 'you're waiting for Bob Hunter to come back, but you're wasting your time. He won't turn up after all this time.'

'He'll be back when he's made something of himself.' To be honest she had just about given up hope of seeing him again, but wouldn't admit that to anyone else. 'He wants to be a teacher, and that takes time.'

'He always did have big ideas, but you mark my words, Ruth Cooper, you've seen the last of him. You'll grow old waiting for him.'

Ruth snorted with laughter. 'I've got a long way to go, Dougie.'

The boy smirked and winked at her. 'You're not only pretty, but you're clever as well. Look at you with your own business. You're gonna make someone a fine wife one day. All the boys are after you.'

'Then they're wasting their time,' she said, still amused. 'Any man I consider will have to have a steady job.'

'Ah well,' Douglas shrugged his shoulders, 'that puts me out of the running, but I'll keep on trying to get you to come out with me. See you, Ruthie.' He walked away, giving her a cheeky grin.

The first hour that day was quiet, and she passed the time chatting to Mrs Law. Ruth was lucky to have got this spot, for the two of them worked well together and it was a comfort to be near her. A trickle of customers began to arrive around ten o'clock, and by lunchtime she had sold two toys, three items of baby clothes, and had an order to make a frock for an eight-year-old girl. Not bad after a slow start.

During a lull she saw John running through the crowds, skidding to a halt by her stall.

He held out a bag. 'Mum said you forgot your sandwiches, and can I stay with you? Mr Hunter is going to look at some more houses and Dad's gone with him. Mum and Sally are visiting the Selbys, and Eddie's playing football.'

'Didn't you want to go with Eddie?'

'No.' John pulled a face. 'Eddie's getting too grown up to want me hanging around him all the time, especially when he's with his friends. And anyway, I'd rather be with you. Can I stay, Ruthie? I can serve and put the stuffing in some toys for you.' He gave her a hopeful look.

145

'Of course you can stay. I do have a couple of toys to stuff and you can certainly help me with customers if we get busy. Want to share my lunch? There's plenty here for two.'

'Yes, please.' He joined her behind the stall, all smiles. 'Mum said we're all doing quite well now and Eddie will be leaving school in a couple of years or so. I don't even have to wear his cut-downs any more.'

'Yes, we're better off now.' She smiled down at her brother. 'And so is Mr Hunter if he's thinking of buying another house.'

Nodding, John munched on a sandwich, a thoughtful expression on his face. 'I wish Bob would come back. I still miss him. Do you think he's all right, Ruthie?'

'I'm sure he is, darling. Bob can look after himself.'

'Suppose so, but he should at least tell us where he is so we won't keep worrying about him.'

'Yes, he should!' This was a sore point with Ruth and she was annoyed at him for being so thoughtless. 'He chose to walk away from us and break all ties, so we shouldn't keep worrying about him.'

Their conversation was brought to an end by a flurry of customers. John loved this and bustled happily around as he tried to help with the serving.

'When you leave school I'll have to employ you,' Ruth joked, as the last customer walked away carrying the parcel John had carefully wrapped for them.

'You don't have to wait that long; I can help you on Saturdays.' Suddenly his bright smile changed to a scowl and he shot in front of his sister, holding

146

out his arms protectively. 'Go away!'

Ruth looked at the people standing by the stall and took a deep breath. Would she ever forget? 'Captain Russell, Mrs Russell,' she said stiffly, then noticed the girl standing with them. She smiled. 'Hello Lilly, how are you?'

'All right.' She rushed up, pushing John aside so she could hug Ruth. 'Did you make all these lovely dolls?'

'Yes, would you like one?'

'Oh, please! Could I have that one in the white dress?'

'Of course. Get it for Lilly, please, John.'

The boy took it from a shelf at the back of the stall and then held it out to Lilly. He stood back in horror after receiving a big kiss. 'What did you do that for?'

'Because I wanted to,' Lilly said, a mischievous grin on her face.

He slid behind his big sister just in case this strange girl tried to kiss him again.

'Coward,' Lilly muttered, still grinning. Then she kissed the doll and hugged it to her. 'Thank you ever so much, Ruth. This is the prettiest doll I've ever had.'

'I'm glad you like it.' Ruth now turned her attention to the captain and his wife, but Mrs Russell was busy inspecting the baby clothes on the stall.

'Oh, darling, just look at this!' She was holding up a christening gown. 'It's absolutely exquisite, and there is a matching bonnet and booties.'

'It's lovely, my dear. Buy it and anything else you need.' The captain smiled at Ruth. 'We are expecting another child in five months.'

147

'I'm going to have a sister this time,' Lilly told them confidently. 'I don't want another brother, unless he likes horses, of course.'

This made them all laugh, breaking the tension, expect for John, who was keeping a wary eye on Lilly. At nearly nine years old he wasn't used to strange girls kissing him.

'Thank you for your letters, Ruth, but I would have liked to hear from you more often.'

'Er . . . Well, I've been rather busy.'

'So I see. We went to your house but no one appears to be in, and as you mentioned the market in one of your letters, we came looking for you here.'

'They're all out today.' Ruth watched in amazement as Mrs Russell gathered up baby clothes.

'These are so beautiful, Ruth, I can't resist them. I'll take them all. How much do they come to?'

John had crept out from behind Ruth as she added up the sale, writing each price down. He already had the paper ready to make a neat parcel.

Ruth handed the captain the bill. 'It comes to one pound, eighteen and sixpence, sir. The christening gown was quite expensive because it took a long time to make.'

He scanned the figures, and then looked up. 'You haven't included the doll.'

'That was my gift to Lilly.'

He nodded. 'That is very generous of you, Ruth, but I hope you have charged us full price for the clothes?'

'I have. The prices are on them so you can check if you want to.'

'Then you are not charging enough,' he said as

148

he handed over a large five-pound note.

'I can't change that!' she gasped.

'Then keep the change.'

'Certainly not!'

Noting the determined glint in her eyes, he took the note out of her hand, found some coins in his pocket and handed them to her. His mouth twisted in a wry smile as she handed him his one shilling and sixpence change.

John had finished tying up the large parcel and he held it out to Mrs Russell, who immediately handed it to her husband. 'I've been so busy buying that we haven't told Ruth why we're here.'

'My mother died two months ago.' The captain took a small black velvet box out of his pocket and held it out to Ruth. 'She left you this in her will. There's a note inside from her.'

Ruth made no attempt to take the box, but looked at it with suspicion. 'I'm sorry to hear your mother has died,' she said politely, 'but why would she leave me anything? I don't think she even liked me.'

'You are wrong,' Mrs Russell told her. 'She was fond of you, and never got over feeling guilty about the way she had treated you. This is her way of saying sorry. Please take the gift.'

The captain placed the box firmly in her hands, and when she opened it she went cold with anger. 'Is this the brooch I was accused of stealing?'

'Yes, it is.'

She snapped the box shut and dropped it on the stall. 'You can't really expect me to take that, surely?'

'Read the note,' the captain urged.

'No, no!' Ruth shook her head. 'Every time I saw

149

a policeman I'd be terrified he was coming for me. No, I couldn't go through that again.'

'Don't you upset my sister again!' John stepped in front of Ruth, bristling with anger. 'She told you she don't want it. Take it away.'

'We're not upsetting her, silly,' Lilly told him, trying to push him out of the way. 'We're only trying to give her a present from my grandma.'

'Don't you call me silly! Go away!'

'Children! Stop shouting at each other,' the captain ordered, his tone of authority silencing them. 'We are just trying to carry out my mother's wishes, John.'

'She hurt my sister, and we don't let anyone do that.' John glared at the people in front of him, especially the girl.

'We know, and she was sorry. My mother was a strong person and inclined to rule any household she was in, so we moved her into the Gatehouse with her own servants. She was much happier there, and the arrangement worked well. When my mother made up her mind she was very hard to overrule. Do you understand, John?'

He pursed his lips as he thought about it, gazing up at his sister, and when she nodded, he said, 'I suppose so, but we won't have you making Ruthie unhappy again.'

'And it is very commendable of you to defend your sister, young man.' The captain turned his attention back to Ruth. 'Can you leave the stall so we can talk in private?'

'Um, well, Mrs Law will keep an eye on it for me. There's a cafe across the road.' She looked doubtful. 'But it isn't your kind of place, sir. It's a bit rough.'

150

'Ruth, I have been in trenches with mud up to my knees, shells bursting all around and men dying at my feet. Do you think I would object to going into a workman's cafe?'

'Sorry, sir, I didn't mean to insult you.'

'You haven't, and do stop calling me sir. From the moment Bob walked into my library and told me to stop drinking, you have all become a part of my life.' He smiled and picked up the box, slipping it into his pocket. 'Come on, I'll buy you a cup of tea and a bun.'

That made her laugh, easing the tension between them. 'All right, I'll just see Mrs Law.'

'There's no need for that, Ruth,' Mrs Russell told her. 'I'll take care of the stall. Everything is neatly priced and John will see I do the job properly. Won't you, John?'

He nodded, and glared at the captain. 'Don't you upset my sister or we'll all be very angry with you.'

Ben held up his hands in surrender. 'I promise.'

The young boy nodded. 'We'll take care of the stall, Ruthie, but you come straight back for me if he don't behave himself.'

'I will, John.'

As they made their way to the cafe, the captain said, 'Fierce little thing, isn't he?'

'He's usually a quiet, sensitive boy, until one of his family is threatened. He might only be small, but I believe he would take on anyone to protect us.'

'You're his favourite, I suspect.'

She nodded. 'We're very close.'

The cafe was crowded, and as they walked in one market trader called out, 'Found yourself a boyfriend at last, Ruthie?'

She clipped him playfully around the ear as they walked past, heading for a vacant table in the corner. 'Mind your own business, George.'

When they sat down the captain was chuckling quietly. 'I'm flattered.'

Ruth ordered tea and buns for them both. 'So am I. Now, what is it you wanted to say?'

'Read my mother's note first, and then we'll talk.' He pushed the velvet box across the table.

She took the note out and started to read, her frown deepening all the time. Then she looked straight at the man opposite her and sighed in exasperation. 'I don't want the brooch, but your mother isn't making it easy for me. I've never held any ill will towards your mother or your wife; they only did what they thought was right. Your world is very different from ours, and I tried to take into account the difference in upbringing and attitude to life. The brooch was found in my room and it never occurred to them that someone else might have put it there. It was the way they dealt with it that was wrong. I was terrified when they accused me of stealing, and to be turned out like that was more than I could stand. I'll never forget it, and it still gives me nightmares now and again. I can't take the brooch. It'd be a constant reminder.'

'It's legally yours now.' Ben stopped her from pushing it back to him. 'If you don't want to keep it then sell it and put the money towards your business.'

She shook her head, shocked at the suggestion. 'Can you imagine the suspicious looks I would get if I tried to sell such a valuable thing? We're in the slums of London, Captain, not a large estate in Kent. People like us don't own valuable jewellery.'

'You have my mother's note to prove it belongs to you, and it is stated clearly in her will. If it will put your mind at ease, I will also sign a declaration to that effect in front of any witness you choose.' He sat back and looked around the busy cafe. 'There are plenty of people here you know.'

She fingered the box and pulled a face. 'That's kind of you, but I don't think I could sell it, and I honestly don't want it. Give it to Lilly.'

'My daughter has more than enough of everything, and it isn't mine to give away.'

'Then I'll give it to her.'

'No! Dammit, Ruth.' His raised voice turned a few heads.

Two of the traders were immediately standing by the table. 'Is he giving you trouble, Ruthie?'

'Everything's all right,' she told them. 'We're having a slight disagreement, that's all.'

They glared menacingly at Ben. 'You be careful, mate.'

'I assure you I have no intention of harming Ruth.'

The men looked startled at Ben's upper-class accent, and the rest of the customers were beginning to take an interest.

'Captain Russell is a friend of ours,' Ruth told the men in an effort to defuse the situation. 'You can relax. We're not going to come to blows. He's trying to help me and I'm being stubborn.'

'Ah, women are good at that.' One of the men smirked and turned his attention to Ben. 'Captain, you say? Fought in the war, did you?' When he nodded, the man asked, 'Where were you?'

'The Somme.'

'Behind the lines, I suppose.'

Ben shook his head. 'I'm only a captain. I was in the front line with my troops.'

'Ah, and a bloody massacre that was.'

There were murmurs of agreement, and the men drifted back to their own table.

'Now, where were we, Ruth?'

'You swore at me. What were you going to say after that?'

The looked at each other and burst into laughter. Ruth found it impossible to dislike this man. 'Eat your bun,' she told him, 'and we'll start again.'

He took a bite, chewed, and then nodded. 'Not bad. I am not used to being disobeyed, so are you going to be more reasonable this time?'

'I'm always reasonable, but you can't expect to win every battle. I can't understand why your mother left me that particular brooch. What on earth did she expect me to do with such a valuable piece of jewellery? I wouldn't like to sell it, and I certainly couldn't wear it.'

'You could always keep it for your wedding day,' he teased. 'Or you could keep it for your sister, Sally. I'm sure she'd love it when she's older.'

Ruth hesitated this time, and sensing a victory, Ben said gently, 'Take it, Ruth. It is Mother's way of apologizing to you.'

'I don't seem to have much choice.' Ruth curled her fingers around the delicate box and looked up. 'But I'll have that signed letter from you. It will make me feel easier. Mrs Law, on the next stall, will witness your signature.'

Ben sat back with a sigh of relief. 'Thank you, Ruth.'

She stood up. 'We'd better get back and see how they've been getting on.'

154

After Ben had paid for the tea and two extra buns for the children, they walked back to the market, stopping once to buy writing materials.

Lilly saw them and came running, still clutching her doll. 'We've sold lots. It was fun.'

Mrs Russell was pointing out the fine stitching on a garment to a customer when they arrived at the stall. She seemed quite at home in the role of market trader.

'My goodness!' Ruth exclaimed when she saw the empty spaces on the stall. 'You have been busy.'

When the customer left carrying her parcel, the captain's wife smiled, her face glowing. 'Do you know, Ben, I think I'm rather good at this, and so are Lillian and John.'

'I've got lots of money, Ruthie.' John patted the bag he had tied around his waist.

'In that case I think you and Lilly deserve a reward.' She took the bag from him and gave him some coins. 'Go to that stall where you bought your wooden toys, and buy something for yourself, Lilly and her little brother. Oh, and you mustn't forget Eddie and Sally. Then when you come back the captain has bought you both a bun from the cafe.'

'Thanks, Ruthie.' He gave her a brilliant smile, and then looked doubtfully at Lilly. 'You'd better come and choose something.'

The girl grinned and clasped his hand as they walked away.

Emma laughed at the sight of the pair of them hand in hand. 'It looks as if he isn't so scared of her now.'

'As long as she doesn't try to kiss him again,' Ruth said drily. 'Now, Captain, you promised me a letter.'

Twenty

Sales that day had been exceptionally good, not even counting the huge amount Mrs Russell had bought. That wasn't normal trade, so Ruth didn't include it in her day's takings. She would put it aside for a rainy day. Her dad's job seemed secure at the moment, but it wasn't wise to take it for granted because so many men were out of work. It was even tough at the market, and that was why she had sent John to buy something from the man who made wooden toys. People were watching the pennies and didn't have anything to spare for luxuries.

John smiled up at her as they made their way home. 'We had a good day today, Ruthie. Thank you for the toys. The man was ever so pleased when we bought so much from him.'

'I expect he was. We must help people when we can. Times are hard.'

The boy nodded. 'Why are some people rich and others poor, Ruthie? It don't seem right.'

'I know how you feel, John, but it's always been like this. A lot of things need to change before it gets better. Men need decent wages and secure jobs. Many of the slum houses should be torn down and new ones built to buy or rent at reasonable prices.'

He pursed his lips thoughtfully. 'Do you think that will ever happen?'

'I hope so.' She placed an arm around his shoulder as they walked along. 'But Dad and me don't intend to wait for that time to come. We're both working hard to get us out of the slums. One day we'll have a nice house away from here, you'll see.'

He smiled again. 'I'll help too.'

'You are helping, John.'

When they walked into the scullery everyone else was home, and there was a lovely smell of cooking from the large pot bubbling away on the stove.

Ruth sniffed appreciatively. 'Smells like your famous suet bacon roll, Mum.'

'I thought you'd both be hungry after a day at the market.' Daisy took some of the parcels from them. 'What on earth have you got here?'

'We've had a good day, Mum,' John told her proudly. 'The captain and his wife came to see us, and they bought ever such a lot of things. Oh, and Lilly was with them, as well.'

'Why were they here?' Steve asked, frowning.

'They came to the house first, but you were all out, so they came across to the market. I'll tell you about it later.'

Steve and Daisy nodded, knowing their daughter would rather talk to them alone.

'What did you think of Lilly?' Daisy asked her youngest son.

'All right, I suppose.' He turned swiftly to Eddie and Sally. 'Ruthie sold so much today she's bought us all a present. I chose them, but the man said we can change them if you'd rather have something else.'

'What did you get me?' Sally was jumping up and down in excitement.

'A little dolls' house, and I got a train for Eddie.'

'Children, take your presents into the other room while I get the supper ready,' Daisy ordered. They scooted off, eager to play with their presents.

157

'John didn't say much about Lilly,' Steve remarked.

'No,' Ruth grinned. 'Don't let him know that I told you, but she kissed him.'

'Oh my goodness,' Daisy laughed. 'No wonder he doesn't want to talk about it. But give him a few more years and he'll change his mind about girls.'

Steve nodded, then turned to his daughter. 'Tell us what the Russells were doing here?'

She took the velvet box out of her pocket and told them all about it. They were astounded as they looked at the valuable jewel. 'I didn't want to take the brooch, but the captain said it was legally mine now. There's a note from his mother to me, but I made him give me a letter signed by him, and witnessed by Mrs Law. I wanted absolute proof that the brooch was mine so there wouldn't be any doubt about it.'

'You did the right thing.' Steve gave his daughter an affectionate smile. 'Not that I believe for a moment that Captain Russell would have lied to you, sweetheart, but having those written proofs of your ownership will give you peace of mind.'

Ruth sighed. 'There was a time when I trusted everyone, seeing only the best in them, but I'm not like that any more.'

'It's called growing up, and we're glad you are more cautious now,' Daisy told her. 'What are you going to do with the brooch?'

'Goodness knows.' Ruth shook her head and laughed quietly. 'I certainly can't wear it at the market. They'll think I'm charging too much for my goods. Can you put it in the rainy-day box you keep in your bedroom, Dad?'

'Of course. You know where to find it if you ever

need to, don't you?'

'Yes, it's under the loose floorboard by the side of the wardrobe. Oh, and you can put this with it.' She handed over the money Mrs Russell had given her for the baby clothes. 'Put that towards the savings for the new house.'

'You don't have to do that, Ruthie,' Daisy told her. 'That's only a dream. It might never happen.'

'Yes it will. Bob always said anything is possible if you set your mind to it. We'll get out of this place one day if we all pull together. The kids need to go to better schools because they're not going to get a good education round here.'

'You're right about that.' Steve stood up. 'I'll go and put these things away safely, while you girls lay the table. I'm starving.'

'Don't be long. It will be ready in five minutes.' Daisy started to set out the plates for dishing up. 'Is Alf joining us?'

The back door opened and their neighbour looked in. 'Love to, if I'm invited.'

'You're invited.' Daisy beckoned Alf in. 'We want to know how you got on today. Steve hasn't had a chance to tell us yet.'

The meal was thoroughly enjoyed, and not a scrap left on the plates. A large pot of tea was made and they settled down to talk. The three youngsters had soon disappeared to play with their new toys, but Ruth was now considered old enough to stay with the grown-ups.

'Did you find another house?' Daisy asked.

'There are plenty to choose from in these hard times, and the prices are reasonable. We saw a couple of possibilities, but the one I liked the best was more than I can afford. If they haven't sold it in a couple of weeks I'll go round and again and make them a lower offer.'

'It'll be worth a try, Alf,' Steve told him. 'It was a sturdy house, and in the same street as your other one.'

Alf nodded. 'I'm in no hurry, so we'll see how it goes. Fancy me talking about buying houses. Who would have thought that the pathetic drunk who came home from the war would be buying houses? It's hard to believe.'

'You're putting your unexpected windfall to good use,' Daisy told him. 'And that's the right thing to do.'

'If you do buy another one will you live in it?' Ruth wanted to know.

'I can't do that, Ruthie. I've got to stay here in case Bob comes back one day. After all, I want him to be able to find me because I'm doing this for him. I want to see he has a secure future.'

'Do you really think he will turn up after all this time?' Daisy sounded doubtful.

Alf's expression changed to sadness. 'To be honest I think he's washed his hands of us, but I still cling to the hope that he will come home. Daft, I know, but I'd like to be able to put things right between us.'

Ruth said nothing. She had adored Bob from a little girl, and in her eyes he hadn't been able to do any wrong. That was no longer how she thought. He had walked away from his dad, leaving him to fight the drink on his own, and what a struggle that had been. She couldn't forget how she had cried out for her friend when the Russells had thrown her out. But he'd run away again, and she didn't think she would ever feel the same way about him again. If he walked in now she would leave the room. That was how low her opinion of him had dropped. He didn't deserve what his dad was doing for him. Of course, she kept all these thoughts to herself.

*　　　*　　　*

'How did you manage to get Ruth to take the brooch, darling?' Emma asked her husband as they settled in the sitting room after dinner.

'It was difficult. She was adamant that she didn't want it, and I understood because it has unpleasant memories for her. I do think Mother could have left her something else, and not that particular item.'

'So do I.' Emma sighed. 'But it was stated clearly in her Will, and if we hadn't taken it ourselves, she would have sent it straight back to us by the next post.'

Ben took the cup of coffee from his wife. 'And then we would have had the unpleasant task of asking Steve Cooper to accept it on his daughter's behalf. Mother put us in a difficult situation—again.'

'I know, but I really think she wanted to make amends, and thought this was the way to do it.' Emma studied her husband carefully. 'You like Steve Cooper, don't you?'

'He's a fine man and deserves better than he's got. I admire him for the way he defends and protects his family. I wish I could get to know him better, but after accusing his daughter of stealing, the gulf between us is too wide.'

'It was too wide even before that happened,' she pointed out.

'You're talking about the class barrier, and I

161

don't agree. The war broke down a lot of the old prejudices, but unfortunately the divide between the rich and the poor is still too great. Why the hell isn't the government doing more for these men and their families? They fought for this country, and what have they come back to? Unemployment, bad housing and poverty. Dear Lord, Emma, what did we fight for?'

Emma didn't get a chance to answer because Lilly came in holding her little brother's hand. She was still clutching the doll Ruth had given her, and Robert had a small wooden train in his other hand.

'We've come to say goodnight,' Lilly announced. 'Robert's very pleased with his toy, aren't you?'

He smiled, toddling straight over to his father to show him.

'I had a lovely day today, Mummy, and it was nice to see Ruth again. Do you think she would come and visit us, and bring John with her? He's a bit bossy, but I liked him.'

'I don't think they would come here, darling,' Emma told her daughter.

Lilly pulled a face. 'I suppose not. We'll just have to visit them. I think I'll marry John when I'm older. Night, night.' She beamed at them both. 'Come along, Robert.'

Ben was laughing quietly as the children left the room. 'Now, that really would break down a few barriers!'

Twenty-One

Where had the time gone? Bob had only intended to stay for a couple of weeks until he found something else, and it had turned into more than two years. His attitude had been that he was just passing through, but had gradually changed as he'd learnt the skills necessary to care for the men. He had quickly discovered that not only was he good at it, but he gained a lot of satisfaction from the work. His respect for the men and everyone who cared for them had grown, and so had his understanding about the suffering the war had caused. So many men without visible injuries were carrying scars inside—like his father and Captain Russell. The work here had been an education, making him look deep inside himself, and questioning his feelings, motives and actions. He didn't always like what he saw.

Bob gazed down at the Thames and felt a sense of peace. That arrogant, judgemental boy no longer existed, and he knew that the most valuable lesson he had learnt was compassion—a quality he had been sadly lacking in previously.

'What's troubling you, Bob?'

He turned at the sound of the soft voice. 'Hello, Sister. What brings you here?'

'I've been shopping and saw you sitting here.' She took the seat beside him on the bench. 'And you haven't answered my question.'

'I was just wondering where the time had gone.'

'It was more than that.'

He gave an amused laugh. 'You are far too

163

perceptive.'

'I've come to know you, except for that inner self you keep guarded. We've never really sat down and talked, so tell me about yourself.'

'Not much to tell really. I've always thought I'd like to be a teacher, but there's not a hope.'

'There's always hope, Bob.' She patted his arm. 'But you still haven't opened that inner door. Do you think you are ready to tell me why a young boy was wandering around the country on his own?'

It only took him a moment to decide, then he nodded and started to explain. It was a relief to unburden himself to this gentle woman he had come to admire and respect. The words he had never been able to voice came easily at last.

'And have you forgiven your father?' she asked when he stopped talking.

'I did that after only a week here.' There was a wry twist to his mouth as he said, 'But forgiving myself is much harder. I walked away from a man who needed my support and understanding. And then I walked away from Captain Russell, who had cared enough to want to help. I was so angry.'

'Are you still angry?'

'No, that burnt itself out long ago.'

'Have you thought about going to see your father and Captain Russell, or at least writing to them?'

'I've thought about it, but what could I say? I couldn't face them. I'm not proud of the way I've acted; in fact I'm ashamed of myself.'

'You don't need to feel like that.' A smile crossed her face as she looked at him. 'Do you believe in Fate?'

'No, I believe we make our own destiny. Our lives are shaped by the decisions we make, and we have to live with them, good or bad.'

'Shall I tell you how I see things?'

'Please.'

'I believe every action you've taken was meant to do one thing, and that was to bring you here. As soon as you walked in I knew you belonged here. And I was right. You have dealt with many of your problems and are growing into a fine man. A complex man, but you have shown yourself to be a man of kindness and compassion. You are excellent at what you can now do, and have gained the respect of everyone. You had to come here because it was the only way you were going to grow to your full potential. I'm not sure if teaching should be your profession, or the work you are doing now. That is for Fate to decide.'

She glanced at the watch pinned to her jacket. 'I must get back now, but may I ask you one thing, Bob? Don't leave here until you are certain which path you should take.'

'You know I can never deny you anything,' he joked. 'I wasn't thinking of going anywhere just yet.'

'That's good, because I believe Fate hasn't finished with you yet.'

He couldn't help laughing softly as she walked away. It had been good to talk freely at last, but she was the only person who could have coaxed him to do so.

Later that day as he was sitting quietly beside one of the men, there was a touch on his shoulder.

'Bob, could you come to my office, please?'

'Can it wait, Sister? I promised Harry I'd stay with him until the end. It can't be long now.'

'He won't know if you leave for a short time.'

Bob shook his head. 'He might, and I gave my

165

word.'

'Of course, you're quite right. You stay then, and I'll see you later. It isn't anything that won't keep.'

Two hours later, Bob stood up, stretched and walked out of the room. This had happened a few times since he'd been here, and he'd learnt to cope with it, but it didn't get any easier. He'd kept his word and now he had better see what Sister wanted.

After knocking on the door he looked in. 'You wanted to see me.'

'Come in, Bob, and sit down for a moment. I want you to meet a good friend of mine, James Morgan. He's a professor of mathematics at Oxford University.'

Bob smiled politely. 'I'm pleased to meet you, sir.'

They talked for a while, but Bob couldn't quite understand what he was doing in Sister's office talking to one of her friends. James Morgan was interesting, though, and he found the conversation stimulating. He was obviously a man of considerable intelligence, and his sense of humour appealed to Bob.

Quite suddenly he turned the conversation round and said, 'I believe you are thinking about becoming a teacher.'

Bob shrugged. 'Thinking about it is as far as I get.'

'Have you given up, then?'

'It's always been a dream—a desire to do something useful, I suppose—without any hope of becoming a reality.' Bob gave an amused grin. 'Sister tells me that nothing is impossible because Fate guides our path.'

The professor gave a low rumbling laugh.

166

'It's no good you two making fun of me,' she said, smiling at them. 'Sometimes we think we should do a certain thing because that's right for us, and then something comes along to change those plans, and we are led in a completely different direction. And that turns out to be what is right for us. I don't believe chance comes into it.'

'And you could well be right, Mary,' James Morgan said, winking at Bob. 'But we have to walk the path that is in front of us.'

'Of course, I'm not saying we should sit around and see what falls into our laps.'

'Indeed not.'

Bob glanced at the clock and quickly rose to his feet. 'Please excuse me, sir, but I must get back to work. It's been a pleasure to meet you.'

'I've enjoyed our talk, young man.'

*   *   *

'What do you think, James?' Mary asked when Bob had left the office.

'Considering his background he's remarkably bright, and appears to have compensated for a bad education by reading a great deal of good literature. That teacher he told you about must have seen to that.'

'That's what I thought. I don't like to impose on our friendship, James, but do you think you can help him?'

He laughed. 'Mary, you know you wouldn't hesitate to impose. Why do you want to help this boy?'

'I like him.'

'Not good enough.'

167

'Oh, you are a difficult man. All right, I believe he has the potential to do something with his life, and I do not like to see talent wasted.'

'Neither do I, but there is a problem with him. He's carrying a lot of mental baggage around and it colours his attitudes and opinions. It could hold him back.'

'I disagree with you. He has changed in the years he has been here, and quite honestly I believe he could achieve a lot now.'

The professor stood up. 'I'll talk with him again in a couple of weeks. Don't let him go wandering off, will you?'

'I'll try, but I have the feeling he's getting restless. His work here is excellent, and I don't want to lose him, but all the time he has this idea of becoming a teacher, he'll be unsettled, no matter what he's doing.'

James Morgan stood up and kissed Mary on the cheek. 'Then we'll have to hope Fate takes a hand.'

They both laughed as he left.

*   *   *

Bob didn't sleep much that night. Ever since he had left home he'd shut out the past, but after talking about it the doors had sprung wide open. He couldn't help wondering what his father was up to now. And what about Ruth and her family?

He tossed and turned. Dammit, he wanted to know, but he couldn't go back to Canning Town. Too much time had passed, and he didn't think he could face them now. But there was one man who might be able to tell him, and Bob owed him an apology as well.

Decision made, he finally dozed off.

The next morning he headed straight for the office and was greeted with a bright smile.

'Good morning, Bob. You're in early this morning.'

'Morning, Sister. I want to ask you if I could take a couple of days off.'

'Of course you can. You are due a break so take a week if you want to.' She studied him carefully. 'Where are you thinking of going?'

'Kent. There's someone there I need to see, but two or three days will be enough. From tomorrow, if possible?'

'That will be quite all right.' She looked him straight in the eyes. 'You will come back, won't you?'

'I promise.'

*   *   *

The house looked exactly the same, and pleasant memories flooded back, bringing a smile to Bob's face. While he was standing there the front door flew open. 'Well, you certainly took your time coming back, Robert Hunter.'

'Hello, Mrs Trent, have you got a room I could have for a couple of days?'

'Of course!'

Bob's grin spread. 'You're just as beautiful as ever.'

'Oh, oh, I see you've learnt the art of flattery while you've been away.'

He laughed and lifted her off her feet. 'It's wonderful to see you again, Mrs Trent.'

'Come in,' she said, as soon as her feet touched

169

the ground again, 'and tell me what you've been up to.'

After making a large pot of tea and producing her famous fruitcake, they talked for more than an hour. Mrs Trent demanded every detail of what he had been doing, but he managed to avoid telling her exactly where he was living, or the true nature of his work.

Finally, Bob sat back, accepted another slice of cake, and said, 'Now it's your turn. I want to know how Captain Russell and his family are.'

'Just fine. He hasn't touched a drop of drink and his family is growing.' Her face lit up. 'The little boy is toddling around now, and Lilly is turning into a pretty girl, but is just as outspoken as ever.'

'I'm glad she hasn't changed,' he laughed, remembering the lively child.

Mrs Trent studied him thoughtfully. 'No, she hasn't, but you have.'

'I'm older.'

'It's more than that. It's hard to explain, but there's a softness about you that wasn't there before.' She tipped her head to one side, concentrating. 'Am I right to feel that you have fought a few battles with yourself and found a measure of inner peace?'

'You could say that.' His smile was wry. 'I was too quick to judge, and so sure I was right. I didn't understand what Dad and men like him were going through. All I could see was that Mum was suffering, and I blamed him. I was wrong. Instead of helping I added to both their burdens. I'm not proud of that.'

She reached out and squeezed his arm. 'You mustn't blame yourself for what happened. You were so young, and the past can't be changed, Bob, no matter how much we wish it could.'

'I know, but it isn't easy to let the regrets go.'

Mrs Trent stood up. 'You've grown into a sensible young man. You can have the same room as before. How long are you staying?'

'A couple of days, and then I must get back.'

'Well, after you've put your things in your room, go and see Captain Russell. Jim's still there and he's married now with a nice little house on the estate.'

'Ah, so you've lost a lodger. Is anyone else staying here?'

'No, so that means I can spoil you. Off you go, but be back by seven for dinner.'

It was strange, but Bob felt as if he had come home as he walked towards the stable block, eager to see if Midnight was still there. He started singing softly as he walked through the door, and smiled when a horse started stamping in the stall. That was Midnight.

'What's the matter with you, Midnight?' Jim called. 'I'll let you out in a minute.'

'He knows I'm here.'

Jim spun round. 'Bob! About time you turned up. Where on earth have you been?'

'Working in Surrey.' The two men laughed with pleasure at seeing each other again. 'I hear you're married now.'

'Eight months ago.' Jim shook his head at the racket coming from Midnight's stall. 'For heaven's sake, go and sing to that animal. He's been nothing but trouble ever since you left.'

Midnight was beside himself with excitement when he saw Bob, pushing, shoving and milling around in the small space. As soon as Bob began to sing, he calmed down, a dreamy look in his eyes.

'Daft animal. We've all tried singing to him, but he didn't like our voices.'

There was a sound of small feet running. 'Is he here? Green said it was him. Where is he? Bob!'

The girl threw herself at Bob, and he lifted her high in the air, pretending to stagger under the weight. 'Who is this grown-up young lady?'

She laughed as he put her down. 'It's me, silly. Why have you been away so long? We thought you weren't going to come back.'

'Sorry, Lilly, but I've been busy and couldn't come before. I'm only visiting.'

'Hello, Bob.'

'Captain Russell.' They shook hands. 'I hope you don't mind me walking into your stables like this, but I couldn't wait to see Midnight again.'

'You are welcome anywhere on this estate. What brings you back after so long?'

'I'd like to talk to you, sir. Can you spare me a few minutes some time? I'll be here for two days.'

'Let's go into the house and we can talk now. I won't keep Bob long, Lilly,' he told his daughter.

Once in the library, Bob wasted no time. 'I've come to apologize for walking out the way I did. You were only trying to help and I should have recognized that. You and your family had been good to me, and I'm sorry I was so ungrateful.'

'No apology is necessary.' The captain sat down, and waited while Bob did the same. 'What have you been doing since you left?'

'Oh, this and that,' Bob said evasively. 'I've been working in Surrey most of the time.'

'But you won't tell me where?' When Bob shook

his head slightly, he said, 'Well, you look well fed, and that suit is expertly cut, so I must assume you are making a decent living.'

'I am, and being so tall I can't buy ready-made clothes, but because of where I work, I've found a sympathetic tailor.'

'This place you work is special, then?' Ben still probed.

'I think it is,' was all Bob would say.

'Then it's no good me offering you work here again?'

'No, sir, I can't stay, but thank you.' Bob stretched out his long legs and relaxed. He hadn't been sure of his reception, but everyone seemed to be pleased to see him. It was a good feeling.

'You've changed,' Ben said, studying him carefully.

'So Mrs Trent tells me,' he laughed. 'I've grown up and learnt a few lessons along the way. I might not have done that if I'd stayed here.' Ben's smile was wry. 'A very kind lady said Fate was guiding me. It's a nice thought, but I don't believe that. It was pure chance I ended up where I did.'

'You like what you do then?'

'It's challenging.' Bob knew the captain was still trying to discover where he was and what he was doing. 'It's no good you trying to find out because that's all I'm saying. Anyway, you'd never believe me if I did tell you.' He changed the subject. 'I was wondering if you have any news of my Dad and the Coopers?'

The captain drew in a deep breath. 'I have, but you're not going to like what I have to tell you. Before I begin can I ask you not to storm off again? It happened more than two years ago, and all is well now.'

'I don't like the sound of this.' Bob sat upright. 'What's been going on?'

By the time the captain had come to the end of telling him what had happened to Ruth, Bob's hands were curled in tight fists. 'I wouldn't have let her be treated like that!'

'Neither would I, but unfortunately for Ruth we weren't here. I arrived back the next morning to find Steve Cooper here, in a towering rage, and determined to clear his daughter's name, which we did very quickly.'

Sadness showed in Bob's eyes. 'Poor little devil. Being accused of stealing must have come as a terrible shock.'

'It did, and I think she will be more likely to question people's motive in the future. I did manage to persuade her to write to us now and again, and we do receive an occasional letter. I don't think she will ever really trust us again.' He looked steadily at the young man in front of him, and then said gently, 'Or you.'

Bob actually flinched. 'Is she all right now?'

'I think so. She is putting her sewing skills to use making toys and children's clothes, and has her own market stall now. Don't you want to know about your father?'

'Is he still off the drink?'

'Yes; like me he's never touched a drop again.'

'That's all I need to know.'

'Are you going to see him?' When Bob shook his head, he asked, 'Will you give me permission to tell him I've seen you and you are all right?'

'You can do that after I've gone.'

'Thank you.' Ben stood up, smiling for the first

time. 'Let's see if you can still ride. Lillian will be getting impatient.'

*   *   *

For the next two days, Bob spent all his time on the estate, and Mrs Trent cooked his favourite food. He enjoyed every minute of his stay, but he had promised Sister he would return, and it was time to leave. But there was one more place he wanted to visit first.

Twenty-Two

After the green fields of Kent, this place looked even rougher than Bob remembered. The dirt and grime made him grimace in distaste, and he wondered why on earth he'd come. But he was here now, so he might as well go in.

When he stepped inside he couldn't believe his eyes, or ears. Children were running around screaming and throwing things at each other. Two teachers were trying to restore order, and another young woman was huddled in the corner with tears streaming down her cheeks. A little girl, obviously frightened, ran towards Bob, and he scooped her up, murmuring soothing words, but never taking his eyes off the chaos. It didn't take him long to spot the ringleaders, and when one of them ran to the door intent on escaping for the day, he locked it and slipped the key into his pocket.

The ruffian tugged at the door in vain, then snarled, 'What you do that for?'

Still holding the girl in one arm he caught the boy by the collar and lifted him over to the man who looked like the headmaster. 'Get your cane ready, sir; it looks as if you're going to need it.'

'Put me down!' the boy yelled, kicking his legs. 'I'll set my dad on you.'

Bob's smile was gleeful. He was now at least six feet six inches in height, and could lift a grown man with ease. 'Your dad can try.'

One of the other boys sniggered. 'He'll knock your dad into next week, Freddy. Just look at the size of him.'

Curiosity had stopped the noise and the kids were mostly silent, eyeing the newcomer with suspicion.

Bob handed the little girl over to one of the teachers, still holding on to the struggling boy. Then he pointed out three others. 'It looks as if these are the four you have to deal with, Headmaster.'

The accused kids all began to shout and blame each other for starting the trouble.

'Quiet!' Bob towered over them. 'You will all be disciplined in one way or another, so if the rest of you don't want the cane you had better get back to your classrooms. And we don't want to hear a sound from you.'

Subdued by Bob's powerful presence, they filed quietly back to their classes.

'Phew!' One of the teachers—a man with greying hair—took a deep breath. 'I'm getting too old for this. I don't know who you are, but thank you for your timely arrival.'

'How did this start?'

'It was my fault.' The woman who had been crying in the corner now dried her eyes, still shaking

176

badly. 'I can't control them and they know it.'

'We'll talk about that later, Miss Greenwood.' The headmaster then turned to Bob. 'Help me with these boys, will you? My office is at the end of the corridor.'

Bob handed the key to one of the teachers so they could unlock the door again, then ushered the four boys towards the office.

When each one had been dealt with and was back in class, the headmaster thanked Bob for helping. 'I'm Mr Edwards. Can I finally ask who you are and why you are here?'

'My name is Bob Hunter and I used to be a pupil here. I was passing by and decided to have a look at the old place.'

'Ah, that must have been before my time, but we are very grateful you happened to be around at that moment. Miss Greenwood is afraid of some of the children and shows it. That's all they need to start bullying her. It's a shame because she's a good teacher.'

'Perhaps she would be better suited to a quieter area.'

'Undoubtedly. Would you like to have a look around now?' He gave a hint of a smile. 'And perhaps you would like to look in on Miss Greenwood's class before you leave?'

'Might be an idea.'

The young teacher had bravely returned to her class and smiled hesitantly when Bob walked in with the headmaster.

'Are they behaving?' the headmaster asked.

'Yes, sir, thanks to this young man.'

'Good.' He surveyed the class. 'Now you all know that disorder of any kind will not be tolerated again.

Mr Hunter was once a pupil here and he is going to talk to you.' With that announcement he sat at a desk right at the back of the class, and nodded to Bob to begin.

This was rather disconcerting. Bob had only intended to have a look round the old place, but he understood the huge problem the man had, so he would want to listen.

He stood to his full height and looked at the sea of faces for a moment, then said, 'As Mr Edwards told you, I was a pupil here and lived only a couple of streets away. Tell me, do you like living in the slums, never having quite enough to eat, and watching your parents struggle to keep a roof over your heads?'

'Course not!' one boy said forcefully. 'It's a bloody disgrace. My dad fought in the war and he can't even get a job.'

'Nor mine!' several others chimed in.

'They was promised a better life,' Freddy said, 'and what a joke that is. Those in charge sit on their backsides and do nothing about us.'

When they all began to mutter, Bob held up his hand for silence. 'I agree that changes need to be made, and you are the generation who are going to see that those changes happen.'

'How we gonna do that? No one takes any notice of us,' someone shouted from the back.

'Then make them. But not by fighting, shouting or swearing. Listen to the way Miss Greenwood speaks and copy her, then study hard. Read as much as you can, and I don't mean rubbish. Your future is in your own hands, but if you carry on the way you are now you'll either end up on the streets, or in prison. The choice is up to you. Is that what you want?'

Every head in the classroom shook.

'Then do something about it, and the time to start is now. And remember, you are all individuals with your own strengths and weaknesses. Help each other as friends.' Bob perched on the edge of the desk. 'Any questions?'

Every hand in the room shot up, including the headmaster's, making them all laugh. 'We'll leave you to last, if you don't mind, sir?' Bob's eyes fixed on the leader of the riot. 'You, Freddy.'

'I took you for a gent, but you're one of us, so how did you do that?'

'I worked hard at school and when I left I took any rotten job I could find. I've dug ditches, been a stable boy shovelling muck, and many others, all hard labour. I've fought a lot of tough battles with myself—some I've lost and some I've won—and I know there are many more ahead of me. But I've always believed that the way we live is up to us. It's a constant challenge, but one I'll keep fighting.' He gazed at each face in turn. 'And you can all do the same.'

For the next hour he patiently answered questions so that everyone had their chance, even the headmaster.

Finally, he stood up and smiled. 'Thank you for listening, and for the many intelligent questions you have asked. It's been a pleasure to meet you.'

The children clapped as hard as they could and there was a completely different atmosphere about the place now. While he had been talking everyone in the school had crowded into the one classroom.

Bob shook hands with the teachers, waved to the children and walked to the door with the headmaster.

'The way you stood up and talked so frankly to the children was just what they needed. Have you ever thought about becoming a teacher?'

'I've thought about it,' was all Bob said, opening the door.

'Will you visit us again, young man?'

'I'll try.' Bob closed the door behind him and walked towards the station. That had been quite an experience. He'd thought that coming here would help to make his mind up about teaching, but honestly, he still didn't know how it would be possible to get the necessary qualifications. What was it the professor had said? We must walk the path in front of us and see where it leads? Well, that's all he could do, and the path he was on now didn't appear to lead to teaching.

*　　　*　　　*

The next day Eddie burst into the scullery, bursting with excitement when he saw everyone there, including Mr Hunter. 'Guess what I've just heard?'

'Stop hopping around or you'll be too out of breath to tell us,' Steve teased.

'I was just talking to Freddy Atkins—'

'I've told you not to go near that boy,' Daisy scolded. 'He's a bad lot.'

'He's all right now. Anyway, he was telling me about a riot at his school yesterday. Just when some of them were about to escape for the rest of the day, this man walks in and locks the door so they can't get out.' Eddie took a deep breath, gulping in air, and then continued. 'Freddy said he made them all go back to class—him and his mates got the cane for starting the trouble, and then this man came and talked to them. He let them ask him all sorts of questions.'

Eddie stopped and gazed at each one, savouring the moment when he told them his final bit of news. 'Freddy said the man was wearing a good suit and spoke well, and he told them he'd been a pupil at that school. He was ever so tall . . . and his name was Hunter.'

There was a stunned silence. The only sound was a knock on the front door.

'Bob was in Canning Town?' Alf gasped.

'It couldn't have been him. He would have come here, surely?' Steve was shaking his head in disbelief.

Eddie shrugged. 'Freddy said it was him. He sort of recognized him, but he was smart and all grown-up, so he couldn't be sure at first. But I knew it was him as soon as Freddy said he was ever so tall.'

'You're quite right, Eddie. It was Bob.'

They all stared at the man Daisy brought in.

'Captain Russell, what on earth is this all about?'

'Sit down,' Steve urged, as they all shuffled round to make room at the table. 'Tell us what you know.'

'Bob turned up at the estate and stayed for two days. I asked him if he was coming to see you, and when he said no, I wanted to let you know immediately. He said I could tell you when he had left. I urged him to stay longer, but he told me there was somewhere he wanted to visit before returning to his job in Surrey. Daisy gave me a brief outline of Eddie's story, so I'm guessing it was the school he wanted to see again.'

'Dear Lord, I don't believe this.' Alf was

perplexed. 'What's the boy up to?'

'I'm not sure.' Ben smiled at Daisy when she put a cup of tea in front of him. 'I couldn't get much information out of him, but he's changed, and if it wasn't for his size and easy way of moving, I might not have recognized him at first.'

'Changed in what way?' Steve asked.

'Well, outwardly he's a couple of inches taller, the suit he was wearing was not of the best material, but it was tailored to fit him well.' Ben paused to drink some tea. 'He was calmer, more in control of himself, and less like the troubled boy of some two years ago.'

'Didn't he give you any idea what he's doing?'

'I'm sorry,' Ben told Alf. 'All I could get out of him was that he was living somewhere in Surrey, and if he told me what he was doing I wouldn't believe him. All I can tell you is that he is well and very grown-up now.'

Alf smiled then. 'That's good to know. Thanks for coming to tell us, Captain, but I'd love to know what he was doing at the school. Do you think he's going to teach soon? It was always his dream.'

Pursing his lips, Ben shook his head. 'I don't think that's what he's doing. I've puzzled over it ever since his visit. His hands were clean and smooth, so he isn't engaged in manual labour, and he's very strong with well developed muscles.'

'That's what Freddy said.' Eddie joined in. 'He picked up one girl to stop her getting hurt, and at the same time caught hold of Freddy and lifted him right off the ground. The kids didn't mess with him after that.'

'I don't suppose they did,' Steve remarked drily, looking at his daughter, who hadn't said a word.

'What do you think about this, Ruth?'

'I think if Bob was in Canning Town, and couldn't bother to come and see us, then I don't care what he's up to. I always loved and respected him, but not any more. He should at least have had the decency to keep in touch with us, but he just walked away. I'm sorry, Mr Hunter, but I don't think I even like him now.'

'Oh, Ruth.' Daisy looked anxiously at Alf. 'She doesn't mean it. She's just upset.'

But Ruth was adamant. 'If he turned up now I wouldn't have anything to do with him.'

Twenty-Three

It was pouring with rain when Bob arrived back in Richmond. When he had first arrived he had stayed in digs for several months, but when it became clear that he was going to stay, he rented the top floor of a house in the same road. He now had a bedroom, sitting-diner, a tiny kitchen, and a shared bathroom. It was good to have his own space, even if he did have to be careful of the sloping ceilings in a couple of the back rooms.

He had just made himself a cup of tea when he heard his name shouted, so he went to the banister and looked over.

'Ah, good, you're back.' Rick waved. He was one of the boys who shared the middle floor of the house. 'We're going dancing tonight. Want to come?'

'All right. What time?'

'About eight.'

'I'll be ready.' Bob went back to his tea. He'd nearly refused, but he was feeling happy about the way things had gone. Everyone at the Russell estate had been pleased to see him, and even Midnight had remembered him. He had enjoyed riding again, and he could hardly believe what had happened at the school. It had taken a lot for him to return to Canning Town, but he was glad he had. He considered it a small victory, and it had shown him that he would be able to handle a class of rowdy kids. But was it really just a childish dream, or something he should pursue? There was a fork in his road and he really couldn't decide which way to go.

He'd see Sister tomorrow and ask her if it would be possible to speak to her friend again. He would be able to point him in the right direction. But tonight he would bring his short holiday to an end by dancing—providing he could find a girl tall enough.

The dance was in a hotel a short walk away. After he had washed, shaved and put on a clean shirt, he joined the boys from downstairs, all of them intent on enjoying the evening.

'Are you back at work tomorrow?' Rick asked.

'Yes, eight o'clock.'

'I don't know how you can work there,' Henry said. 'I don't think I could do it.'

Bob smiled. 'And I'd go mad sitting in an office all day.'

'I expect you would, but I will be a lawyer one day.' He looked up at Bob and grinned. 'Anyway, we haven't got a chair that would hold your weight.'

Bob made a lunge for the boy, who dodged nimbly out of the way, and they were all laughing when they reached the hotel.

It was already crowded, and they stood on the side of the dance floor studying the girls.

'Phew! There are some pretty girls here. Have you seen anyone you fancy yet?' Rick asked Bob.

He shook his head. 'I'm waiting for them to stand up. It's awkward dancing with someone who only reaches my chest. I feel as if I'm dancing by myself, and I hate talking to the top of their heads.'

Rick chuckled. 'Being so tall does have some disadvantages then?'

'A few . . .'

Henry was nudging Bob in the ribs. 'Look at that one, she's taller than me.'

Bob placed a large hand on top of Henry's head. 'Is that difficult?'

'Ha, ha.' Henry ducked out from under him. 'Hey, boys, Bob's in a funny mood tonight. Wonder what he's been up to this last three days?'

'Who knows, but don't upset him,' Greg, the other one of the group, said. 'You know we only bring him along for protection.'

'You fight your own battles, boys!' Bob walked away, laughing, to see if that blonde Henry had pointed out would like to dance with him.

'How can a bloke that tall move so smoothly and look so elegant?' Rick mused.

'Blowed if I know.' Greg sighed. 'Makes you sick, doesn't it?'

*   *   *

'Welcome back, Bob. We've missed you.' Sister gave him a bright smile. 'Have you enjoyed yourself?'

'Very much, thank you. Can I have a quick word

with you when you have a moment, please?'

'Now would be convenient, before we start the day.'

He followed her into the office and said straight away, 'I was wondering if I could talk to the professor again?'

'As a matter of fact, I saw him yesterday and he asked me to give you this.' She held out a large envelope.

Bob opened it, frowning as he flicked through the document. 'These are exam papers.'

'No, James has set them himself. He wants to find out how good your general knowledge is. Complete as much as you can, without cheating, and he said he'll be here sometime next week to have a look at the work you've done.'

'But why?' Bob was completely mystified by this.

'He wants to see how good—or bad—your education was.'

'I told him it had only been elementary.' He studied a couple of the questions and shook his head. 'If these are university standard questions, how on earth does he expect me to do any of this?'

'All he asks is that you try.' Sister indicated that he should sit down. 'James Morgan is a family friend of many years, and a busy man, but I asked him to take an interest in you. He's offering help, Bob.'

Hardly able to believe this was happening, Bob was silent, not able to find the right words to thank this fine woman.

When he didn't speak she held his gaze and smiled. 'When Fate holds out a guiding hand, take it, Bob. This may lead to something, or it may not, but if you turn away you will regret it for the rest

186

of your life. You will always wonder if you did the right thing.'

He finally found his voice. 'Of course I'll see if I can complete any of this paper.' Amusement glinted in his grey eyes. 'If you keep on like this I'll start believing in Fate.'

*   *   *

That evening Bob settled down to have a good look at the questions. Each sheet covered a different subject, and at first glance he didn't hold out much hope of answering many of the questions, but he had promised to try.

For the next two hours he worked, and to his surprise he had managed to answer a few of the questions, and he was again grateful to that teacher who had made him read a wide variety of books. He'd always had a good memory and that was serving him well now. However, he hadn't even completed a third of the paper, so he would be busy for some nights to come. But enough for one night, it was time to get some rest because there was a busy day ahead of him tomorrow.

'How did you get on?' Sister asked him the next day.

He grimaced. 'Some of the questions might as well be in a foreign language. I've managed some of it though.'

'Good. Do what you can, that is all he's asking of you.'

For the next three nights he laboured over the questions, refusing calls from the boys downstairs to go out with them. When he'd done as much as he could, he was sure Professor James Morgan wouldn't bother with him again.

For the next week he carried on with his work and hardly gave the document a thought. Then when he was called to the office he found James Morgan there drinking tea with Sister.

'Have you got the paper with you?' he asked, the moment Bob stepped into the room.

He nodded and handed it over.

'Good, good, I'll go over this and see you in about an hour.'

Knowing he had been firmly dismissed, Bob went back to his work. He wasn't anxious because he was certain he hadn't done enough to interest a man like Professor Morgan, but he'd tried. Most of the paper had been way above his level of knowledge.

It was a very busy day and he didn't take any notice of the time passing, so he was surprised when one of the other helpers tapped him on the shoulder and told him he was wanted in the office.

James Morgan was alone and beckoned him in. He had pages of written notes on the desk in front of him. 'Sit down, young man. The questions I set you were intended to give me an indication of your knowledge and how your mind works. You've made a valiant stab at answering as much as you could, and where I've asked you to say how you feel about something, you are articulate. Now we will go through this together.'

Bob drew in a deep breath, preparing himself for the bad news.

'History—good.' He looked up. 'Your favourite subject?'

'Yes, sir.'

'Mathematics—adequate, but needs further

study. Geography—poor. However you could have looked on a map for the answers, but you didn't, and I'd give you marks for that.'

'I was told I mustn't cheat,' Bob told him.

'Correct. Your writing is good, so is your English. Politics ...' The corners of his mouth twitched. 'You are quite well informed, and have strong opinions on what needs to be done. You are particularly scathing about most of the politicians.'

'I know what it's like to struggle every day to put food on the table and keep a roof over our heads.' Bob leant forward, elbows resting on his knees. 'We were promised that things would be better after the war, but it still hasn't improved. Men can't find jobs, and not enough is being done for those who fought for this country. It's a bloody disgrace. Pardon my language, sir.'

'And you believe you can help by becoming a teacher in the poor areas?'

'Well, I don't know what sort of a contribution I could make, but I do believe that education is the key to the next generation having a better chance in life.' Bob then told him about his visit to his old school. The paper was forgotten as they talked, the discussion deep and wide-ranging.

Suddenly, Bob caught sight of the clock and stood up. 'I'm sorry, sir, I'm wasting your time, and I must get back to work.'

'Sit down,' he ordered. 'Mary has your job covered. I'm going to send you to a friend of mine who teaches boys out of school hours who need extra help. I've already spoken to him about you.'

'I can't afford private tuition,' Bob protested.

James Morgan waved his hand dismissively. 'We know that. If he thinks you have potential, William

189

Jackson is prepared to charge you one penny a week.'

'That's ridiculous!' he declared, beginning to think this man was playing some kind of joke on him.

'Yes, isn't it?' The professor smiled broadly. 'But don't look so insulted, my boy. This is not the time to let pride get in the way. He's a first-class teacher, and if Mary is convinced you are worth the trouble, then he will take you on.'

Bob was stunned, but James Morgan was right to point out that pride had no place in this arrangement. 'I'd be a fool to turn this opportunity down. Will it help me into a teaching career?'

'William will give you an education up to elementary teacher standard, but what you do with it will be up to you.' He wrote a local address down and handed it to Bob. 'Go and see him when you finish work today. I shall be keeping an eye on your progress, so good luck. You have a lot of hard work ahead of you.'

* * *

The house on Richmond Green was impressive and Bob decided that William Jackson must do very nicely teaching pupils who were lagging behind in their studies.

'Are you coming in, Robert Hunter?'

While Bob had been standing there gazing at the house the door had opened, and he was surprised to see that the man standing there could not be more than thirty.

'How did you know who I was?' he asked, walking towards the door.

'James described you to me, and I hope you are going to ask more intelligent questions than that,' he said drily. 'You would hardly get lost in a crowd.'

'I suppose not.' Bob grinned, liking the teacher already.

'What do you prefer to be called, Robert or Bob?' He urged Bob in and led him to a room set up for teaching.

'Bob, sir.'

'Mr Jackson will do. Sit down and I'll go through the rules with you. I will expect you here twice a week to begin with. I know your working hours are irregular, so we won't set days. You will let me know each week when you will be able to come. Each lesson will last for two hours, and I shall expect you to work hard. I will set you homework and you will bring it—completed—with you at each lesson. If at any time you fail to keep up with the work-load, or show any sign of disinterest, then I shall terminate our arrangement.' His gaze was direct. 'Is that clear?'

'Perfectly, Mr Jackson. I can assure you that I'm not going to throw this chance away. Where else will I get private tuition for only a penny a week?'

William Jackson smiled and sat on the edge of the large desk that dominated the room. 'Indeed!'

'Do you and Professor Morgan consider me a charity case?' The paltry fee still rankled with him. He might not have much, but he was fiercely independent.

'We consider you a special case, and don't be offended. I do take pupils who can't afford to pay anything. I happen to believe that a good education is the right of everyone, not just the rich. I told James that I would be happy to take you on without

191

a fee, but he said I must charge you something or you probably would not come. Your pride would not allow you to take charity. I believe he summed you up correctly?'

Bob nodded his head in acknowledgement; satisfied with the answer he had been given. 'Thank you for that explanation, Mr Jackson.'

'Now we understand each other, Bob, let us begin straight away.'

Twenty-Four

It was bitterly cold and Ruth stamped her feet and flapped her arms to keep the circulation going. 1923 had arrived on a blast of cold air, and hadn't let up. In fact March was even colder. How she longed for spring! There were a few hardy people walking round the market, but generally most people were only venturing out when absolutely necessary. Once it warmed up a bit trade would, hopefully, pick up again. Her takings had dropped terribly, but that was the same for all the traders. Not only was it cold, but also the unemployment queues were long and many people were having a hard time keeping warm and fed. Those who could manage it were helping the old and frail in their street. Mr Hunter and her dad were also doing what they could for the unemployed ex-servicemen with young families. Everyone would breathe a sigh of relief when this winter was over.

'Don't think we're going to do much trade today, Ruth.' Mrs Law was wearing so many clothes her face was hardly visible.

'No, you're right. We must have been crazy to even turn out today.' Ruth gazed around at the empty stalls. 'Most of them have got more sense than us. We might as well pack up.'

'Good idea.' Hannah Law began to clear her stall when she looked up and frowned. 'Your brother Eddie's in a tearing hurry.'

Ruth followed her gaze to see Eddie running towards her, waving his arms frantically. She could hear him shouting but he was still too far away to understand. From the way he was running it was clear that something had happened. She began to hurry towards him.

When they reached each other, Ruth was alarmed. Eddie was gasping for breath and tears were streaming down his face. Fear gripped her. 'What's happened?' she demanded.

Her brother doubled over trying to catch his breath, and then he straightened up, distress showing clearly in his eyes. 'There's been an accident at the docks, and Dad's hurt bad. Mum said you must come home at once.'

Without saying a word she ran back to the stalls. 'Mrs Law, can you pack up the stall for me, please? There's been an accident and Dad's hurt. I've got to get home!'

'Off you go, Ruth. I'll see to everything, and you let me know if there's anything I can do.'

'I will, and thank you.' Grabbing her distressed brother's hand, they ran all the way home, tumbling through the scullery door out of breath and worried sick.

Sally and John threw themselves at her, their faces wet with tears, and eyes wide with fright. Ruth gave them a quick hug, told Eddie to stay with the children and put the kettle on. Then she climbed the stairs, feeling faint with fear, and praying that it wasn't as bad as Eddie believed.

The door to the bedroom was closed so she turned the handle carefully and pushed it open. Her mother was sitting beside the bed, head bowed, and a doctor was bending over the bed.

'Mum,' she whispered, moving to stand beside her and placing a hand on her shoulder. The sight of her much-loved father tore her apart, and it took all of her self-control not to cry out. His eyes were closed, his face completely colourless, and his body was cut and bleeding. They waited in silence for the doctor to finish his work.

Finally he stood up, his expression grim. 'I've given your husband something to make him sleep, Mrs Cooper. When he wakes he will be in considerable pain and will need more of the medication I've left for you. Don't touch the bandages, and try to stop him moving around. He should have been taken straight to the hospital, not brought back here, but I can't take the risk of moving him again. He's been crushed by the falling machinery, and to shift him now would be far too dangerous.'

'What are his chances of coming through this?' Daisy asked, her voice trembling with fear.

'I'm not going to lie to you, Mrs Cooper. Your husband's chances of living through the night are not good. I'll be back in the morning.'

When the doctor left, Ruth stooped down and took hold of her mother's shaking hands. 'He will live, Mum. He's a strong man and he won't leave us without a fight. Why don't you go down and comfort the kids? They are very frightened. I'll stay

194

with Dad, and we'll take it in turns through the night. He won't be left alone for a second.'

Daisy nodded and allowed her daughter to steady her as she stood up. 'Thanks, Ruthie, we must be strong for him, mustn't we?'

'We will be.' She watched her leave the room and sat in the chair. She wasn't going to cry—he would hate that—so instead she forced a smile. 'Now, Dad, you didn't survive the war to lose your life in a silly accident. Do you hear me? We need you, so you'd better make up your mind to get through this. We are all going to help and support you, so you rest now and heal quickly.'

'He can't hear you.' Eddie was standing in the doorway, a cup of tea in his hands.

'We don't know that, Eddie, and it might help him to hear our voices.'

'You think so?' Eddie handed her the cup, sniffed, and wiped his hand over his wet eyes.

'Yes, pull up another chair and tell him what you've been doing today.' Ruth didn't know where her strength was coming from, but her dad needed her and she wouldn't let him down.

During the long, terrible night, Daisy and Ruth stayed by Steve's side. They had agreed to take it in turns, but neither of them could bear to leave him. Twice they had given him medication when he'd woken up in pain, and they prayed, willing him to live. When dawn broke he was still with them.

Alf arrived early and took charge. 'You two are exhausted. You take a break and I'll sit with Steve until the doctor comes.'

When they started to protest, he said firmly, 'Daisy, you've got three more kids who need you as well. Now, do as I say. I'll call you if there's any change.'

They reluctantly left the room, but knew that Alf was right.

*   *   *

During the next week, with Alf's help, there was always at least one of them beside Steve's bed. He was in and out of consciousness, but one time he woke up when Alf was there alone with him.

'I'm in a mess, mate,' he gasped. 'What's going to happen to Daisy and the kids?'

'Don't you worry about that,' Alf assured him. 'I'll see they're all right until you're back on your feet. It's my turn to help you, so just you concentrate on getting better.'

Steve grimaced. 'I don't think I'm going to make it, and if I do I'm not going to be much use to anyone. I can't feel or move my legs. That bloody machinery fell on my back.'

'Now don't you go thinking like that! Your legs are numb because of the medication they've given you. Once you don't need it things will be normal again.'

'You never were a good liar, mate . . .'

'Dad!' Ruth came in and hurried to the bed. 'I thought I heard him talking to you, Mr Hunter.'

'He was, but he's gone to sleep again.' Alf patted the worried girl's arm. 'He's getting a bit better every day.'

There was no way he was going to tell her what Steve had actually said. 'He just asked if everyone was all right. I told him you were all fine, and he wasn't to worry because I would be looking out for you until he was back on his feet again. He said,

196

"Thanks mate," and went back to sleep.'

'Oh.' She gave a tremulous smile. 'That's good, isn't it?'

'Very good.' Alf didn't like stretching the truth like this, but this family were exhausted, and nearly out of their minds with grief. He would keep his word if his friend didn't make it, and he would look after them.

'You'd better go off to work, Mr Hunter. Mum's got breakfast waiting for you downstairs.'

'Shouldn't you be on your stall, Ruth?'

'Mrs Law is looking after it for me. There isn't much trade in this cold weather, and I can't leave Dad.'

'She's a kind woman,' was all he said, knowing it would be useless at this point to remind her they didn't have any money coming in. Thank goodness he had a job.

'Yes, she is.' Ruth smiled at him. 'And so are you. I don't know what we'd do without your help.'

'He's my friend.' Alf looked at the man in the bed, his heart heavy with sorrow. 'I'll do what I can for him, and all of you.'

'And we're grateful.' Ruth bowed over her sewing, settling in to keep her vigil.

Before going to work, Alf went to the market. Hannah Law was just setting up when she saw him coming. 'How are things, Alf?'

He shook his head. 'Not good, Hannah, but don't tell any of the Coopers that.'

'Won't say a word. Terrible business; he's such a fine man and loves his family. Is he going to make it?'

'Only time will tell. I tried to suggest to Ruth that she came back to work, but she won't leave his side.

If Steve does come through this it's going to be a long job, and it might be better if she has something to keep her occupied.'

'I agree, but give it a bit longer. She might feel she can leave him when he begins to recover. It will dawn on her quite soon that she's the breadwinner of the family now and has got to work.'

'I've got a little put aside and will see they don't go without.'

Hannah looked doubtful. 'They won't want to rely on your money for too long, and it wouldn't be right. If Steve Cooper dies, or lives but can't work any more, they are going to have to make their own way in life.'

'I know, but all they can think about at the moment is Steve.' Alf sighed sadly. 'Let's just hope he makes a full recovery.'

*   *   *

Searching through the morning's post, Ben frowned. 'Ruth hasn't written for weeks.'

'I expect she's busy, darling.'

'Not in this weather she isn't.' He walked over to the window and gazed out, deep in thought. Although they were into April now it was still very cold, but the daffodils had bravely shown their faces to let them know that better weather was on the way. He didn't know why, but he had a feeling of disaster, and it was so strong he couldn't ignore it. 'I think I'll go and see if they are all right.'

Emma looked up from the newspaper she was reading. 'Don't forget you have an appointment to see that horse you're keen on. Your meeting is at two o'clock.'

'I'll be back by then.'

She smiled at her husband. 'Make sure you are or he might sell the animal to someone else.'

'I won't be late.' He kissed her and hurried out of the door.

Canning Town was a bleak enough place in good weather, but the low grey cloud seemed to turn everything the same colour. Only the blue of the Coopers' front door gave a little brightness. He knocked and waited.

When Daisy opened the door he was shocked. She had lost weight, had dark rings under her eyes and looked as if she could hardly stand. He knew immediately that his premonition of disaster had been correct. Something bad had befallen this family.

He reached out to steady her. 'What's happened?'

'Come in, Captain Russell, but keep your voice down, please.' She led him to the scullery. 'Would you like tea?'

'No. Tell me what's going on, please. Is Ruth all right?'

'Yes, I am.'

He spun round at the sound of her voice. Ruth was standing in the doorway, and was in the same exhausted state as her mother.

'Dad's asking for you, Mum.'

Without a word Daisy hurried from the room and ran up the stairs.

Ben made Ruth sit down and stooped in front of her. 'Tell me,' he ordered.

'There was an accident at the docks and Dad's been badly hurt.'

'How bad? And when did this happen?'

She was struggling to get the words out, but finally her mouth set in a grim line, and taking a deep breath, said, 'He was crushed by crates of falling machinery. His back might be broken or too badly damaged for him to ever be able to walk again. It happened four weeks ago.'

'Oh, hell, I'm so sorry. Why didn't you let me know?'

'Erm . . .' She looked at him, puzzled. 'I never thought about it. We've had a lot to do.'

'Well, I'm here now, so what can I do? How are you managing for money?'

'We're all right. Mr Hunter is looking after us.' She raised a ghost of a smile. 'After the accident the doctor didn't think Dad would live through the night, but he did. He's getting stronger and fighting to get better. He really is, and we won't let him give up.'

'Can I see him?'

She shook her head. 'Not yet, wait a while longer. He doesn't like anyone to see him like this.'

'Ruthie.' Daisy appeared again. 'Sit with your dad while I go for more medicine. I've just given him the last.'

'You'll forgive us, Captain.' Ruth stood up. 'But as you can see we don't have time for visitors. I'll write when I can.'

'I understand.' He stood up, not wanting to leave, but he wasn't family and would only be in the way. 'Promise me you'll let me know if there's anything I can do for you.'

Daisy had already left and Ben found he was talking to an empty room. Reluctantly he left, but before catching his train he went to the docks. It was about lunchtime and he needed to talk to Alf

200

Hunter. He was in luck, for men were streaming through the gates and Alf was one of them.

'Hello, Captain.' Alf saw him but kept on walking. 'I can't stop. I've got to pop in on Steve, and I've only got an hour.'

'I've just come from there.' Ben fell into step beside Alf, matching his hurried stride. 'Tell me what Steve's chances are—and I want the truth.'

'The doctor said he'll most likely live now he's survived the last couple of weeks. But we don't know if he's ever going to walk or work again. Only time will tell.'

Ben swore, hardly able to believe it. Steve had survived the war only to have this happen to him. 'I offered to help, but was firmly refused. Is there anything I can do?'

Alf stopped. 'Yes, you can find that bloody son of mine. He should be here to help. I can't give up my job because we need the money, and Daisy and Ruth are wearing themselves out. But, by God, we're going to get him through this, whatever it takes.'

'Let me give you some money—'

'Not your problem, Captain. We'll manage this ourselves.'

'This is no time for damned pride, Alf!'

'It's good of you to want to help, but we take care of our own. Now, if you'll excuse me . . .'

Ben could only watch helplessly as Alf strode away.

He arrived home just in time to buy the horse he wanted so much, but the pleasure had gone now. All he could think about was the struggle going on in that tiny house. He liked Steve Cooper and his family, and knowing they were in such terrible trouble was hard to bear. He wanted to help ease their burden and pain, but they wouldn't let him, and he couldn't force them to accept his offer.

Emma was waiting for him when he walked into the drawing room. 'You were only just back in time. Did you buy the horse?'

He nodded and sat down, closing his eyes.

'What's the matter, darling, are you unwell?'

He sat up, opened his eyes again, and began to tell her about Steve. When he had finished speaking she was white with shock.

'Oh, Ben, what a tragedy, is there anything we can do?'

'I offered, but was refused. The only thing Alf asked was that I find his son, as they needed him.'

'Then that's what you must do.'

He looked at his wife in amazement. 'And how the hell am I supposed to do that? That boy didn't give much away while he was here. All he said was that he was living in Surrey. The work he was doing was challenging, and if he told me what it was I would never believe him.'

'Well, he gave you a few clues, so put your mind to it, darling. I'm sure you'll discover where Bob is.'

Twenty-Five

'I'm leaving school now!' Eddie lifted his chin in defiance. 'I've already got a job at the grocers in the High Street as errand boy.'

'Why are you doing that?' Ruth couldn't believe what she was hearing. Eddie had always liked school, so why this sudden decision to leave early?

'It's daft to leave before you have to. Mum, tell him he can't do it.'

But Daisy was too tired and grief-stricken to answer. More and more decisions were being left to Ruth. 'Eddie, you mustn't leave school.'

'I've got to. Don't you see, Ruthie? Dad isn't going to work any more; you won't leave him long enough to get back to the market, and we can't always live on Mr Hunter's money. It isn't right. We've got to start looking after ourselves and earn some money or we'll starve! I'm going out to work and you can't stop me!'

Ruth sat down with a thump and gripped the edge of the table for support. Her brother was right. The little money they had put away for a rainy day was nearly gone, and it was still pouring. The doctor's fees and medicines were draining them, but she hadn't given it a thought. The only thing on her mind, and that of her mum, had been keeping Dad alive. Everything else had been ignored— even her brothers and sister had been looking after themselves. What was the matter with her? Why hadn't she faced this before?

'Oh, Eddie, I'm so sorry. Of course you're right. I must get back to the market, and I'll pawn the brooch. That will see us through for a while.'

'But it won't be enough,' Eddie insisted. 'We've got to have regular money coming in. It's only six weeks since Dad had his accident and we've used everything from the tin box. Dad is going to need medication for a long time. We've got to face it, Ruth, it's up to us.'

He sounded so grown-up, and with a heavy heart she finally accepted the seriousness of their situation. Seeing her darling father helpless and in

203

pain had wiped all sensible thought from her mind.

'Don't look so sad, Ruthie.' John's little face was unusually troubled. 'We've talked about this with Eddie. He's got a job and me and Sally will help you with the sewing.'

'I can do lots now,' Sally told her. 'I've been watching you.'

'Thank you all,' she said with a catch in her voice. 'Dad's been telling me to get back to the stall, but I haven't been listening. I can see now that he's worrying about how we're going to manage now he isn't working, and that won't help his recovery. I'll have a word with him and tell him what we are going to do.'

Eddie nodded. 'We've got to see that we can pay the rent and not starve, Ruthie, and you'll have to take over the family because Mum's not able to make any decisions at the moment.'

Daisy had gone back upstairs, taking no part in the conversation; hardly even aware it was taking place. It was as if her whole world was in the bedroom upstairs, and nothing else registered with her.

'I'll start right now, Eddie. You take that job with my blessing. Sally and John, there are toys in the front room to be finished off, and material torn up small to make stuffing. I'll be back on the stall in the morning.' She hugged each one. 'I'm proud of you.'

There hadn't been much reason to smile just lately, but now all three children's faces lit up with relief. Sally and John disappeared into the other room and Eddie shot out the door to see how soon he could start the job as errand boy.

Ruth stood up, took a deep breath, and walked

up the stairs. Her mother was in her usual place beside her husband, looking frail and worn. It was time to start giving orders.

'Mum, enough! Go to bed. You need sleep.' Ruth literally lifted her out of the chair.

'What are you doing?'

'Making you get some rest. If we're going to survive this terrible time then changes have to be made. Eddie's starting a job, Sally and John are helping me, and I'll be back in the market tomorrow.' Steve was watching his daughter taking charge, and she said, 'I'm sorry, Dad, but we can't go on like this. I'm taking over or we'll all end up in the workhouse.'

'Oh, thank God! I'm worried half out of my mind. You do what you have to, Ruth, and to hell with me. I'm useless now.'

'No, no, Steve, you mustn't say that.' Daisy was distraught. 'You're going to get better; it's taking time, that's all.'

He reached out and took hold of her hand. 'We've got to face the facts, darling. I might never be able to work again, and I'm not going to get any better if I lie here worrying about the rest of you. Do what Ruth says and get some rest.'

'Come on, Mum.' Ruth guided her out of the room and to the bed made up for her in Sally's room. 'Rest, because we're no good to Dad like this. He's got to know the money is coming in, and that we can manage while he's ill.'

Daisy sighed and was asleep as soon as her head touched the pillow.

Steve held out his hand when she went back to him. 'Good girl, now tell me the truth. How much money have we got left in our tin box?'

'Six shillings, but I'll take the brooch to the pawn shop tomorrow. That will help, and you don't need so much medication now, so that's a saving. Mr Hunter has been wonderful, but there are a lot of us and we are a drain on him, and although he won't admit it, I reckon we've used all the money he'd saved. The doctor and medicine have cost an awful lot, Dad,' she told him gently, 'but we couldn't see you in such pain.'

'Oh, hell!' Steve closed his eyes in anguish, and then opened them again to search his daughter's face. 'What are we going to do, Ruthie?'

'We're going to fight, Dad!'

'That's what I like to hear.' Alf came into the room. 'Want to sit up for a while, Steve?'

'Please, I'm sick of looking at the ceiling. It needs a coat of paint.'

Smiling at the feeble joke, Alf eased his friend into a sitting position, resting him against the pillows Ruth had put in place. 'How's the back?'

'Can't feel a bloody thing now. Wish I could.'

'The feeling will come back when you're properly healed,' Alf said cheerfully. 'Don't you worry about a thing; you just concentrate on getting better. The rest of us will take care of everything. Won't we, Ruth?'

She nodded and smiled, hoping to stop her dad from fretting.

'Ruth's just told me how the kids are rallying around to help, and I know you're looking after them for me, Alf. I'm more grateful than I can say, but you mustn't beggar yourself for us—and that's an order. Ruth and Eddie are going to see we don't starve.'

'Now you listen to me, Steve. You and your

family stood by me when I needed help, and now it's my turn to repay your kindness. I would never have made it without you. We're all going to come through this—including you. Like Ruth said, we're going to fight, so I don't want to see you retreating into hopelessness. When your ship went down you must have struggled to stay afloat and live. Didn't you?'

Steve nodded, and Alf leant over his friend. 'Well, you swim now, mate. Our boat might be floundering, but by hell not one of us is going to drown. Do you hear me?'

'I hear you, Alf.'

'Good.' He patted his friend's shoulder and grinned. 'That's enough lecturing for today. You rest now while Ruth and me get the supper ready.'

'Thank you,' Ruth said when they reached the scullery.

Alf's expression was grim. 'We mustn't let him give up. I've seen men do that, and once the will to live is gone that's the end. Steve's a proud man, always providing for his family, but now he can't and doesn't even know if he'll ever be able to again. That's a hard burden to bear, and he could easily sink. We mustn't let him.'

'I know we'll have to be firm and appear more cheerful around him.'

'And you also need to shake your mum out of her stupor. It's hard, I know, Ruth, but it's got to be done.'

'I've already started by making her go to bed. She hasn't allowed the kids to do more than tiptoe into the room and see Dad, but I'm going to encourage them to sit with him and chatter about the things they've been doing.'

'Just the thing; their lively talk will help him. He must be bored to tears confined to that room with only grim faces around him.' Alf removed his jacket and rolled up his sleeves. 'Now, what can I do?'

'Peel the potatoes, please.' She put the sausages on to cook, feeling as if she was back in the world again. Dad was alive, and that was the only thing that mattered. Whatever the future held they would face it together.

*   *   *

Ben had gone over and over every word Bob had said. He could see his tall figure in his mind's eye striding along, riding Midnight, laughing with the other men, and teasing Lilly. He had been fit, well dressed and more relaxed than he had been the last time he had been here. And it had been clear from the fine condition of his hands that he hadn't been doing manual labour. Where had he been, and what had he been doing since he walked away from here?

'Damn you, Bob, where are you?' Ben cursed as he made his way to the stables, knowing there was one man who he might have talked more freely to.

'Good morning, Captain. Have you come to see how the new stallion is settling in?' Jim greeted him, smiling with pleasure. 'He's a fine animal, but a little restless.'

'Ah, I expect he is. Put him in the large paddock and let him have a free run. I'll look at him later.'

'Yes, sir.' Jim was about to walk away to carry out his orders when Ben stopped him.

'Leave that for a moment. I need your help, Jim. When Bob was here did he say anything about

208

where he was living?'

'He didn't say much.'

'Think, Jim. I must find him. Steve Cooper's had a terrible accident, and Bob's father said they need him there to help the family.'

'How bad?'

'About as bad as it can be. Steve might never walk or work again, and the Coopers are in a desperate situation. Alf Hunter is doing what he can, but they need all the help they can muster. I hardly recognized Ruth and her mother. They won't take help from me after the way we treated Ruth, and that's sad, but understandable. They have their pride and don't want to be beholden to me.'

'Oh, damn, I'm sorry to hear that. Bob would want to know because he did say to me once that the Coopers were like family to him.'

'Can you think of anything he said that might give us a clue to his whereabouts?'

Jim leant on the paddock fence, deep in thought. 'All I can recall him saying was that he lived in Surrey and was earning enough to rent the top floor of a house on a hill.'

'Ah, I haven't heard that before. Keep thinking, Jim. What about his job?'

'Challenging. Something he never thought he could do. He said he would have walked away if it hadn't been for a remarkable woman who is in charge there.' Jim looked at his boss. 'He seemed to think a lot of her, but he never went into details.'

'A woman who is in charge? He obviously said more to you than me. Was there anything else you can remember?'

The head groom was shaking his head, and then

stopped suddenly, frowning. 'At the time this didn't make sense, but he did once refer to her as his sister, but I know he's an only child.'

'He might think of Ruth as his sister. Was he talking about her?'

'No, I'm sure he was talking about the woman he worked for.'

Ben straightened up suddenly. 'No, Jim, that's her title! She's a Sister. He's working in a hospital of some kind. I noticed that his hands were smooth and well cared for, and with his strength he would be invaluable in lifting patients. My God, if he is doing that kind of work it's even more important that we find him!'

'You might be jumping to the wrong conclusion, sir.'

'That's possible, except for one thing. He said to me that if he told me what he was doing I would never believe him.'

'Supposing you're right, sir, Surrey is a large county and he could be anywhere.'

'I know.' Ben slapped the fence in frustration. 'Let's consider what we've got. He's working with someone he calls Sister . . . He's living in a house on a hill. Did he say anything about the area?'

'Hmm, only that it was a nice place, and sometimes, when he's off duty, he sits on the terraces and looks at the river below.'

There was silence as Ben digested this information, his mind going over every possibility. An idea was forming, but it was too unlikely to believe. But there was no getting away from the fact that all the clues fitted the place.

'I think I know where he is, Jim. He's in Richmond, and I've a fairly good idea where he's working. If it's true, then he was right to say that I wouldn't believe him. I'll go there straight away. Thanks for your help.'

'Good luck, sir,' Jim called to the hastily retreating figure of his boss.

Twenty-Six

Gazing down on the River Thames, Ben nodded to himself. Yes, this must be the place. Even if he had been able to discern the kind of work Bob was doing, he would never have come here if he hadn't mentioned this spot. Injured servicemen were being cared for all over the country, but the boy was here, he had to be!

He saw her as soon as he walked into the building. She was younger than he would have expected, around thirty perhaps, and nothing striking about her, until she smiled. Then there was nothing ordinary about her.

'Can I help you, sir?'

'I am Captain Russell and would like to have a word with Robert Hunter, if at all possible. It's very important.'

'Of course.' She caught a man who was walking past. 'Ask Bob to come to my office as soon as he's free, please.'

Ben felt a surge of relief. He was here!

'You can wait in my office, Captain Russell. It may take Bob a while before he can come. Would you like tea?'

'No, thank you.'

He was just about to sit down when the door

211

opened again. The smile on Bob's face died the moment he saw who was waiting for him, but he quickly recovered.

'What brings you here?' he asked politely.

'I'm sorry, Bob, but I had to find you. I have bad news. There was an accident at the docks and Steve Cooper is badly injured. He might never walk again, and the Coopers are having a rough time. Your father is helping all he can, but medical fees are expensive, and they are in dire trouble. I have offered financial help, but they won't take it from me. I thought you should know.'

The news hit him hard, and that was plain to see. Bob drew in a deep breath and looked at the woman.

'You must go, Bob,' she said gently. 'The skills you have learnt here could be of help to the man.'

He bowed his head for a moment then straightened to his full height. 'I might not be able to come back for some time.'

'I know.' She smiled again. 'But I want you to know that there will always be a place here for you. Come and see us when you can, and if there is anything we can do you mustn't hesitate to contact us.'

'Thank you, Sister. I'll see William Jackson before I leave, but would you thank Professor Morgan for his kindness, please?'

'I will. Now go and see Jack, and tell him that I've given you permission to take any lotions and equipment you think you might need.'

'That is kind of you.' He looked straight at Ben. 'I have things to take care of here first, but I'll be in London some time today.'

His expression was now completely composed;

giving no indication of his feelings, though Ben was aware he was making painful decisions.

'I'll accompany you back.' He thanked the Sister and stepped outside the office to allow Bob to take his leave in private.

In only a couple of minutes, Bob strode out of the office and into another room. The captain followed. Bob was talking to a man of medium height and a ready smile. They were loading jars and bottles into a bag.

'Oh, Captain, this is Jack Beamish,' Bob said when he saw he had been followed. 'He's the physiotherapist here and I have been working with him ever since I arrived.'

'Delighted to meet you.'

When the bag was packed, they left the building, and their first stop was a fine house on Richmond Green, where Bob shook hands with a man and thanked him, then walked away, giving no hint of his feelings again. Then it was back up the hill to a three-storey house. They climbed to the top floor where Bob packed his belongings. On the way down he caught one of the boys who lived on the next floor down.

After hearing that Bob was leaving, he said, 'Oh hell, I'm sorry. But if you ever need a place to stay you can move in with us.'

On the ground floor he saw his landlady, paid whatever he owed, and said goodbye.

All the time Bob said nothing to the captain, and he could only watch with deep sadness as the boy systematically dismantled the life he had built up here. He knew he wouldn't be coming back for some time.

Bob spoke for the first time when they were on

the train. 'How did you find me?'

'I put two and two together and came up with the correct answer. Who was that man you said goodbye to at the house on Richmond Green?'

'A teacher. I was improving my education.'

'I'm almost sorry I found you because you seem to have built up a good life for yourself here, but the Coopers are in terrible trouble, and I didn't know what else to do. If they had let me help I probably wouldn't have come for you.'

'You did the right thing.'

'I hope so.'

For the rest of the journey they remained silent, each one lost in their own troubled thoughts.

When they reached the street, Bob told him with a wry smile, 'You had better come in with me and explain what I'm doing here. I might not be welcome, and they can blame you while I find out how bad things are.'

They went straight to Alf's house and Bob tossed his bag of belongings on a chair, and still holding the other, he vaulted over the fence. Ben followed again.

Daisy was the only one in the scullery, washing up after lunch, and was startled when Bob walked in after a brief knock on the door. She stared at him, hollow eyed. 'Bob?'

'Hello, Mrs Cooper, or can I call you Daisy now?'

Suddenly the grim boy had vanished and Ben could hardly believe the transformation. He was smiling, relaxed, and had a teasing tone in his voice as he kissed her cheek.

'Er . . . yes . . .' She looked confused.

'All right, Daisy.' He had removed his jacket,

placed it on the back of a chair, and rolled up his sleeves. 'Now, where's this husband of yours?'

'Upstairs in the bedroom.' She eyed him with alarm. 'Bob, what are you going to do?'

'Hopefully make Steve more comfortable and see if I can help him.'

'But ... but ...' She looked helplessly at the captain. 'I don't understand?'

'Start heating up plenty of water, Daisy.' Bob called as he took the stairs three at a time.

Panicking now, Daisy rushed up after him, and Ben followed. They entered the bedroom just in time to hear Steve saying, 'What the hell are you doing here?'

'I'm here to help you.' Bob pulled back the bedcovers. 'You can curse me all you like. I'm used to it, so let's have a look at you.'

When Daisy went to stop him, Ben caught her arm. 'He knows what he's doing, Mrs Cooper.'

'I'm going to turn you over, Steve, so I can take a look at your back.'

'Become a doctor since you left us, have you?' Steve tried to fend off the strong boy.

'No, a masseur, and it's no good you fighting me.' Bob grinned. 'You're not going to win.'

Steve stared at the tall, powerful boy in disbelief. 'A masseur?'

'Among other skills. Now, let me have a look at you,' he said gently, lifting the man with ease and placing him face down.

They watched as Bob went to work, his long-fingered hands moving over Steve's back, probing, soothing.

'Oh, that feels good,' Steve groaned.

After a while, Bob lifted Steve back, sat him up

215

in the bed, and then he pulled over a chair and straddled it. 'I'm not making any promises; your back is damaged but not broken. If you'll let me work on you we might be able to get those legs working again. It's going to be a long job, though.'

For the first time since the accident, hope flared in Steve's eyes. 'You think so?'

'I'll do my best, but you'll have to do as I say.'

'Yes, sir!' Steve actually smiled when he said it.

'Right.' Bob stood up and swung the chair back against the wall. 'First thing we're going to do is make you more comfortable. Daisy, get that water going while I bring the tin bath up here, then we'll change the bed and have clean pyjamas. Captain, I'll need your help.'

Ben was already rolling up his sleeves, eager to be of some use after following the boy around all day and feeling helpless. An assortment of emotions was rushing through him. Not only did this boy know what he was doing, but also he knew how to deal with Steve and Daisy. He had sensed there was something special about Bob when they had first met, and now that instinct was being confirmed.

The bath was soon in place and they were running up and down the stairs with hot water to fill it. While this was being done Daisy put clean sheets on the bed, then left the men to it.

Steve looked apprehensively at the steaming bath. 'How are we going to manage this?'

'Easy.' Bob removed Steve's pyjamas, lifted him out of the bed and eased him into the bath.

The captain was drying Steve's hair when the door burst open, and Alf stood there, unable to believe his eyes. 'What the hell . . . ?'

'Hello Dad.' Bob glanced up briefly. 'You're just in time. There's a large sheet in my bag over by the window. Take the pillows off the bed and spread it out for me, please.'

Absolutely shocked to see his son, Alf was too dazed to argue. The bag held all manner of things, bottles containing liquid of some sort, a bedpan and the sheet. He spread it out as ordered, still reeling from the fact that his son was here, and giving the orders.

Bob carried Steve to the bed and laid him face down on the bed. Then he opened one of the bottles, poured some of the liquid into his palms and rubbed them together. Bending over the man on the bed he began to massage his back and legs.

Tearing his gaze away from his son, Alf whispered to the captain. 'Should he be doing that?'

'He's been trained to work on injured men, so don't worry. Let's empty the bath and I'll tell you all about it.'

While they carried buckets of water out to the backyard, the captain told Alf what his son had been doing, and how he had managed to find him. By the time the water had been thrown away, they went back to find that Ruth and her brothers and sister had arrived home.

'Hello, Captain Russell,' she frowned when she saw him with his sleeves rolled up and the front of his shirt wet. She opened her mouth to ask what they were doing, when Bob appeared carrying the tin bath.

'Bob!' the youngsters squealed.

'Hello kids. Talk to you later. I'm busy now.' He walked past Ruth, dropped a quick kiss on her cheek, and said, 'You look awful.'

She watched him go out to the yard, her expression one of utter disbelief. 'What's he doing here?'

He soon returned, and ignoring the expression of hostility on Ruth's face, said, 'Daisy, set a place for Steve at the table because he's going to join you for supper. He needs to feel a part of the family again, not shut away all the time in that room.'

'But how's he going to get down here?' Daisy asked.

'I'll carry him.' He glanced at everyone in the room. 'And I don't want to see any long faces at the table. All of you talk about your day, and any funny stories will be good. Let me know when you're dishing up the food, Daisy, and I'll bring him down.'

Ruth turned to her mother as soon as Bob had gone upstairs again. 'He turns up after all this time and starts ordering us around? He's got no right to do that!' She glared suspiciously at the captain. 'Did you find him?'

'I did, and if anyone can help your dad, then it's him, Ruth. He knows what to do, and he's given up a lot to come here.' The captain explained about Bob's work. 'He'd made a good life for himself, but he didn't hesitate when he heard about the accident. I stayed with him so we could come back together, and it tore me apart to see him dismantle the life he had there. He has received good training, and also had a professor and a top-class teacher interested in him. All that's gone now, and I haven't heard one word of complaint from him. He's done this because he knows it will be a long job, so he's staying. When we got on the train I was desperately sorry I had found him, but after seeing him in action, I know it was the right thing to do.'

Daisy turned to her daughter, showing the first spark of life since the accident. 'I know you've never forgiven him for not being around when he was needed in the past, but don't you go giving him a hard time. Your dad needs the kind of help Bob can give him, and I thank God he's here. Thank you for finding him for us, Captain.'

*   *   *

Upstairs, Bob was sitting beside the bed. Steve was clean and refreshed, and he sighed with relief.

'I expect you're feeling tired now.'

'Just a bit.' He smiled at the boy—no, a man now—sitting beside him, the worried expression returning to his face. 'I've got to be able to go back to work again, Bob. What are my chances?'

'I'm not a doctor, but as far as I can see you are healing well, Only time will tell how complete your eventual recovery could be, but if at all possible, I'll get you walking again. I can't make any promises though, Steve.'

'Are you staying then?'

Bob nodded, then grinned. 'You're not getting rid of me until you can run up and down the stairs.'

'Thanks.' Steve gasped and closed his eyes.

'Where's your medication?'

'In the bedside table drawer, but there's only a couple of tablets left. I'm keeping them in case the pain gets too bad any time. It's taken all the money we had, and your dad's, to pay for the doctor and the medication. I won't have my family going without just so I can have more pills. I told them I don't need them any more.'

'Take these now and I'll get you some more.'

219

Bob held out a glass of water, watching while Steve took the tablets. 'Now rest because I'm taking you down to have supper with the family later.'

Steve was already dozing so Bob slipped the empty bottle into his pocket and went down to the scullery. 'He's comfortable and sleeping now, so don't disturb him.'

The captain put on his jacket. 'I must be going, but if you need anything, Daisy, you must let me know.'

'Oh, we'll be all right now, Captain.'

'I'll walk with you to the station.' Bob picked up his jacket and then they left the house. As they walked along, he said, 'Thank you for tracking me down, Captain. I shouldn't have been so secretive about where I was living, and I could have come as soon as this happened. I'm sorry about that and many other things I've done.'

'Don't be. If you had stayed at home or with me you wouldn't now be in a position to help Steve.'

Bob chuckled. 'Fate, was it, Captain?'

'Seems that way. Who knows?'

Bob nodded, a faint smile on his face.

Twenty-Seven

With a new box of Steve's pills in his pocket, Bob made his way back to the house. His return had been greeted with disbelief, and he had sensed hostility from Ruth, but he felt fairly confident that his dad was pleased to see him. He hadn't had much chance to talk to him, but he must find time as soon as he could.

The scullery was bustling with activity when he walked in. Everyone, except Ruth, was pitching in to help prepare the meal and lay the table. There was no sign of her.

Daisy smiled. 'Steve's resting peacefully after his bath. We'll let him sit at the head of the table in his usual position. Is that all right, Bob?'

'Perfect, but I'll get one of the chairs with arms on from the front room. He'll be more comfortable in that.'

'I'll get it.' Eddie hurried to get the chair.

John and Sally were gazing at him in wonder as if he was some stranger, and he supposed he must seem like that to them. 'How long will supper be, Daisy?' he asked.

'Half an hour.'

'That will give me time to get something from next door.'

Once in his old room he removed the mattress from the bed, slung it on to his shoulder and climbed back over the fence. 'Make way,' he called, before entering the scullery.

Alf immediately grabbed an end of the bulky mattress. 'Here, let me help you.'

'Thanks, Dad.'

Ruth appeared and stepped quickly out of the way as they manoeuvred their way towards the stairs. 'What on earth is that for?'

Bob lowered his end and looked at her over the top. 'I'm going to sleep in your dad's room so you and Daisy can get some proper rest. You both look exhausted.' She spluttered a protest that he ignored. 'All right, Dad, up we go.'

Steve was awake when they carried the mattress into his room. 'I'm going to make up a bed on the

221

floor,' Bob explained. 'I'm a light sleeper so if you want me during the night you just call. Your wife and daughter can have a good night's rest now.'

'Oh, that's a relief. I've been so worried about them.'

'You can stop fretting now,' Alf told him with a touch of pride in his voice. 'Everything's going to be all right now my son's here.'

'We've still got a lengthy fight on our hands,' Bob warned, not wanting them to get too confident.

'Ah, we know that, son, but it's good to have you back, isn't it, Steve?'

'It certainly is. My back feels easier since you massaged it, Bob.'

'Good, I'll do that twice a day at first, and then we'll see how it goes.' He laid the mattress in the only spot large enough, against the wall near the door.

Daisy appeared holding sheets and pillows. 'You'll need these.'

'Oh, thanks.' Bob jumped up and took them from her, then made up his bed.

'Supper's about ready. We've got your favourite sausages, darling,' she told her husband. 'Ruth brought them home with her.'

'Lovely, I'm looking forward to those. I'm starving.'

When she left, Bob said to Steve, 'Would you like to get out of those pyjamas and wear trousers and a shirt for a change?'

'Please, if you can manage it? My underclothes and shirts are in the chest of drawers, and trousers in the wardrobe.'

'Give us a hand, Dad.' It didn't take long for the two big men to dress Steve, and they were all smiling with pleasure when it was done.

'Right, how are we going to do this?' Alf asked when his son lifted Steve off the bed.

'You walk backwards in front of us. The stairs are so narrow I'll have to go down sideways.'

It was tricky, but Bob was determined that Steve should eat with his family. He knew how important it was for him to feel a part of ordinary life again. With Alf walking backwards with arms outstretched to support Bob, they made it down successfully.

Steve breathed a sigh of relief when he was safely in the chair. 'Blimey, I don't know how you did that, Bob. You must have muscles of steel now.'

'He has grown taller and filled out a bit.' Alf was smiling happily at everyone in the scullery. 'How tall are you now, son?'

'About six feet six, I think.'

'Sit down everybody,' Daisy ordered. 'Ruth, help me dish up.'

It was a lively meal with the kids chattering away, obviously happy to have their dad with them again. Steve asked Ruth how the market was doing, and she told him every detail, but never once did she speak to Bob.

He watched her as she laughed and was struck by how pretty she had become. She was clearly angry with him, and he wasn't surprised. He would have to make his peace with her when he had time, but for the moment, Steve must come first.

They were all still too busy talking to Steve to ask Bob any questions, and that suited him just fine. He said very little, intent on watching the man at the table, and he recognized the moment when it was becoming too much for him.

Pushing back his chair, he nodded slightly to Alf

223

who instantly stood up as well. 'Steve will have his tea upstairs, Daisy,' he told her cheerfully, bending to lift Steve out of the chair.

Going up was easier than coming down and they soon had Steve settled back in bed. 'Oh hell, I'm tired, but that was good. Thank you both.'

Father and son stood side by side, both tall strong men. 'No thanks are needed, mate.' Alf slapped his son on the back. 'Let's go and get our tea.'

'Is he all right?' Daisy asked anxiously when they came down.

'He's tired, but fine.' Bob sat at the table. 'Why don't you take him up a nice hot cup of tea?'

Ruth had disappeared, but all the other kids were there, eager to talk to Bob.

'I've still got my dictionary.' John pulled it out of his pocket. It was falling apart now and he'd put a piece of string around it.

'Looks as if I'll have to get you a new one.'

John shook his head. 'I like this one, and I think all the pages are still there. Will you read to me again, like you used to, please? I've got lots of new books. Ruthie gets them for me from the market.'

'I'd love to, John, but you must give me a few days to see to your dad.'

He nodded solemnly. 'Is he going to be all right?'

'I can't say for certain, but I hope he will.'

'The doctor told Mum he couldn't do any more for him,' Sally told them. 'I heard him say he needed another kind of doctor, but it would cost a lot of money.'

'I didn't know that,' Alf exclaimed. 'Daisy should have told me. I'd have raised the money somehow, even if it meant selling my house.'

'Mum said we weren't to tell you because you'd already used all the money you'd saved for another house.' Eddie sat next to Alf and rested his arms on the table. 'None of us have got any money left, and that's why I've left school early.'

'I know.' Alf's expression was grim. 'But Daisy should have told me. Have you got enough for the rent this week, Eddie?'

He nodded. 'Ruth pawned the brooch the captain's mum left her, so we're all right for the moment, but that money won't last long.'

'Hold on a minute.' Bob was mystified. 'The captain told me about the brooch, but what's all this about buying houses, Dad?'

'It's a long story, and I'll tell you when we have time,' Alf told him, dismissing the subject firmly.

Daisy came downstairs again. 'He's asleep and too tired to even finish his tea.'

'That's only natural.' Bob took the tray from her and placed it by the sink. 'We'll have to take it steady at first, but I want to get him out of that bed as much as possible. What we need is a wheelchair, so I'll see if I can get hold of one, and then I'll be able to take him outside if it's a nice day.'

'They cost a lot of money, don't they?' Daisy frowned. 'We're only just managing on what we've got coming in.'

'Don't worry. I'll get one somehow.'

'Oh.' Daisy looked relieved to leave it to Bob. 'It would be good for Steve. Thank you very much.'

'You don't have to keep thanking me, Daisy. Now, you kids nip upstairs and say goodnight to your dad, but only stay for five minutes.'

The three of them rushed out and Bob glanced at the clock so he could make sure they didn't overtire Steve. He was already worn out.

'Do I have your permission to go up as well?'

'There's no need to be sarcastic, Ruth.' She was standing in the doorway when he turned to face her. 'You've made it very plain that you don't want me here, and if I can get Steve on his feet again, I won't bother you any more. Of course you can go up.'

'Ruth!' Daisy was livid. 'What's the matter with you?'

'Well, who does he think he is, coming in our house and giving orders?'

'Dear Lord, you have changed. I've never known you to be spiteful before. Haven't you seen the difference in your dad already? He's laughed for the first time since the accident. Doesn't that mean anything to you? How can you be so ungrateful?' Tears were streaming down Daisy's face. 'Get out of my sight!'

Bob stepped forward to comfort the distraught woman. 'Please don't upset yourself. I don't care what your daughter thinks of me. I didn't expect everyone to be pleased to see me after the way I left.'

'But you still came.' She wiped her eyes and glared at Ruth, who hadn't moved. 'You wanted to see your dad, so why are you still here?'

Ruth fled.

'Since that business with the brooch she's become bitter. And I think in some silly way she blames you. In her mind it wouldn't have happened if you had been there to stand up for her.'

'I understand, but you mustn't let it upset you,' he said gently. 'The kids have had their five minutes, so you go and chase them out, and then sit

226

with Steve for a little while. Then I want you to go to bed and rest because I'll be with him all night.'

'I'll do that.'

Bob went through to the front room. Ruth was sitting on the floor surrounded by pieces of material, but she was just staring at them, making no attempt to do anything.

He sat beside her. 'We've got to declare a truce. You can hate me all you want, but don't let it show. Your mother is at the end of her strength, so watch your tongue. I have been working with injured men ever since I left the captain's estate, and have received good training. Steve needs the kind of skills I now have. That's why I came. I'm sorry if you believe I've let you down, but we used to be friends, Ruth, and I hope we can be again. If you love your family then you'll keep your nasty remarks to yourself.'

Uncurling himself he stood up, looking down at the forlorn figure. It hurt him to be unkind to her, but it had to be done. If he had read the signs right then Daisy was about to break. When she said nothing he turned and walked out of the room, out of the house, and jumped over the fence. His dad was clearly pleased to see him, and they had worked well together, but he still owed him an apology.

'How did it go?' Alf asked his son as he walked in.

'I told Ruth to keep her hostility out of the way when she's with her family because her mum can't take much more. I think she'll be careful now. Being accused of stealing has really disturbed her, hasn't it?'

'I'm afraid so, but she's a good girl and will come

to her senses eventually.'

'I hope so.' Bob sighed. 'We have been friends for a long time, and it's hard to know she dislikes me now. If I could change some of the things I've done in the past I would.'

Alf nodded. 'We haven't had a chance to talk, Bob, but thanks for coming. When I asked the captain to find you I never thought he would. He said you had made a good life for yourself and you left it all to come and help Steve.'

'I've also come back to say how sorry I am for leaving you. I didn't understand, but I shouldn't have walked out.'

'Yes, you should.' Alf smiled at his son, so grown-up now. 'The shock of losing you made me fight to pull my life together, and if you hadn't ended up in Surrey, you wouldn't have the experience to help Steve. No apologies are needed. What you did has been for the good of us all.'

Bob was stunned by such a gracious reception after what he had done. 'It's good of you to say that, and I can tell you that it's a great relief to know you feel like that. I didn't like being so hard on Ruth, but if Steve is going to make any progress, he mustn't worry about anything.'

'That's a tall order. Steve's used to providing for his family, and he can't do that now.'

'I know, and that's why we have to put a cheerful face on things. Now, what's all this talk about houses?'

Alf told him about the Imperial War Museum, avoiding all mention of the book, and saying only that he had been able to help them and they'd paid him some money.

They talked for nearly an hour, and then Bob

stood up. 'It's good to see you, Dad, and I'd like to talk again soon, but I must get back to Steve now.'

'Of course. Goodnight, son.'

Twenty-Eight

It was getting late and Ruth was still in the front room, her emotions in turmoil. This man who had walked in and taken charge was a stranger to her. He wasn't the boy she had grown up with, and he had changed almost beyond recognition. Not his physical appearance, although he was slightly taller, but there was something very different about the way he acted. There was an air of confidence about him, a quiet self-assurance that frankly frightened her. She had lashed out at him, not understanding why.

The scullery door opened and she listened to the stairs creaking as Bob made his way up to her dad's room. Mum had gone to bed some time ago, exhausted, and still upset. She swiped away tears of remorse and shame for the way she had acted. Bob was right; she should have been more careful. They had enough to cope with without her acting like a stupid child.

Scrambling to her feet she straightened up, and then crept up the stairs to the room she now shared with Sally and her mother. 'Are you awake, Mum?' she whispered.

The woman in the bed moved her head.

'I'm so sorry I upset you. I didn't mean to. I don't know what came over me.'

'You had no right to be rude, Ruthie. Bob didn't

229

have to come, but by God we need him. I couldn't have carried on like this for much longer, and neither could you. Have you apologized to him?'

She shook her head.

'Then you make sure you do. Now get some sleep.'

*   *   *

Sleep was elusive as Alf gazed up at the ceiling with eyes wide open. He was so happy to see and talk to his son. He didn't know why he hadn't said anything about the book, but somehow it hadn't seemed to be the right time. Steve was all that mattered at the moment.

He turned over and closed his eyes, bringing his thoughts back to their situation. While Steve healed they had to survive. There were a lot of people to feed and the two youngest kids must not go without. All the money he had saved towards buying another house had gone on doctors and medicines, and he didn't begrudge a penny of it. He still had the one house, of course, but if he sold that then he would have to turn the Selbys out, and that wouldn't be right. They were so happy and grateful to be there. He couldn't do that, and he was absolutely certain that Daisy wouldn't want him to either, no matter how desperate the need. There had to be another way . . .

He finally drifted off to sleep, the problem still unresolved.

*   *   *

The next evening, when Daisy was upstairs with

Steve, Alf gathered Ruth and Eddie around the scullery table and tried to work out how they were going to get through the next couple of weeks.

'The traders at the market are giving me some vegetables and a little fruit at the end of the day, and Mrs Law gave me the sausages we had last night. I don't like taking from them, but they understand the difficulty we are in and want to help. Everyone is being so kind.'

'I'm earning enough to pay the rent,' Eddie said, looking at Alf. 'And you are buying us groceries each week. Now we don't need to pay for the doctor or medicines we are managing—just.'

'But now you have me to feed as well.' Bob strode into the scullery and put some coins on the table. 'I'll contribute each week for as long as I can.'

'You can't do that!' Eddie protested. 'You are looking after Dad, and it's only right we should feed you.'

'Eddie, there's a long struggle in front of us, with no guarantees that Steve is going to make a complete recovery, so we've all got to help out.'

'You're right, of course.' Eddie pushed the coins towards his sister. 'Buy what we need at the market tomorrow, Ruthie.'

When Ruth put the money in her purse, Bob was satisfied.

'How's Dad today?' she asked.

'Resting peacefully. But I'm about to disturb him. Help me get the bath ready, Dad, and when he's warm and relaxed I'll have another go at his back.'

Ruth touched Bob's arm and whispered, 'I'm sorry.'

He bent and kissed the top of her head to show

his acceptance of her apology. 'Thanks, Ruthie.'

The two youngsters were in the front room stuffing toys for the stall, but everyone else pitched in to help get the bath ready. Daisy wandered into the bedroom and Bob was pleased to see her looking calmer, and hoped she would continue to improve. They would really be in trouble if she collapsed, and he made sure he was always cheerful and confident when she was around.

The bath was filled and Bob ushered everyone out of the room, except Alf, who watched intently the way his son handled Steve, and was fascinated to see the long-fingered hands moving over his back and legs. The boy was good, and he sent a prayer of hope that his friend could be helped.

By the time Steve was back in bed and resting again, they began the trek up and down the stairs to empty the bath and put it away again in the outhouse.

Bob sniffed the air and smiled. 'Smells like something's cooking, and I'm starving.'

'You haven't changed then—you always were!' Alf laughed.

*　　　*　　　*

The next morning Bob found himself alone with Daisy. Alf had gone to work, so had Eddie and Ruth, and the kids were at school. She was looking more rested, but tension still radiated from her, and he didn't like the withdrawn look in her eyes. That worried him because it hadn't been there yesterday.

'Steve's looking better,' she said, trying to smile, but her bottom lip trembled.

'He's more comfortable.'

232

'I wanted to get the help and medicines he needed,' she blurted out, 'but he wouldn't let me. He said if I brought anyone in he would refuse to let them touch him, and he didn't need the pills any more. But I know he does . . .'

Making her sit down, he stooped in front of her and gripped her hands. 'He knew you couldn't afford it. He was thinking of you and the kids.'

'We'd have found the money somehow.' She held tightly to Bob's hands.

'You don't need to worry about the pills because I've bought those for him, and I'm going to help as much as I can. I know it's hard, but I want you to stop fretting because it won't do Steve any good to see you in such a state. Ruth, Eddie and Dad will see we don't starve, and I'm asking you to trust me.'

'I do . . .'

'No you don't. You look at me and see that kid who resented living the way we do, and who had big ideas about changing things.'

She gazed at him with a stricken expression. 'I'm trying, Bob, and I know they're all saying you know what you're doing, but how . . . ? I don't understand . . . I don't know what to do. What's going to happen to us?'

Bob hauled her to her feet and wrapped his arms around her. This is just what he had feared would happen. 'Shush, Daisy, take deep breaths—that's the way. We are going to win this battle. A kind lady told me that nothing is impossible, and you must believe that. Don't let hope die.'

As he comforted and calmed her, an idea came to him. It might be the way to help her trust him with her darling husband, the man she had prayed for all through the war, only to have this happen to

233

him when she had believed him to be safe.

'What's the matter?' Ruth rushed in and tried to get her near hysterical mum away from Bob. 'Is Dad all right?'

'He's fine.' Bob spoke quietly, and allowed Daisy to go to her daughter for comfort. 'She has finally broken down, Ruth. I'll put the kettle on for a strong, sweet cup of tea.'

It took nearly an hour, and several cups of strong tea before Daisy was coherent again. Bob urged Ruth out of the back door so they could talk in private. 'Your mum doesn't really trust me; though she's grabbed at any chance to help Steve. She needs to be convinced that her husband is safe with me, and there's only one way I can give her that assurance. Can you stay here for the rest of the day? I want to take her to where I worked.'

'Can I come too?' she pleaded. 'Eddie's got a half-day off and will be home soon. He'll stay here, and Mrs Law is looking after the stall for me.'

He thought for a moment, and then agreed. After all, Ruth had apologized to him, but he doubted that she trusted him either, and it might calm Daisy to have her daughter with her. 'Get her ready and we'll go as soon as Eddie gets here.'

No sooner had he said Eddie's name before he appeared round the side of the house. After explaining what had happened, he readily agreed to stay with Steve until they got back.

'We'll be as quick as we can,' Bob told him. 'I've given him a tough session today so he'll probably sleep most of the time.'

'That's all right. I know how to look after him.' He looked anxiously at his mum. 'You go.'

A train was just pulling into the station when they got there, and Bob was glad they didn't have to wait. Daisy was quiet now, but her mental state was fragile, and he wasn't sure he was doing the right thing. But something had to be done for her, and he couldn't see any other way. If she could see that he could be trusted not to harm her husband then she might relax more.

It was a pleasant day and Daisy seemed to enjoy the walk up the hill. Before going to the home, he took her to see the view of the river.

'This is nice.' Daisy spoke for the first time. 'But what are we doing here? I should be with Steve.'

'Eddie is looking after him.' Bob turned her to face him. 'I'm going to show you where I worked.'

'Oh.' She gazed around, distracted. 'Mustn't be long. Got to get back home.'

'We'll be quick, I promise.' Placing a guiding arm around her shoulder they continued walking.

As soon as they stepped inside the door someone shouted, 'Bob, where the blazes do you think you've been? Roll up your sleeves, there's work to be done!'

He grinned at the man in the wheelchair. 'Hello, Stan, missed me, have you?'

'Now why would we do that, you great hulking brute?' Stan propelled himself over, a broad smile on his face. 'I see you've still got the pretty girls flocking around you.'

'Of course. This is Mrs Cooper and her daughter, Ruth. Ladies, meet Stan.'

'Nice to meet you.' He turned his attention back

235

to Bob. 'How long you staying?'

'This is just a quick visit.'

'Ah, shame, but come and say hello to the men. They'll be pleased to see you.'

Bob promised and he went on his way giving them all a cheery wave. 'Bye, ladies, and don't believe a word he tells you.'

'Bob, how lovely to see you. Will you introduce me to your friends?'

'Hello, Sister.' As he introduced Daisy and Ruth to Sister Headley, he could see she had already spotted what the trouble was with Daisy.

'And you've come to have a look round, have you?'

Ruth was clearly uncomfortable. 'Bob thought it might help Mum.'

'I'm sure it will. Both of you come with me while Bob goes to see everyone. We all miss him very much.'

'He's a good boy.' Daisy was beginning to look a little more alert. 'But I'm not sure he can look after my husband . . . It's very worrying . . . you know?'

'Indeed I do.' Mary smiled gently at mother and daughter. 'But you need have no concerns about Bob's capabilities. Come, let us walk around and you will see that the men like, respect and trust Bob, as I do.'

Mary turned and smiled at Bob as she led them away, then he hurried off to visit some of the men he had come to know so well while he had worked here.

Twenty-Nine

The journey home was quiet. Daisy was so worn out she was sleeping with her head on Bob's shoulder, and Ruth didn't know what to say. She was thoroughly ashamed of the way she had reacted to his return. She had acted like a silly child, and he must despise her now. Walking around the house, seeing him joking with the men, showed her that he had left a job he loved to come and help them. And she was positive he wouldn't have taken them there if her mum hadn't broken down. The Sister had praised him and his skills, saying that they hoped to have him back with them one day so he could continue with his training as a physiotherapist. That place was special to him; she had seen it in his eyes, and also the flash of regret when they had left.

They reached home and Daisy was put to bed at once, then Bob went straight up to Steve, relieving Eddie.

'How's Mum?' he asked anxiously as soon as he saw his sister.

'Calmer now, but we've got to see she has plenty of rest. That was frightening, Eddie. Mum's always seemed so strong, but this is more than she can handle.'

'We'll take good care of her. Did the visit to the home help?'

Ruth nodded, tears filling her eyes. 'It helped both of us. It has been hard to imagine that Bob knew how to look after Dad, but he does, and after what we've seen and been told about him, we can be grateful he's with us.'

'Good.' Eddie placed an arm around his sister. 'One invalid in the house is enough, Ruthie, so you hold in there. We all need you to be strong.'

'I know.' She wiped the tears away.

'Let's hope Mum'll be all right now. I thought she trusted Bob right from the start, but deep down she must have had doubts about him.' He looked intently at Ruth. 'Just like you did.'

She nodded. 'When he arrived back it was like looking at a stranger. But I don't have any doubts about him now. I watched him dealing with Mum, and everyone we saw today spoke very highly of him.'

'He's always been like another brother to us, but he's grown-up now. And don't forget that we haven't seen him for a long time, so of course he's changed. I expect he thinks the same about us. But now you've told me all this I feel much more confident that everything is going to be all right. We mustn't give up hope, Ruthie.'

They stopped talking when they heard Bob coming down the stairs.

'How is she?' he asked Ruth, as soon as he walked into the scullery.

'She's fast asleep.'

'Good, that's what she needs, but keep an eye on her, please.'

'I will.' Ruth took a deep breath, her nervousness showing. 'Thank you for what you did today. We wouldn't have known what to do. It was frightening to see Mum in such a state.'

He inclined his head in acknowledgement, slipped out of his jacket and began to roll up his sleeves.

Eddie was immediately on his feet. 'Oh, are

you going to work on Dad's back? Can I help you, please? I won't get in the way, but I'd love to see what you do.'

'All right, but you mustn't talk. I want Steve to relax.'

'Promise.'

'Come on, then.'

The back door burst open and John and Sally tumbled in from school. Ruth shot to her feet. 'Oh my goodness, is that the time?' She hastily cut them a slice of bread each and grabbed jam out of the pantry. 'There, that will keep you going while I get supper ready.'

'Where is everyone?' Sally asked. 'And why aren't you at the market, Ruthie?'

'I've been out with Mum so Mrs Law has looked after the stall for me. Eddie's upstairs, and Mum's taking a nap.'

'That leaves us to do the cooking.' John finished the last of his bread. 'What do you want me to do?'

She opened her purse and handed him some coins. 'I want you to run to the butcher's and get me as much mincemeat as that will buy. It's nearly closing time so he'll be selling some meat off cheap. Give him your best smile, John. We've got vegetables so I'll make a shepherds pie.'

'Lovely!' John disappeared through the door with Sally tearing after him.

'Do those two ever walk anywhere?' Eddie grinned as he came into the scullery.

'I don't think so. How's Dad?'

'Asleep now, and he does look a lot better. He has a better colour in his face and is more relaxed. He still can't move his legs, but Bob's working on those.'

Ruth frowned. 'The longer this goes on the harder it is to believe he's going to recover completely.'

'What did we say a while ago? We mustn't give up hope. We've just got to do the best we can, and whatever worries we have must be kept hidden, because our family needs us, Ruthie.'

'That's all any of us can do.' Bob strode into the room, peered in the teapot and poured himself a cup of tea.

'That's stewed.' Ruth began to fill the kettle. 'I'll make you a fresh pot.'

'This will do just fine.' Bob thirstily drained the cup. 'Let me know when supper's ready and I'll bring Steve down. I want Daisy at the table as well or Steve will start to worry.'

'Suppose she doesn't want to get up?' Ruth's voice shook slightly.

Bob studied her for a moment, noting how shaken she was by her mother's breakdown. 'Then you call me and I'll talk to her.'

'I'll do that.' She put the kettle down with a thump and bowed her head. 'I'm sorry for being so useless, but now Mum's sick as well, I'm frightened. We are putting a great strain on you, and it isn't fair.'

He turned her to face him and tilted her head up so she could look at him. 'I know this is frightening, but these bad times will pass. If there's anything you can't cope with you come straight to me. My shoulders are broad enough to take the load.'

Eddie laughed and Ruth managed a faint smile.

'That's better. Let's take it one day at a time and we'll get through this.'

The back door swung open and the two

youngsters ran in with huge smiles on their faces. They were both holding packets. 'Look what the butcher gave us!' John put his packet on the table and made his sister do the same. 'We've got loads of mince and he gave us a ham bone to make soup, and some lamb scraps he said would do for a pie. And we've still got two pennies left,' he declared proudly.

'My goodness, you must have both smiled very nicely.' Ruth took the change from her brother and put it back in her purse.

'It was Sally who did that,' John giggled. 'She's prettier than me.'

As laughter filled the scullery, Ruth's tension drained away. They were a close family with good friends around them. They would be all right whatever the future held for them.

'What's all this noise?' Alf asked when he arrived. 'I could hear you halfway up the street,' he joked.

'Mum!' Eddie saw Daisy first and helped her to a chair. 'Did we wake you?'

'Yes, but it's lovely to hear laughter again.' She smiled up at Bob and caught his hand. 'Thank you.'

He smiled at her. 'You're looking better.'

'I am. Everything suddenly became too much for me, but I'm feeling calmer now.'

'Good. You're not on your own, Daisy, you must remember that.'

'Mum, you don't have to worry about anything now because Bob said his shoulders are broad enough to take the load.'

This sent the kids into shrieks of laughter as they looked at the size of him, making everyone else join in as well.

'If you're going to make fun of my size, I'm going back upstairs.' Bob put on a mock hurt expression, causing more hilarity.

He took the stairs two at a time back to the bedroom.

'What on earth is going on down there?' Steve was smiling.

'They are having fun at my expense. I'll get you dressed and then you can join in. See if you can manage some of the dressing yourself. You do what you can and I'll finish the rest.'

Between them the job was soon done, but Steve's mood had plummeted. 'Why aren't I recovering, Bob?'

'You are making progress, but you have been badly injured and it takes time.'

'I've got to provide for my family.' Steve thumped the end of the bed. 'I've got to get back on my feet. I must!'

Bob watched Steve rile against his disability, and this was what he had been expecting. 'Do you want to try and stand?' he asked briskly. 'I'll support you.'

'Let's give it a try.' Steve's mouth was set in a determined line.

Lifting him off the bed he let Steve's feet touch the floor. 'Any pain?' he asked.

'A bit in my lower back, but it feels strange to be upright again.' Steve struggled to take a step, finally admitting defeat. 'It's no good, I'm bloody useless.'

When he was back on the edge of the bed, Bob sat beside him. 'I asked you to do that because I wanted to find out how much pain you would be in when standing. It wasn't too bad, so that's an improvement, but we can't rush things. Don't look so despondent; smile. They are cheerful downstairs, so let's keep it that way, shall we?'

*　　　*　　　*

Later that evening, Bob slipped next door to have a word with his dad.

'Hello, son, is Steve asleep?'

He nodded and sat down. 'Do you know how much money Ruth's making at the market? The bit of money I brought with me isn't going to last much longer, and they certainly can't exist on what Eddie's earning.'

'I gather trade is slow, and with so many out of work, that's understandable. I help as much as I can.'

'I know, but you can't support us all. I haven't said anything to them, but there's no sign of Steve getting back the use of his legs again.'

'Oh, damn!' Alf swore. 'If that's the case what the hell are we going to do?'

'I'm going to concentrate on making him as independent as possible. I'll do a tour of the pawn shops in the morning and see if I can get hold of a cheap wheelchair.'

'That might be a help. What else can we do?'

'We'll need to fix something over the bed so he can pull himself out and into the wheelchair on his own. And ...' Bob paused for a moment. 'The family aren't going to like this, but we'll have to turn the front room into his bedroom.'

'That's sensible.' Alf's expression was grim. 'But as soon as we tell them this they'll know there isn't much hope left.'

'It can't be helped. Steve's got to learn to cope

243

with his disability so he doesn't have to have someone with him all the time.'

'If you can help him manage on his own will you go back to your job? I think you were happy there.'

'I was, and I will go back there, but not yet. The Coopers are in dire trouble, and with the two of us helping we might be able to keep a roof over their heads. I'm afraid all this is going to land on Ruth and Eddie's shoulders because Daisy's in no mental condition to be of any use at the moment.'

Alf ran a hand through his hair in agitation. 'So you're saying that we've got to stop thinking Steve will get better and plan for a future with him in a wheelchair?'

'I don't want us to give up hope, but the way things are going, I think it would be wise to make it possible for him to do as much as he can on his own. I'm going to need your help, Dad.'

'Of course I'll help.' Alf's eyes misted over. 'Poor devil. When are you going to tell him?'

'Tomorrow evening. I'm sorry I haven't been able to do more.'

'You don't have to feel like that, son. No one could ask more of you.'

Standing up, Bob laid a hand on his dad's shoulder. 'I wish there could have been a better outcome. Goodnight, Dad. Try and get some sleep because we've got a rough day in store for us tomorrow.'

Thirty

A search of the pawnshops was fruitless. Bob was unable to find a wheelchair he could afford. The only one he saw would have taken all the money he had left, and that wouldn't be wise. Frustrated, he returned to the house to find Daisy wandering aimlessly from room to room.

'Oh, there you are. I thought you'd left us.'

'I've only been out for a couple of hours, Daisy. Steve's quite comfortable.' He smiled reassuringly, hoping she wasn't slipping into her confused state again. 'What are you going to get us for lunch? Steve will be hungry.'

At the mention of her husband she seemed to wake up, and immediately began to rummage in the larder. 'There isn't much here.'

'I bought eggs and a loaf of bread while I was out, so how about scrambled eggs on toast?'

'Oh, yes.' She smiled, nodding. 'Steve likes that.'

'I'll leave you to it then.' Seeing she was now occupied, Bob returned to the bedroom.

'How's Daisy?' Steve asked as soon as Bob walked in. 'She came in to see me, but she couldn't sit still. I'm worried about her.'

Sitting on the edge of the bed he knew it was time for plain speaking. 'I'm afraid Daisy's at the end of her strength. She needs plenty of rest, and Ruth has taken over the responsibility for the family until your wife recovers.'

'Oh, Lord, what a mess.' Steve looked intently at Bob, distress showing plainly in his eyes. 'I'm not going to walk again, am I?'

'I don't know. I'm not a doctor, but it's time we made arrangements in case that is so. I want to make you as independent as possible.'

'How the hell are we going to do that?'

He listened as Bob outlined what he thought should be done, and when he had finished, the man in the bed nodded. 'Whatever you think is best. Talk this over with Eddie as well as Ruth. He's a sensible boy.'

'I'll do that. There's one more thing I want to do, but I need your permission. You must have a wheelchair, but I haven't been able to find one I can afford. Dad told me that Captain Russell offered help but you all refused.'

'Of course we did. I won't take charity from a family who treated my daughter so shamefully.'

'So you'd rather see your wife and kids end up in the workhouse, would you?' Bob asked bluntly.

'That won't happen!'

'Maybe not. You could always move in with Dad if you can't keep up with the rent.'

'What the hell are you doing? Are you trying to frighten me?'

'No, I'm trying to make you face the facts. Ruth, Eddie and Dad are keeping the family afloat at the moment, but Daisy is incapable of making decisions, and there's also John and Sally to consider. That's a lot to feed, and I'm sure you don't want them to go hungry.'

'You know I don't.'

'Then don't be too proud to take help when it's offered. Let me go and see the captain. He's a good man and wants to help, but I won't do it without your permission. Swallow your pride for the sake of your family, Steve.'

He was now fighting to keep the tears of despair at bay, but he eventually nodded. 'Do what you must. But, hell, boy, you can be tough!'

'Sometimes it's necessary.' Bob stood up and pulled back the covers. 'Now, let's try and ease your back, shall we?'

'What's the use? I'm a bloody cripple and useless to my wife and kids.'

'You can curse all you like.' Bob lifted him over. 'But don't you dare start feeling sorry for yourself. They all love you very much, so you're a lucky man, and don't you ever forget that.'

'Sorry,' Steve muttered, and grunted as Bob's hands began their work. 'There's still hope, isn't there?'

'There's always hope,' he said, quoting Sister again. 'You just relax and leave everything to me.'

*   *   *

It was seven o'clock before Alf arrived home. Daisy was with Steve and the two youngsters were sitting at the table stuffing toys. Eddie and Ruth were also working on things for the stall.

'You're late. I've kept your supper hot for you.'

'Thanks, Ruth.' Alf sat down and started to eat. He gave his son a quick questioning glance, and nodded, indicating they should get this over with.

'I need to talk frankly with you.' Bob sat at the table and looked at the four Cooper children. 'Your dad is not improving as much as I had hoped, and I think it's time we tried to make him as independent as possible.'

Sally stopped what she was doing and her eyes filled with tears. 'Isn't he going to get better?'

247

'I don't know, Sally, but at the moment there is no sign of him getting the feeling back in his legs.' He looked at each one in turn. 'I'm not saying a full recovery is impossible, I'm just saying that we should help him to do more for himself. I've spoken to your dad so he knows what I want to do. If we move his bed to the front room and I get him a wheelchair, he will be able to move around down here and become part of the family again.'

'Shouldn't we be talking to Mum about this?' Ruth asked.

'I'm afraid she's too sick to be able to make decisions. It's hard, I know, but you and Eddie will have to take on the responsibility until she's better. Steve is going to explain this to her, as we thought it might be better coming from him.'

'Well, I think it's a good idea,' John declared, sounding very mature. 'He can then help with running the stall, Ruthie. You know he likes that.'

'Yes, he does.' Ruth smiled at her little brother. 'Dad's isolated upstairs, and even if he can't walk he can still help us.'

'That's the spirit.' Alf smiled with relief. 'Your dad has to feel he's needed, and that will help with his recovery.'

'We'd better start making room for the bed.' Eddie was on his feet, ready to marshal everyone into action. 'When do you want to move it down, Bob?'

'Sunday, when we're all here, but we can push the furniture back before then,' he suggested, seeing they were all eager to get on with it. 'If we put the bed by the window he will be able to look out and see people walking by.'

'We're going to need your help, kids,' Alf

248

declared, 'because we're also going to rig up something over the bed so your dad can pull himself up and into the wheelchair. Bob knows what we need.'

He nodded. 'We're going to have to build a frame over the bed.'

'You'll need wood then. There's the Wilson scrap yard. You might be able to get what you need there.'

'Good idea, Eddie, and they might have some strong rope as well.'

'Right.' Alf pushed away his empty plate. 'Let's see how much space we can clear.'

'That went well,' Bob said to his father as they all trooped into the front room. 'It hurts them to think that their dad might not recover fully, but they're a sensible bunch of kids, aren't they?'

'And thank goodness for that. Let's hope Steve has been able to make Daisy see the sense in this move, but I don't think she'll mind if it's for her husband.'

For the next hour they pushed furniture against the wall, carried smaller pieces upstairs, until they had enough space for the bed, frame and wheelchair.

'Where are we going to get a wheelchair from?' Eddie asked when they returned to the scullery for a well-earned cup of tea.

'I'll find one somewhere. You leave that to me.'

The two youngest were very tired by now so Ruth packed them off to bed, and after deciding that they had done all they could for the moment, it was time for all of them to have an early night.

Before Ruth went upstairs, she turned to Bob and Alf. 'Thank you—both of you. We really wouldn't know what to do for Dad or Mum if you weren't here.'

The two men watched her leave, sadness in their eyes. 'We've got to make this work, Bob.'

'All we can do is our best. Goodnight, Dad.'

Bob listened to Steve's steady breathing, wide awake. He hated to see the Coopers suffering like this, and as much as he yearned to be back at his job, he wouldn't be anywhere else at the moment. After his mum had died, the Coopers did everything for him while he had been too consumed with grief and anger to think clearly. He'd never forgotten that, and this was his chance to repay the debt of gratitude. It was a relief as well to see that Ruth no longer disliked him. That had hurt more than he had shown, because their long friendship meant a great deal to him. As he had said to his Dad, they could only do their best, and he was determined that their best would make a difference to all of them.

*　　　*　　　*

The next morning, after he had made Steve comfortable, Bob sat on the edge of the bed. 'How did Daisy react to the idea of moving you downstairs?'

'She thought it was a good idea, so I left it at that. I didn't tell her we were going to the captain for help.'

'I didn't tell the kids either,' Bob admitted. 'They were all enthusiastic about trying to help you live as normal a life as possible, so I thought it best to keep this to ourselves for a while. I was told once that there are times when we shouldn't let pride get in the way. This is one of those times, Steve.'

'I know, so do what you have to. My family is my life, and if I can move around on my own I might be more help to them.'

'I agree.' Bob stood up. 'I still hope you will get some use back in your legs, but if that doesn't happen, you mustn't think your useful life is over. Adjustments will need to be made, but I'll help you. You have full use of your arms and shoulders, so there is a lot you will be able to do.'

Steve nodded. 'I'm trying to come to terms with what has happened to me, but it's damned hard. And watching my wife and kids suffering is tearing me apart. If you hadn't turned up, I don't know what state I would be in now.'

'You're a strong man, Steve, and you would have managed. The sooner we get you a wheelchair the better. Daisy seems calmer this morning, so will you be all right for a while? Eddie will pop in at lunch time.'

'I'll be fine.'

Bob wasted no time and was soon on the train to Kent.

The first person he saw was the captain returning from his morning ride and heading back to the house.

'Bob, it's good to see you, but I hope it isn't bad news that brings you here. Is Steve all right?'

'There isn't much improvement, I'm afraid. I'm here because Dad said you once offered to help and they refused to let you. Well, I'm not refusing.'

'Good, come in and tell me what you need.'

As soon as they were settled with a trolley of refreshments, Bob told the captain what they planned to do for Steve. 'I need to buy a wheelchair, but we are almost out of money. Trade at the market is slow at the moment, and Eddie brings in precious little as an errand boy. In fact we're all struggling. Mrs Cooper can't help much because she's had a breakdown.'

'This is dreadful.' Ben was dismayed by the news. 'I'm glad you came to me. Of course I'll help in any way I can. Green!' he called, and the butler arrived at once. 'Send someone to the Gatehouse and bring the wheelchair back here, please.'

'Yes, sir.'

'Mother used a chair towards the end of her life. You can have that if it's right for your purpose; if not I'll get you another one.' He opened the drawer of his desk and took out several five-pound notes. 'This will help the family for a while.'

Bob gazed at the money on the desk. 'No, sir, I can't take that. If I arrive back with plenty of money in my pocket they will want to know where it came from.'

'Ah, the Coopers don't know you're here?'

'Only Steve and Dad. It's very generous of you and I appreciate your kindness, but at the moment we are scraping through. I only came to ask your help in buying a wheelchair.'

Captain Russell was clearly disappointed that Bob wouldn't take the money. 'Will you at least let me pay for your fare today?'

'Thank you, that would be welcome.'

There was a knock on the door and Bob couldn't believe his eyes. He had expected the chair to be a relic of the past, but this was one of the latest models. When he'd looked it over, he said, 'This will be perfect, Captain, but it's a very expensive chair. Could I borrow it until we can buy a cheaper one?'

'It's yours.' When he saw Bob hesitate he became exasperated. 'Dammit, you won't take my money so at least take the chair as my gift to Steve. I like the man and I care what happens to him and his family.'

Bob shook hands with him, accepting the generous gift. Then he sat in the chair and manoeuvred it around the room, smiling with pleasure. 'This is just what Steve needs. It will get him out of that bed and give him a degree of freedom.'

'I'm happy to see it put to good use. Now, you said Steve has shown no sign of improvement, so have you spoken with his doctor?'

'Yes.' Bob got out of the wheelchair and sat in an armchair. 'I did that as soon as I arrived back because I didn't want to risk doing any damage to him. He told me that he'd been crushed under heavy boxes of falling cargo. When I explained what I had been doing, he told me to go ahead as there was nothing else he could do for him.'

'Did they seek a second opinion?'

'They couldn't afford to. The medical bills had already drained them dry.'

'If I sent a doctor at my expense would they see him?'

'I doubt it,' Bob told him. 'And I'm sure Steve wouldn't let another doctor in the house. They are all finding life very difficult at the moment and Daisy's mental health is very fragile. She will recover in time, but I don't want her disturbed in any way.'

'Then we mustn't do anything to upset them. What about bringing Steve here and we'll put him on a horse?'

'Good heavens!' Bob looked at him in amazement. 'I never thought of that. It might help, and it would certainly give him a sense of freedom. But could he sit on a horse, I wonder?'

'We could ride either side of him and hold him in the saddle.'

A broad smile spread across Bob's face. 'Captain, you're a genius! Now all I've got to do is get him to come here.'

'Don't tell him where you're taking him.'

Bob tipped back his head and laughed. 'You're devious, as well.'

'When I have to be.'

Bob folded the wheelchair and picked it up. 'Any chance of a lift to the station?'

'Green!' The butler appeared. 'Ask Jim to take Bob to the station now, please.' Then he scribbled a number on a piece of paper and handed it to Bob. 'We do have a telephone and that's the number. Phone and let me know when you're coming and I'll arrange for you to be collected at the station. You'll need money for fares, and don't you dare argue about it,' he ordered, as he placed money in Bob's hand.

Knowing that he would need the fare money, Bob nodded and placed it in his pocket, thanking Captain Russell. 'I'll let you know when to expect us.'

Thirty-One

'Where did you get that?' Eddie shot to his feet when Bob walked in with the wheelchair. 'It looks brand new!'

'I had a bit of luck,' he said, setting up the chair. 'I'll bring your dad down so he can try it.'

Heading for the stairs quickly to avoid answering questions, he left the boy inspecting the chair. Daisy was sitting by the bed doing some sewing, and smiled when he came in. 'What are you making?' he asked, pleased to see her doing something instead of just sitting.

She held up a small garment. 'I'm helping Ruthie. She's got an order for this.'

'That's lovely, and she needs all the help she can get to keep the stall going. You're both very good at needlework, aren't you?'

'I used to do it before we were married.' She smiled affectionately at Steve. 'And I taught Ruth when she was very young, but she's better than me now.'

'I don't believe that, darling.' Steve squeezed her hand. 'Ruth's good because she had an expert to teach her.'

She studied the work she was doing and nodded. 'I am still quite good, aren't I? If I didn't come up to Ruthie's standards then she wouldn't ask me to make clothes for her stall. She's very fussy, you know, and has a good reputation for doing beautiful work.'

'And I'm sure she wouldn't do anything to lower those standards,' Bob told her. 'Now, I'm going to take Steve downstairs, Daisy. I have a surprise for the both of you.'

'Oh, I wonder what it can be? I'll go down and put the kettle on.' She gathered up her sewing and left the room.

'How are you?' he asked Steve when they were alone.

'All right. Eddie's been up to see to me. How did you get on this morning?'

'Captain Russell has given us a wheelchair his mother used. It's practically new. We'll go down now so you can try it.'

The chair was just what was needed, and Steve stayed downstairs learning how to move himself around. Some pieces of furniture had to be rearranged to allow him a clear run, but he soon got the hang of it.

Bob watched for a while and then placed a hand on Steve's shoulder. 'That's enough for now. Rest for a while.'

'Oh, yes, I mustn't overdo it at first, but it feels so good to be able to move around.'

'Once your bed is down here and fixed up with the frame I'll be able to show you how to get in and out of bed on your own. Then we'll rig something up in the outhouse so you can manage that as well.'

'That would be wonderful.' His expression was full of gratitude. 'I know what you gave up to come here, Bob, and I want you to know that we are all very grateful to you. You are throwing away the best chance you have had of becoming a teacher.'

'You don't have to thank me, Steve. We help each other and that's the way it's always been. And as for becoming a teacher, well, my path seems to be going in a different direction, and it's one that

256

feels right. The future will take care of itself; we have to deal with the here and now.'

'You've become quite a philosopher,' Steve joked.

'You can blame that on Sister Headley. She's a great one for putting things in their proper perspective.' Bob smiled as he changed the subject. 'If the weather's good tomorrow I'll take you out somewhere.'

'Would you? I'd like to go to the market and help Ruth on the stall. I need to feel useful, and that's something I could do, isn't it?'

His enthusiasm was heartening, and Bob was delighted to see he was beginning to take an interest in doing things again. It was a good sign, and he would give him all the encouragement he could. If he was going to remain in the wheelchair then he had to begin reshaping his life. 'You could certainly help on the stall. We'll start slowly and gradually build up until you're strong enough to do a full day there. That will give Ruth more time to make goods for sale.'

'Yes, yes,' he nodded, pleased at the prospect. 'And I promise I won't try to overdo it at first.'

'You won't have a chance because I'll wheel you straight back if I think you're looking too tired.'

*   *   *

The next day dawned bright and clear, just right to take Steve out for the first time since the accident. They hadn't told Ruth they were coming because Steve wanted to surprise her. She saw them long before they reached the stall, and ran to meet them, taking the wheelchair from Bob so she could push it.

'I've come to help you,' he told his daughter.

'Lovely! You can serve while I get on with some sewing. I've just received an order for a christening gown, and you know how much work there is in one of those.' She smiled at Bob, thanking him silently with her eyes.

'I'll be back for you in two hours,' he told Steve. 'I'm just going to have a walk round.'

'All right.' Steve wheeled himself into position, and was already talking to people looking at the baby clothes. He was obviously happy to be out of the house and involved in something.

Bob was satisfied with what he saw, knowing how important this was. He left them and headed straight for the junkyard. Eddie had mentioned it, so it must still be there.

It was, and it hadn't changed at all. It was still piled high with junk of every kind. He should be able to get everything he needed here.

'What are you looking for, mate?' a man asked Bob while he was moving old doors to get at something he thought might do for making the bed frame.

'I need some pieces of strong wood.' He hoisted more junk out of the way.

The rag-and-bone man watched as heavy items were tossed aside as if they weighed nothing. Bob finally reached the wood he was after and pulled it free, examining it carefully to make sure it was sound. 'How much do you want for this?'

'Five bob to you,' the man said with a perfectly straight face.

'Do I look daft? I'll give you a shilling.'

'I'll go out of business if I charge prices like that.

Half a crown.'

Dusting off his hands, Bob looked thoughtfully at the pile of wood he had gathered together. 'Got any rope?'

'There's some in that box over there.'

He strode over, tipped the large box upside down and began sorting through lengths of rope until he found some suitable pieces. After tossing the rest back in the box, he walked back and dropped the rope on top of the wood.

The man was still watching him with interest.

'I tell you what I'll do. If you take the wood and rope to my house for me I'll give you two shillings.'

'Sixpence for the delivery.'

'Two pence only.'

The man sighed. 'You're not easy to do business with, mate, but I'll do it for that price as long as you load it on to my cart, come with me and unload it at your place.'

'Done!' Bob handed over the money, lifted the wood on to his shoulder, headed for the cart and tossed it on. 'Where's your horse?'

'On a bit of spare ground behind the shed.'

'All right. Hitch him up because I'm in a hurry.'

The man was soon back, leading an ancient but sturdy-looking animal.

After patting the horse, Bob began to fix him into his harness.

''Ere, you know what you're doing, don't you?' A calculating look came into his eyes. 'Strong devil too, aren't you? I could use someone like you.'

'Are you offering me a job?' Bob couldn't keep the amusement out of his voice.

'Might consider it. You interested?'

'Not right now.' He patted the horse again as it

nuzzled him.

'Shame. I've only got one son and he's hurt from the war. Can't use his right arm no more.'

Bob was about to get in the cart when he stopped. 'I've been working with injured men. Would your son let me have a look at him?'

The rag-and-bone man gave him a doubtful look, then shrugged and shouted, 'Dave!'

A young man in his late twenties came out of the shed, and Bob studied him carefully as he walked towards them. He was around five feet nine, with dark hair, and when he reached them amusement was showing in his dark eyes.

'You called, Dad?'

'Let this bloke have a look at your arm.'

His mouth twitched. 'Which one?'

'Stop mucking about, son. The one what's hurt, of course.'

The young man still had a sense of humour, Bob noted, and that was a welcome sign. He said nothing while Dave looked him over.

'You a doctor?'

'No, but I've been trained to look after injured men. I haven't got anything to prove to you that I'm a physiotherapist, but I've been taught by one of the best. I might be able to help you. No promises though.'

'Go on, Dave,' his dad urged. 'Can't do no harm to let him have a look.'

Giving a shrug, he removed his jacket and unbuttoned his shirt to allow Bob to examine his right arm and shoulder.

After carefully going over the badly scarred limb, Bob helped Dave back into his shirt and jacket. 'Well, as far as I can see, your shoulder is all right,

260

so that's good, but the arm needs work to loosen it up. If you come to my house this evening around eight, I'll see what I can do for you.'

Dave rubbed his arm, looking at Bob with interest. 'That feels better already. I'll be there, but what are you charging?'

'Nothing. If I can help anyone who has been hurt in the war, then I'm happy to do it.' Bob jumped in the cart. 'Your dad will tell you where I live.'

As the cart rumbled out of the yard, the young man called, 'What's your name?'

'Bob Hunter,' he called back.

As soon as the wood was stacked in the back yard, Bob returned to the market. He found Steve laughing with Hannah Law, but looking rather tired. 'Time to go home,' Bob said. 'That's long enough for your first outing.'

'I am feeling a bit tired, but it's been good to be out again.'

Ruth kissed her dad. 'Thanks for helping; it's been lovely to have you here.'

'I'll come again, won't I, Bob?'

'Of course.' He said goodbye to everyone, and then pushed Steve towards home.

*   *   *

When Eddie and Alf saw the wood they suggested that the bed be moved downstairs at once, instead of waiting for the weekend, then they could make a start building the frame.

Everyone joined in to help with the moving. Even John and Sally were trotting up and downstairs, getting in everyone's way, but no one said anything to the youngsters who were so eager to help. Daisy

261

had pitched in with enthusiasm and was even giving orders about where things should go, appearing to be much more like her old self.

Alf and Bob struggled to get the heavy iron bedstead down the narrow stairs, but they eventually managed it. Daisy and Ruth made up the bed, and then they all sat down to have a rest.

'That calls for a nice cup of tea.' Daisy filled the kettle, obviously relieved something was being done to make her husband's life more bearable.

There was a knock on the front door and Daisy went to answer it. When she came back, she said, 'Here's a young man to see you, Bob. He said you're expecting him.'

'Oh, Dave!' Bob jumped up. 'I didn't realize it was so late.'

Dave stood in the doorway and his gaze swept over the people in the crowded scullery, then rested on the man in the wheelchair. 'You look as if you've all been busy. I'll come another time if it's not convenient, Bob.'

'No, stay.' Bob introduced the young man to everyone, and gulped down the tea Daisy had just handed him. 'Right, let's go next door and see what we can do for you.' They made their way back to the Hunters' house.

'Take off your shirt,' Bob ordered, when they were in his scullery, 'and get on the table so I can work on you more easily.'

Leaving Dave, he ran up the stairs and came back with a large bottle. After rubbing some of the oil in his hands, he set to work.

Half an hour later he stopped. 'That will do for this session. How does it feel?'

Dave sat up and was astonished when he could

move his arm a little. 'That's bloody marvellous. Look, I can lift my arm about six inches, and even curl my fingers slightly. I couldn't move it at all before.'

'I've managed to loosen it a little, and with more sessions you might be able to get some more movement back.' Bob helped him off the table. 'But don't expect miracles. Your arm will never be as good as it was before this happened to you.'

Dave nodded. 'I know that, but anything would be a blessing. Can I come again, please?'

'Come three times a week and we'll see how it goes.'

'Thanks.' Dave put his shirt back on. 'What are you intending to do with the wood you bought today?'

Bob explained about trying to make Steve more independent by building a frame over the bed.

'Have you got a pencil and paper?'

They both sat at the table and Bob watched as Dave began to draw a frame in great detail, using his left hand. 'That's brilliant, Dave! It will be a help having it set down on paper.'

'Not as good as I used to be able to draw. I'm right-handed really, but I've had to learn to use my left.'

'What's this bit sticking out from the bed?' Bob was still studying the drawing.

'I thought it might make it easier for Steve if he had something extra to hold on to when he gets in and out of the wheelchair.'

'I see . . . yes, you're right. I don't think I've got enough wood for that though, because I want to build a frame in the outhouse as well.'

'I'll get you anything else you need. No charge.

It'll be my way of thanking you for helping me.'

The two of them talked for a while, and then went back to the others to show them the drawing.

Thirty-Two

Thank goodness Mum was getting better, Ruth thought. It had been awful to see her lose control like that, and heaven knows what they would have done without Bob's steady, calm help. He seemed to know just what to do. She had stopped looking for the young boy she had grown up with, and now accepted him for the person he had become. This big, confident man was nothing like the boy she remembered, and it saddened her to realize that she had lost that special friendship. They had both grown and moved on in life, and it was useless to keep hankering after the past. There was one thing that couldn't be denied though: they needed him, they needed the man he had become.

Drawing in a ragged breath, Ruth looked at the crowded market. The long winter was over at last and people were strolling around, enjoying the warmth of the sun. She smiled, hoping to attract customers to her stall. They were struggling to manage, and every penny she could make was needed.

Her thoughts turned back to last evening, remembering how they had all worked together converting the front room into a bedroom. It would be much better for their dad, and once he was in the wheelchair he could move around on his own. And Bob was helping another man, Dave Wilson, as well. They all knew his dad, of course, but she hadn't realized he had a son. He seemed quite nice and had an easy smile. She liked him.

'Ruth!' Hannah called, laughter in her voice. 'Look what's coming.'

She turned her head and waved at the group of people. John was pushing their dad, helped by Bob, who was guiding the wheelchair as well. But the most welcome sight was that of her mum with them, and they were all laughing. Seeing them like that brought tears to her eyes. She swiped them away quickly before they reached her.

'We've come to help,' John said, leaving the chair and coming to greet her.

'What, all of you?' she laughed.

'Bob's thrown us all out while he and Alf build their contraption,' Daisy told her. 'They don't want me to see the mess they're going to make.'

'That's right. We'll be ankle deep in sawdust by the time we're finished,' Bob exaggerated.

John began to tug at Bob's sleeve. 'There's that man who came last night.'

Following John's outstretched arm, Ruth saw Dave striding towards them, a big smile on his face.

'Morning, everyone. Lovely day, isn't it?'

They all said hello and agreed that it was.

'I thought you might be here, Bob. Dad's put some more wood round the back of your house for you. It should be enough to build both frames.'

'Thanks. What did he say about you giving away his wood?'

'Not a word when I showed him this.' David curled his fingers round the largest of Ruth's dolls, and even managed to pick it up. He bowed when they all applauded. 'Not too bad, eh? I still can't hold a pen, but with Bob's help, I'm hopeful now.'

Ruth smiled with approval, feeling drawn to the man with the infectious grin. Her family liked him too, she could see. He might come from a line of rag-and-bone merchants, but they were hard working, and she approved of that. And the drawing he had done last night was very good indeed, so he obviously had talent. Perhaps that was why he was so anxious to be able to hold a pencil in his right hand again?

'When are you going to start on the bed frame?' he asked Bob.

'Right now. Dad's already started sawing the wood into the required lengths.'

'I'll give you a hand if you like. Left one, of course.'

Both men laughed, and Bob nodded. 'Any help gratefully accepted.'

'Don't bother coming back for us,' Daisy said. 'I can manage the wheelchair.'

When he looked doubtful, Steve said, 'We'll be all right, Bob. I'm getting the hang of this thing now.'

'That's true, but if you need help send John along to get me.'

'We'll do that. Now off you go.'

Ruth watched them walking away, already deep in conversation. They appeared to have quickly formed a friendship, so perhaps she would see a lot more of Dave Wilson.

*   *   *

'I've brought some help, Dad.'

'Thank goodness! I hope you two know how to

build this thing, because I'm blowed if I do.'

Dave nodded. 'I built a bridge during the war, so I'm sure we can rig this up between us. You'll have to carry the wood though, and I'll be the foreman.'

Alf snorted. 'I thought you said he was here to help.'

'I can make the tea with one hand.'

'Ah, that's all right then.' Alf glanced at his son, a look of disgust on his face. 'Where did you say you found him?'

'In a junk yard.'

Dave just stood there grinning, thoroughly enjoying himself. 'I'll have you know I was training to be an architect before the bloody war put a stop to that. You need me if you're going to make this thing work.'

'An architect?' both men asked, looking at him in amazement.

He nodded, serious now, a flash of disappointment showing in his dark eyes. 'A London firm of architects had taken me on.'

'Why didn't you go back there after the war?' Bob asked.

'They said they couldn't take any trainees, but I knew it was because my right arm was useless. At first my drawing with the left was terrible.' Dave shrugged and his smile was back again. 'So, are you going to build this thing, or spend the day thinking about it?'

'Put the kettle on.' Alf gave Dave a gentle push towards the scullery. 'And we'll start getting the wood in.'

Alf hoisted a thick plank on his shoulder and muttered, 'Bloody war. That boy laughs and jokes, but he's hurting inside.'

'I know that, and I'll do what I can for him.'

For the next two hours they cut wood, hammered and nailed it into place, with Bob and Alf doing all the hard work, and Dave giving advice.

'Time for a break.' Bob sat on the edge of the bed, mopping his brow, and Alf did the same.

Dave took that opportunity to inspect the work they had done so far. 'Hmm, not bad. We make a good team.'

Alf nudged his son. 'Team? Do you see any sweat on his brow?'

'Not a drop.'

'I know what you two giants need.' Dave grinned, completely ignoring their teasing. 'Food, so I'll pop out and get us fish and chips.'

'Good idea.' Alf started fishing in his pocket for some money.

'No you don't.' Dave held up his hand. 'This is on me.'

'You can't do that,' Bob protested. 'You've already given us more wood without charge.'

'That's nothing. You two have given me much more. Won't be long.'

'What do you think he meant by that?' Alf asked his son when they were alone.

'Not sure, but I have a feeling that for all his cheerful attitude he's hurt and lonely, like so many men who fought in the war. He's surprising, and must have had a good education to be taken on by a firm of architects. Junk is obviously a good business.'

'Must be.' Alf gazed at the half-finished frame and sighed. 'I hope to goodness this works.'

'It will, but Steve's going to have to build up his strength to be able to use it properly. Spending all this time in bed has weakened him.' Bob ran his hands through his hair. 'It's just one blasted battle after another, and it's time we started winning a few.'

'That will come; it must.' Alf's face broke into a huge smile when Dave appeared with the fish and chips. 'Ah, lovely, did you put plenty of salt and vinegar on them?'

'Of course.'

Starving, they all settled down, unwrapped the paper and tucked in, not bothering with cutlery.

'Ruth Cooper seems a nice girl.' Dave licked the salt from his fingers. 'Pretty too.'

The other two men nodded, still eating.

'Er . . . Bob?'

'Hmm?'

'Are you and her courting?'

'No.' He popped a chip in his mouth, chewed and swallowed. 'Why?'

'I just wondered if I'd get a bashing from you if I asked her out. Only you're too big to get on the wrong side of.'

Alf chuckled. 'You don't have to worry about him, Dave, he's quite gentle really.'

'I'd rather not take that chance.'

Finishing the last of his chips, Bob screwed the paper into a ball and tossed it at Dave. It whizzed past his ear.

'You sure he's gentle, Alf?'

'Well . . .' He put on a thoughtful expression. 'I might have exaggerated a bit.'

'Fancy her, do you?' Bob asked, keeping a perfectly straight face.

Dave grinned and nodded. 'Not only is she pretty, but she's clever enough to run her own business, and she's so young. How old is she by the way?'

'She must be eighteen by now.' Bob stood up and wiped his hands on the sides of his trousers. 'I've always looked out for her since she was a toddler, so you be careful you don't hurt or upset her.'

'I'll remember that.' Dave's face lit up. 'So, I can ask her to come out with me, can I?'

'You can try.'

*   *   *

'How on earth do you expect me to be able to get in and out of bed using that contraption?' Steve shook his head in disbelief.

'I agree it isn't very pretty, but it works. I'll show you.' Bob hoisted himself on to the bed and off again. 'It's strong enough for someone of my size and weight, so it's quite safe. Have a go.'

After several attempts, getting more and more frustrated, Steve gave up. 'You've wasted your time. That's impossible.'

'It's just a case of getting used to it,' Alf said encouragingly. 'You'll manage it after a while. Let me have a go.'

'Don't bother!' Steve spun the wheelchair away from the bed and stormed out of the room.

Alf looked at his son, who was completely unfazed by Steve's outburst. 'I've never seen him behave like that before. He's always been a calm and controlled man.'

'Don't let it worry you, Dad. The reality of his disability is dawning on him. He's fighting with frustration, and is also terrified about the kind of future in front of him. This is going to be a very difficult time for him.'

Sitting on the edge of the bed, Alf ran a hand over his eyes. 'Isn't there something else we can do? What about finding him a doctor who specializes in back injuries? I've still got the house and could possibly scrape the money together.'

'And you're going to keep it,' Bob told him firmly. 'You've got needy tenants, and you can't throw them out.'

'No, of course I can't. I'm just trying to think of a way to help Steve and his family.'

'I agree something needs to be done.' Bob placed an arm around Alf's shoulder. 'I'll give it some thought. Come on, let's join the others.'

A sea of worried faces met them when they walked into the scullery. 'Dad's really angry,' Eddie told them. 'When we asked him what was the matter, he told us to mind our own business, and then he went out into the yard.'

'He wasn't able to use the hoist, and it made him furious.' Alf stood by the window and gazed at the man sitting forlornly outside.

Without comment, Bob walked outside and stood slightly in front of Steve, gazing up at the sky.

'What do you want?' Steve snapped.

'Just admiring the view.' He turned his head and smiled. 'There's a touch of pink in the sky so that means it's going to be nice tomorrow.'

'Where did you learn that nonsense?'

'While I worked on the Russell estate. The farmers were very good at predicting the weather. It's surprising how often it turns out to be true. Of course it's clearer there without all the London smoke and grime.'

'Well, why the hell don't you go back there and

271

leave me in peace?'

'And what would you do if I did leave?' Bob turned slowly to face the angry man. 'You don't need to answer that because I have no intention of giving up on you. If it makes you feel better you can curse and swear at me all you like, it won't bother me, but you've just upset your family. They love you and don't deserve to be spoken to so rudely.'

'Oh God!' Steve bowed his head, tears falling silently down his cheeks. 'What am I going to do, Bob?'

'I'll think of something.'

Thirty-Three

It had turned out to be a lovely day without a cloud in the sky. Bob finished talking and left the phone box. He had spent a restless night trying to decide what to do to raise Steve's spirits again. After his outburst he had apologized to his family for upsetting them, but he remained withdrawn, refusing to try the hoist again. Bob knew the signs: he had given up. The phone call he had just made was the only thing he could think of doing, and he wasn't sure if it would help. Something had to be done though, because progress of any kind would be impossible in Steve's present state of mind. He had hesitated about making that call, but he had been told to go to them if he needed help of any kind, and he really needed it now.

Striding back to the house he got Steve washed, dressed and in the wheelchair. 'We're going out for the day,' he told Daisy.

'Oh, in that case, as it's a lovely day I think I'll go and help Ruthie on the stall.' She kissed her husband. 'You have a nice time.'

He didn't tell Steve where they were going, and it wasn't until they were on the train that he even bothered to ask. 'You'll see when we get there. I told you it was going to be a lovely day, didn't I?'

Steve didn't bother to answer and the rest of the journey was spent in silence, and Bob knew it wouldn't help to try and force conversation out of him. He also knew that Steve was sinking fast into a state of despair, and there would probably be trouble when they reached their destination.

Not a word was spoken until he pushed the wheelchair through the door, then it was as if Steve woke up from a deep sleep. 'What the hell are we doing here?'

He didn't answer but smiled at a woman coming towards them. 'Hello, Sister, it's so good of you to let me come. I seem to keep turning up, don't I?'

'Of course you do, Bob, you belong here, or haven't you realized that yet? And we did tell you to come to us if you need help or advice.' She turned her attention to Steve. 'Doctor Vickers is waiting for you.'

He glanced up at Bob in horror. 'You're not leaving me here?'

'No, but the doctor has agreed to have a look at you, and let me know the best way I can help you.'

'Have you lost your mind?' Steve demanded. 'You know we can't afford anything like this!'

Mary laid a hand on his arm. 'There will be no charge for the examination, Mr Cooper. Our reasons for helping Bob are completely selfish. If we can get you back on your feet, then we can have

Bob back with us again. We need him as well, you know.'

'And I want to see him finish his training to become a qualified physiotherapist.' A lean man came towards them, hand outstretched, and a smile of welcome on his face.

They greeted each other with obvious pleasure, and then the doctor shook hands with Steve. 'Right, Mr Cooper, come with me and let's have a look at you.'

Steve was by now lost for words and could only gaze from one person to the other. Bob noticed and thought wryly that at least bringing him here had shaken him out of his lethargy.

There was another man in the consulting room. 'Ha! I knew you wouldn't be able to keep away from us.'

'Hello, Jack. Steve, meet the best darned physiotherapist in the business.'

Jack winked at Steve. 'He's still got a good line in flattery. Now, let's see what we can do for you. Give us a hand, Bob.'

Before Steve knew what was happening he was stripped and face down on the table.

The examination took some time with quiet discussion going on between the three men. Steve breathed a sigh of relief when he was dressed and once again in the wheelchair.

The young doctor sat on the table, swinging his legs. 'What fell on you, Mr Cooper?'

'Cases of machinery. It was bad luck really because I was only walking past, but they had been badly stacked and they fell just at the wrong moment.'

He nodded. 'Well, your body took a beating, but

274

I can find no indication of anything broken, which is something to be grateful for.'

'Meaning?' Steve asked hesitantly.

'Nerves and muscles take time to heal completely, but you are doing well, and in time you might get some use back in your legs.'

'Might?'

'I can't say more than that. You have been badly injured, and only time will tell how complete your eventual recovery will be. But there is a small hopeful sign. You flinched a couple of times during the examination, so there is some feeling there. Bob is doing exactly the right thing for you, but if there is still no improvement in two months, then I'll see you again.'

'Doc!' A head appeared in the doorway, and then disappeared just as quickly.

'I must go.' He jumped off the table. 'Nice to meet you, Mr Cooper, and don't give up hope. Bob, you come back soon.' Then he was gone.

'I must get back to work as well.' Jack then placed his hands on Bob's back. 'Work this area more, and don't be afraid to be strong about it. Like this.'

'Ouch!'

'That's the place, now you'll remember where it is.' Jack grinned and slapped him on the shoulder. 'Don't you desert us, my lad. You've got sensitive hands and a real talent for the work. Forget about being a teacher. This is where you can do the most good, and as Sister is continually saying, this is where you belong.'

Turning to Steve, Jack shook hands. 'I know it's hard, Mr Cooper, but try to have patience, and do as Bob tells you. Make the most of his talent because he's only on loan to you.'

Steve could only watch with his mouth open as Jack left the room. 'They like you, don't they?'

'They're a good crowd. Now we've finished here I'm going to show you my favourite place before we go home.'

There was no sign of Sister so Bob left a note of thanks on her desk.

A few clouds were appearing now, but they weren't rain clouds, and it was still pleasantly warm. Bob's first stop was the butcher for two of his famous pies, and after that he wheeled Steve to the Terraces. They sat there admiring the view and enjoying their pies.

'How could you bear to leave here and come back to Canning Town?' Steve asked quietly, sighing deeply as peace settled over him. 'This is such a lovely spot.'

'You have always been like family to me.' Bob tore his gaze away from the view and looked directly at the man beside him. 'That's why I returned.'

'Will you come back here when you've done all you can for me?'

'Yes.' Bob wasn't surprised by how quickly the answer had come. No doubts. This was where he wanted to be.

'Why did you bring me here?'

'You were losing heart, and I needed to find out if I was doing you more harm than good. I was afraid I had been pushing you too hard. I trust the people here to tell me the truth about your chances of recovery.'

'And what exactly did they tell you? Because I'm damned if I'm any the wiser.'

'There is a chance you will walk again, but probably not without something to support you. However, as far as I'm concerned, that is not good enough! I won't be happy until you can walk without any aid, so don't you damned well give up!' Bob looked at Steve, determination written on every line of his handsome face. 'I'll be wasting my time if you don't cooperate. So, are you up to it?'

For the first time that day Steve smiled, his eyes misted with emotion. 'I'm with you all the way. Here's to victory!'

They clasped hands to seal their unity for the struggle ahead, and Bob sighed with relief. If Steve had given up there wouldn't have been a chance, but if he could stay in a positive frame of mind they might just win. Steve didn't know exactly what Doctor Vickers and Jack had told him, and he wouldn't tell him in case it came to nothing, but there was more than a glimmer of hope.

The journey back to London was more cheerful. They didn't speak much, both lost in their own thoughts, but they were relaxed, and it was good to know he had done the right thing in coming here.

*　　　*　　　*

Dave came after tea for Bob to work on his arm again. This would only be the third time, but it was already showing signs of improvement.

'Have you asked Ruth out yet?' Bob asked as he worked.

'Not yet.' Dave grimaced when a tender spot was located. 'I'm waiting until I can use my arm more.'

'Don't wait too long or someone else might beat you to it.'

'You, for instance? Ouch!'

'I wouldn't stand a chance. She's never forgiven me for walking out after Mum died.'

'Ah, yes, I read about that. Must have been tough for you.'

Bob stopped working. 'You read about it? Don't you mean someone told you about it?'

'No, I read it in your dad's book.' Dave turned his head. 'You finished?'

'Stay where you are. What book?'

'It's in the Imperial War Museum. Are you telling me you don't know?'

'No, I damned well don't!' Bob worked in silence for a while longer, then stopped. 'That will do for tonight. How does it feel?'

Sitting up he moved his fingers. 'Wow, look at that, I can almost close my fist, and there's more movement in the arm. Thanks, Bob.'

'Glad I can help. Now, tell me about this book.'

Over a cup of tea Dave explained about Alf's memoirs and how the museum had had them made into a book for anyone to read.

'So that's how he managed to buy that house.' Bob was stunned. 'But why hasn't anyone told me about this before now?'

'Alf's not one to brag. You ought to have a look at the museum some time.'

'I will.' And he'd find that book as well. His dad was bound to have been given a copy, so it must be somewhere in the house.

'Er . . . Bob, I've got a mate who was injured as well, and he's having a tough time. I was wondering if you'd have a look at him? The doctors have given up on him, just like a lot of us.'

'What are his injuries?'

278

'Left leg and hip.' Dave fidgeted awkwardly. 'When he saw how my arm was improving he said he'd be grateful if you'd see him. I know I shouldn't ask, but I told him what kind of job you'd been doing, and he begged me to ask you.'

'Bring him round with you tomorrow evening, but I'm not promising anything.'

'He knows that.' Dave smiled in gratitude. 'Thanks, Bob.'

The door burst open and Alf rushed in. 'Bob! Come and see. Steve's used the hoist and got on the bed without any help.'

'He didn't try it with no one there, did he?' Bob was already on his feet.

'No, I was beside him all the time.'

'That's good. I'll come now. I was just about to search for a book Dave's been telling me about.' He gave his dad a pointed look. 'But it can wait. I expect it's in your bedroom, isn't it?'

'Ah.' Alf gave Dave a hard stare.

'I didn't know you hadn't told him,' he protested.

'What's the secret, Dad?'

'No secret. I have a copy for you, and I intended to give it to you one day. I just haven't got around to it yet.'

Noting his dad's uncomfortable expression, Bob smiled. 'I look forward to reading it, and well done.'

'Thanks.' He laughed nervously. 'But Steve did all the hard work and dragged me to the museum. I'd never have done it without him, and I owe him and his family more than I can ever repay.'

'You're repaying that debt now. Let's go and make sure Steve doesn't try to get out of bed while we're not there. Come on, Dave, let's all go and congratulate him. I want us to give him all the

279

encouragement possible.'

Steve was sitting on the bed with everyone clustered around him, smiling and happy about this big step forward.

'Isn't it wonderful?' Daisy said as soon as they walked in. 'He did it all by himself.'

'Well done.' Bob stood beside the wheelchair. 'Now, can you get out again?'

'I'll try.'

'Take your time and don't worry if you can't. You've crossed the first hurdle, and it will get easier with each attempt.' He gave Steve a sly wink, making his mouth twitch in amusement. On the way home they had agreed not to tell anyone where they had been today, not wanting to raise false hopes. For the moment this would be kept between the two of them.

It took three attempts before he was back in the wheelchair, but he had managed it without their help. Mopping his brow he smiled in acknowledgement of the applause.

Bending down so no one else could hear, Bob said, 'That's victory number one, but don't you dare try that when I'm not here. I'll tell you when I think you are expert enough to use the hoist on your own.'

'I won't, sir!' he said smartly, and burst out laughing, flushed with success.

*   *   *

Later that evening when everyone was in bed, Alf gave Bob the book he had been keeping for him. 'It isn't pretty reading, son, but I think it will explain a lot of things.'

'I'm sure it will.' He was still sleeping on the

280

floor in the same room as Steve. 'I'll read it before going to sleep tonight.'

'You know I can't believe the difference in Steve. Yesterday he seemed to have given up, but now the fight is back in him.' Alf gave his son a questioning look. 'Just what did you do to him today?'

Bob shrugged. 'I shook him up a bit.'

'And that's all you're going to say?'

'For the moment.'

'Hmm.'

*　　　*　　　*

Bob read well into the night, unable to put the book down. War on the front line came to life, giving him a much clearer understanding of why so many men were still suffering nightmares and other problems. But when he read the final chapter he couldn't stop the tears of remorse running down his face. Why hadn't his mum told him? He would have understood then.

Without giving the time of night a thought he left the house, jumped the fence, and went to Alf's room. He shook him awake.

'Eh? What?' Alf sat up, startled. 'What's happened? Is Steve all right?'

'He's fast asleep.' Bob sat on the edge of the bed. 'You knew Mum was dying.'

'She told me as soon as I arrived home, knowing it wouldn't be long, you see. I had been longing to get home and back to normal life, and all my hopes were ripped away in a moment. I was already struggling and that tipped me over the edge. I couldn't handle it, and to my shame, I lost control.'

281

'You should have told me.'

'Your mum didn't want you to know. She had seen a doctor and knew there was no hope of her recovering, so she thought it best not to tell you. I didn't agree, but she was firm and wouldn't hear of it, making me promise not to say a word about it to you. It was hard watching your love for me turn to hate, but I'd promised and I couldn't go back on my word.'

He now understood the pain Alf must have been going through, and the difficult position he had been put in. 'I wouldn't have left the way I did if I had known.'

'No, son, you did the right thing. I would probably still be drinking if you had stayed. It has all worked out for the best. Don't hold on to regrets. All the misunderstandings between us have been cleared away, and that's all that matters now.'

'You're right. What's done is done.' Bob stood up, squeezed his shoulder, and said, 'Night, Dad, sleep well.'

Thirty-Four

'Hello, Dave.' Ruth smiled as the young man stopped by her stall. 'How's your arm?'

'Feeling good, thank you. I couldn't move it at all, but now I can lift it about six inches. Bob's massaging is making a difference.'

'I can't imagine him being a masseur. It's not the sort of thing I would ever have expected him to do.'

'Oh, he's more than a masseur. The training he's been receiving is in physiotherapy. You

282

couldn't have anyone better to look after your dad. Someone my dad knows is in a home for the badly injured—not where Bob worked, but he was able to find out a few things for us.' Dave gave her a speculative look. 'Don't underestimate him.' Dave grinned. 'But I didn't come here to sing Bob's praises. Would you come out with me, Ruth? We could go to the pictures, or dancing, whatever you fancy.'

Taken by surprise, she hesitated for a moment, and then nodded. She liked him, so why not? It was time she started to go out on dates, just like all the other girls. 'I don't mind what we do. When?'

'Wonderful!' He beamed with pleasure. 'I can't make it tonight because I'm bringing a mate round to see Bob, but tomorrow would be fine. If that's all right with you I'll come for you at seven o'clock?'

'I'll be ready.'

'Nice boy, Dave Wilson,' Mrs Law remarked, watching him disappear into the crowd. 'His dad made sure he had a decent education. There's money in junk, so the family's not short of a bob or two. The lad made it to sergeant in the army as well. You could do quite nicely for yourself there, Ruth.'

She burst out laughing. 'I haven't even been out with him yet, and I'm far too busy to get serious about anyone, Mrs Law.'

'How many times have I told you to call me Hannah?'

'Sorry, I keep forgetting, Hannah. And here's Alf coming to see you.' Ruth hid the smile as Hannah patted her hair into place. This Saturday afternoon visit was becoming a regular thing, and she couldn't help wondering if there was a romance blossoming between them. If there was then she was pleased. Hannah had lost her husband during the war, and Alf had been through a lot, so they both deserved a bit of happiness.

'Ruthie.' John suddenly appeared, ducking through the crowds and pulling Sally behind him. 'Mum told us to bring you a sandwich, and could you get a loaf of bread, please. And can we help you? We won't be a nuisance.'

'Of course you can both stay.' She smiled as her young brother and sister took up positions by the stall, smiling at the people walking by and urging them to come and see what they had for sale. They really enjoyed doing this.

'Hello, Mr Hunter.' Both of the kids waved to him on the next stall. 'Bob isn't taking Dad out today because he's tired after all the excitement yesterday.'

'Is he all right?' Alf frowned, concerned. He had come to the market straight from the docks, and was wondering if he should have gone home first.

'Oh, yes.' John nodded. 'He's been talking to Bob, but they wouldn't let us hear.'

'They've got secrets,' Sally told them, 'and I heard Dad say "you must be joking" and they both laughed.'

John nodded, pursing his lips. 'They're up to something, Mr Hunter. Do you know what it is?'

'I've no idea.'

John looked hopefully at his big sister. 'Dad's much happier. Do you think he's getting better?'

'They haven't said anything to me, but whatever they did yesterday has certainly cheered Dad up. Do you know where they went?' she asked Alf.

'Not a clue, but I know Bob didn't like the way

he was acting, and wanted to cheer him up. He's certainly done that.'

Customers came to the stall, putting an end to their conversation, and for the rest of the day they were quite busy. In fact when it came time to pack up, she was able to send the children to get the bread and also some sausages for a treat.

*   *   *

'How did you get on with Dave's friend last night?' Steve asked Bob.

'His leg is a mess, I'm afraid, but I'll see what I can do for him. I've given him some gentle exercises to try, and I'll see him again next week.'

'You go on like this and they will be queuing up outside the door to see you.'

'I don't mind helping.' He shrugged and changed the subject. 'Are you up to an outing today?'

'You're not thinking of the horse-riding you mentioned yesterday, are you?'

Bob grinned. 'It's a lovely day for a ride in the country.'

'Is it going to do me any good?' Steve asked, looking rather doubtful.

'We won't know until we try, but it will be fun, anyway.'

'I'm not sure I agree with your idea of fun, but let's give it a try.'

'Good, we'll catch the nine thirty train. I've already let the captain know that we're coming.'

'Ah.' Steve's mouth twitched in amusement. 'So I really didn't have a choice?'

'None at all.'

Jim was waiting at the station with a brand-new car, and when both men admired it, he told them that the captain only got it yesterday.

'And he's letting you drive it?' Steve asked. 'That's very trusting of him.'

'He insisted, saying it would give you a smoother ride than the old horse and buggy. Come on, in you get.'

As they drove away Steve watched the passing scenery, sadness almost swamping him. 'Last time I came here I walked from the station.'

'Wait until you've ridden a horse a few times, Mr Cooper, and you might be able to do it again.'

'I hope so, Jim.'

Captain Russell was waiting for them in the stable yard, with Lilly at his side, as usual.

She ran to meet them, all smiles. 'Daddy said I can ride with you if I behave myself. I will, I will!'

'Lovely.' Bob swept her off her feet, making her squeal in delight.

'I've got a sister now, but she's too little to ride yet, and Robert doesn't like horses. How can you not like horses?' she asked, looking thoroughly puzzled. She stopped chattering and went up to Steve in the wheelchair. 'Hello. We've got a lovely quiet horse for you.'

'You remember Ruth's father, don't you, Lilly?' And when his daughter nodded, Ben shook hands with Steve. 'It's good to see you looking so well.'

'Thanks, but I'm not sure about getting on a horse. Bob seems to think it will help me.'

'You'll be all right,' Lilly told him seriously. 'We won't let you fall off.'

'I'm very glad to hear that.' Steve cast an apprehensive look at the horses being led into the yard. 'I hope you're not going to try and put me on that big black one. He's got an evil look in his eyes.'

'No, he's mine.' Bob whistled, sending Midnight stamping with excitement, making him difficult for the groom to control.

'He'll be calm when Bob gets on him,' Lilly giggled. 'The chestnut is yours. She's very docile.' She ran to her own pony and mounted with ease.

Captain Russell then mounted his own horse and held on to Cherry. A block was placed the other side for Bob to stand on as he put Steve in the saddle. Jim and the captain held him securely while Bob jumped on Midnight's back then took his place beside Steve, who was gripping the saddle fiercely.

With Lilly leading the way they walked out of the yard and into the open fields of the estate.

They walked the horses for about half an hour, and as Steve began to relax, Bob nodded to the captain and they slowly released their hold on him. He was beginning to enjoy being out in the fresh air and lovely countryside, and didn't even notice they weren't holding him in the saddle any more. Bob was elated. Steve was balancing well, and this was a very encouraging sign.

They stopped on a rise to admire the view and Midnight began to prance, impatient at the slow pace.

'Take him for a gallop, Bob, or he'll be nothing but trouble for the rest of our ride. We'll wait here for you.'

Seeing that Steve was quite happy, he let Midnight have his head. As he raced across the fields he felt a peace he had never known before, and for the first time in his life he knew where he was going and what he was going to do. The dream of becoming a teacher had been a childish desire to do something useful. It wouldn't have been right for him, but the kind of work he had stumbled into *was* right for him. As soon as Steve could manage without him he would return to the home and continue his training. He would also see William Jackson again, but just to improve his education, not so he could become a teacher.

Laughing with a sudden feeling of freedom, he turned Midnight, and they sped at full gallop back to the others.

*　　　*　　　*

'Where have you two been all day?' Daisy asked the moment they arrived home. 'It's six o'clock, and I was getting worried.'

'Sorry, darling.' Steve pulled her down so he could kiss her. 'I've been horse riding! Can you believe that? And I stayed on all by myself. Didn't I, Bob?'

'No trouble at all. Next time we'll have you trotting.'

Steve couldn't stop smiling. 'Captain Russell and his wife have had another daughter. Lilly insisted we have a look at her, then they insisted we stay for lunch.'

The kids were all staring wide-eyed as he told them, in great detail, about their day.

'You've been to Kent?' Daisy asked when she could finally get a word in.

'Yes, Bob said it was the captain's idea that I should try riding.' It was only then Steve realized that someone was missing. 'Where's Ruth?'

'She's making herself all posh.' Eddie's face showed his disgust. 'She's going out with Dave.'

'Ah, so he finally got around to asking her.'

'You know about this, Bob?' Steve's smile had faded.

'He told me he wanted to take her out, but don't worry, I told him that if he didn't behave himself he'd have me to deal with.'

Daisy laughed. 'In that case he won't do anything to upset Bob. And don't look so worried, darling, it's about time our daughter began to take an interest in boys.'

'I suppose you're right. I still keep thinking of her as a little girl.'

'How long before supper, Daisy?' Bob asked.

'An hour.'

'Right, that's just time to give you a massage, Steve, or you'll be stiff from the riding.'

*　　*　　*

It was eleven o'clock! Bob prowled over to the window, gazing out as he listened to Steve's steady breathing. His day had tired him out, but it had been good to see him laughing and enjoying himself again.

Ah, there she was. If they'd been much later he would have had a word with Dave. Spinning away from the window, he swore under his breath. What on earth did he think he was doing? He wasn't Ruth's father, and she wasn't a child who needed looking out for any more. She didn't want or need his protection now. She was grown up. There was no doubt about that!

Thirty-Five

With Christmas less then three months away, Ruth was receiving more and more requests for gowns. Once the quality of the clothes on her stall had been recognized, her reputation as a dressmaker had been spreading, and she was now making clothes for more of the middle-class. In fact she was working all hours to keep up, but she didn't dare turn anything down. Demand would drop after the festive season, and she was determined to earn as much as she could. Eddie was now working behind the counter at the grocer's, and the small increase in wages was welcome. Mum was much better and helping with the sewing as much as she could, but her main concern was still her husband. They had all, reluctantly, accepted that he would probably never walk again, and that meant he wouldn't be able to work again either.

She sighed. How her heart ached for him. Nearly six months after the accident and she still had to fight the tears to see him so helpless. He had always been an independent man and hated relying on other people all the time, but there was nothing else he could do. Bob had been wonderful by showing him how to do things on his own, and she dreaded to think what his life would be like now if Bob hadn't arrived with his special skills. Her mum wouldn't have coped, that was for sure, and the strain on the rest of them would have been terrible. He had brought a feeling of strength and stability to their lives when it was so badly needed.

'Ruthie.' John opened the door of her bedroom

and peered in. 'Mum said supper would be ready in ten minutes. Are you going out with Dave tonight?'

She shook her head. 'I'm too busy.'

'Oh.' He edged into the room, being careful not to tread on the lovely material draped all over the floor. 'What are you making?'

'A wedding gown, and I've only got a week to finish it.'

'It looks as if it's for a posh wedding. Is it?'

'Very, and it's important that I make a good job of it.'

'Sally's helping Mum. She likes cooking.'

'She's a good girl.' Ruth folded the gown carefully and laid it on her bed, then smiled at her brother. 'In fact you've all been very brave and helpful. I'm proud of you all.'

'Dad's not going to walk again, is he, Ruthie?' This was a question he was constantly asking, probably hoping that one day he would get the answer he hoped for.

'We don't know, but Bob doesn't give up trying, and I'm sure he hasn't given up hope. So we mustn't either.'

Disappointment showed on his expressive face, then he brightened. 'Bob's been showing me and Eddie how to help Dad, because he's got lots of other men coming every day to see him, but he doesn't leave Dad's side for long. Mr Hunter says Bob should charge for what he does, but he said the men he sees haven't got any money. We're all right, though, aren't we, Ruthie?'

'We're doing fine. I'm getting more work than I can handle really, but Hannah is looking after my stall when I can't get there. And you, Sally and Mum are helping as well, so we're making enough money to get by.'

John nodded. 'I'm ten now, and when I leave school and get a job, you and Eddie won't have to work so hard.'

'That's true,' she agreed, 'but you mustn't worry about that now. We'll manage while you finish your schooling. It's very important, you know.'

'That's what Bob says. Do you know that before he came home he was having special lessons from a university teacher? A professor arranged it for him.'

'Really?' She was being constantly surprised by the things Bob had been doing. 'He's never said anything about it.'

'Captain Russell told Mr Hunter. He said Bob was really upset about giving it all up, but he tried not to show it. As soon as he told him about Dad though, he came immediately.'

This news upset her. Had he been close to fulfilling his dream, and walked away from it because they needed help? In that moment every doubt she'd held on to about him drained away. The accident had changed all their lives.

'Mum's calling.' John tugged at her sleeve. 'Come on, I'm hungry.'

While they were sitting around the table, Ruth studied Bob carefully when his attention was elsewhere. If she looked very hard she could still see small signs of the boy she had known so well, in the way his grey eyes never seemed to miss a thing, and that slightly crooked smile was still the same. He was older, of course, and even better looking, but she felt the biggest change was inside. As a boy he had been quite volatile, intolerant, but now there was a sense of calmness about him. Since he had come back she hadn't once seen him lose his temper; even when her dad had been depressed and at his most difficult, it had not appeared to touch him. She didn't know what difficulties and trials he had faced during the last few years, but he certainly wasn't the same person who had walked away from here so full of anger. She couldn't help wondering if he saw great changes in her as well, and perhaps he didn't like what he saw. That was an uncomfortable thought, for although they got on well now, she couldn't forget how rude she had been to him at first. How childish he must have thought her to be, and he would have been right.

There was a knock on the front door and she was about to get up to see who was there, but her mum beat her to it.

Daisy was soon back. 'Bob, there's a woman asking to see you and she has her husband with her. He's on crutches and she begged me to persuade you to see them.'

Without a word Bob was on his feet and heading for the front door.

Alf was shaking his head. 'Better keep his supper warm, Daisy, because we won't see him for a while. Word is getting around and they keep turning up now, don't they?'

'Some men are desperate for help, and most living around here can't afford expensive medical treatment.' Daisy put Bob's plate in the oven on a low gas.

'I know, but he can't take on everyone. He's working continually and not being paid a penny. Even when it's offered he won't take it.' Alf finished his meal and stood up. 'I'd better see if he needs any help.'

'They've become very close,' Steve remarked when Alf left the scullery. 'It's good to see.'

*   *   *

Nearly an hour passed before they returned, and as soon as they were settled Daisy put Bob's meal in front of him again. 'It's dried out a bit, but I've put some fresh gravy on it.'

'Thanks, Daisy.' He immediately attacked the food.

'Were you able to help that man?' Ruth asked, curious, because he said very little about the men who came to him.

Bob swallowed before speaking. 'Can't say at this point. I need more information about his injuries, and after that I'll do what I can.'

Ruth persisted. 'How many men are coming to you now?'

'I'm not counting, Ruth.' He finished his meal just as there was a thump on the back door. It opened a few inches, then a few more to allow a face to peer in.

'Hello everyone.' Dave gave them his wide grin. 'You ready, Bob? Er . . . I've brought someone with me.'

'Not another one,' Alf muttered, watching his son's mouth twitch at the corners. 'Is he taking them off the streets?'

The door opened a touch more so Dave could get his head right in. 'They keep coming to me, Alf, and I've got a soft heart. I can't say no.'

'Hmm. There's nothing wrong with your hearing either, is there?'

Dave shook his head, still smiling, shoulders

295

inside now. 'Hello, Ruth, have you got any time for me yet?'

'Sorry.' She shook her head. 'I'm still too busy.'

'You ought to be careful you know, because I might find someone else.'

She burst out laughing at his false hurt expression. 'You've already got them lined up, Dave Wilson.'

'I can't help it if the girls find me irresistible.'

'The conceit of the man,' Steve said, and they all laughed.

Bob got to his feet. 'I'll take him out of your way.'

But Dave was standing right inside the scullery now. 'I've got some good news.'

'You're not going to bring Bob any more injured men?' Alf asked, drily.

'Not that, but I won't have as much time after this week.' He looked smug. 'I'm starting work with a firm of architects so I can finish my training.'

'Oh, that's wonderful!' Ruth was applauding and everyone else joined in. 'Well done, Dave.'

'Thanks.' He looked almost shy for a moment, his eyes full of gratitude when he looked at the tall man standing beside him. 'I'd never have been taken on if it hadn't been for Bob. I can hold a pencil now and draw as well as I ever did. He's worked a damned miracle on me, and given me the chance to do the job I really love.'

'It was your own determination,' Bob told him dismissively. 'I'm glad you are going to be gainfully employed instead of making a pest of yourself. Now, let's see the man you kindly brought along with you.'

Both men were laughing as they left.

'Isn't it wonderful news?' Daisy said as she began to clear the table. 'Bob must be so pleased to know he's been able to continue his training.'

'I'm sure he is.' Steve looked at his family, serious now. 'But we can't keep him here much longer. He never says anything, but I know he's longing to return to his job. I've told him he's to go after Christmas.'

There was a tense silence, and Daisy was the first to speak. 'I know you're right and we must let him go, but we are going to miss him terribly. How will we manage without him, darling?'

'I'll be all right. He's been teaching Eddie how to help me, and Alf will be around as well. I can do quite a lot for myself now.'

'I can even massage Dad's back,' Eddie told them proudly. 'Bob said I'm quite good at it, didn't he, Dad?'

'You most certainly are, and you've had a good teacher.'

'How long has this been going on?' Ruth asked. She had known her brother was interested in what Bob did, but she had no idea he had been learning how to do a massage. She had been so busy trying to earn enough money for them to live on, that she hadn't had time to take an interest in what everyone else was doing.

'Oh, ages,' her brother said. 'We just haven't mentioned it, that's all.'

'You mustn't worry, Daisy,' Alf assured her. 'We've been working towards making it possible for Steve to do things for himself, and Eddie and I can take care of anything he can't manage. We can't keep Bob much longer; it wouldn't be fair on him.'

'No, of course you're right. We've asked a great deal of him and it's been good of him to stay this long.' She brightened up. 'He'll be here for a while yet, but you'll miss your riding. You enjoyed that.'

'I can still go. Alf and Eddie are going to take me.' Steve chuckled. 'Captain Russell said he would get them both on a horse as well.'

'We'll see about that,' Alf smirked.

'What's he going to do about all the other men, Mr Hunter?' John wanted to know.

'He's going to come back once a month to see them, and he plans to stay for two days each time.'

'You sound as if you've been planning this for some time.'

'We have, Ruth.' Steve nodded. 'I've been telling him to go back to his work for quite a while now, and he's finally agreed to go after Christmas. They want him to return so he can finish his training and I know he wants to do that. He's done enough here; we can't keep him forever.'

Daisy sighed. 'That's true enough, but it's a comfort to know he will come back to see us regularly.'

Everyone agreed, and so did Ruth. The thought of him leaving made her unhappy, for he was going back to a life that didn't include her, and she was desperately sorry about that, because she very much wanted to be with him. She had always loved the boy, but she now loved him in a very different way.

The realization came as quite a shock.

Thirty-Six

'The weather is getting too cold for you to ride now, Steve.'

'That's a shame. I've really enjoyed this, and I can even trot now.'

'You're welcome here any time.' Captain Russell steadied the chestnut horse while Bob lifted Steve off. 'If Bob isn't around then you bring Eddie and Alf, as we agreed.'

'Thanks, I know Eddie's looking forward to coming, but I'm not too sure about Alf.' He grinned at the thought as Bob put him back in the wheelchair, then he started to rub the top of his left leg.

'What's the matter?' Bob asked immediately.

'My leg aches . . .'

'Does it?' Bob began to run his hands over Steve's legs.

'Ouch!'

Bob surged to his feet. 'I need somewhere to examine Steve, Captain.'

'Follow me.' Ben took them into the house and up the stairs to one of the bedrooms. 'Will this do?'

'Perfect.' He laid Steve on the bed.

'Anything I can do?'

'No thanks, I can manage.'

'What have I done?' Steve asked, agitated. 'I've ridden lots of times and never hurt myself.'

'I don't think you've hurt yourself, but I need to make sure.'

For the next half an hour Bob said nothing as he worked, massaging and manipulating Steve's back and legs.

The silence finally became too much for Steve. 'Tell me what the hell's happened.'

Bob sat him up again and smiled. 'The feeling is coming back to your legs. Try moving your toes.'

Steve studied his toes, concentrating hard, and when one moved slightly he yelled, 'Look at that! Oh dear Lord, am I going to walk again? Please tell me I am, Bob.'

'Don't get too excited.' Bob laid a restraining hand on him. 'There's an improvement at last, but we don't know how good it will get. What I'm going to do is exercise your legs more to strengthen them.'

Steve was nodding eagerly. 'Anything you say. Get me on my feet by Christmas.'

'Steady on there, that's only four weeks away,' he pointed out. 'But don't worry. If there's a chance you're going to get some feeling back in your legs, I'll stay on after Christmas.'

'Oh, thanks, Bob.' Steve clasped his hand in gratitude. 'You've done so much and I hate to ask you to stay longer.'

'You're not asking, I'm offering.'

There was a rap on the door and the captain came in. 'Do you need a doctor, Bob? I can get one here quickly.'

'No, thanks, everything is all right.'

'Look!' Steve pointed to his feet. 'I can move a toe, and there's some feeling coming back to my left leg. All that horse riding must have done some good.'

'That's wonderful!' The captain spun to face Bob, a questioning look on his face. 'Is this the start of a steady improvement?'

'All I can say is that this is the most hopeful sign we've had so far.'

'I want to get back on my feet by Christmas,' Steve insisted, 'even if it's on crutches. It would be the best present my family could have, and Bob has arranged to go back to his job in the New Year. I don't want to delay him; he's already spent far too much time with us.'

Lilly peered in the room. 'Mum said would you like tea up here, Daddy?'

'What do you think, Bob?'

'No, we'll come down.'

'Tell Mummy we'll be down soon. And Lilly, do you remember Grandpa's walking stick? The one with the horse's head in silver?'

She nodded. 'It's in the stick stand by the door.'

'Bring it here for me, sweetheart.' The captain thought for a moment. 'You're going to need crutches as well, but I'm not sure if we have any of those. Perhaps the servants . . .' He strode to the door and shouted for the butler.

Green soon appeared. 'Sir?'

'Have we got any crutches around the place?'

'I believe there is a pair in the stables. One of the lads sprained an ankle last year and he used them.'

'Send someone to see if they are still there, and if so, bring them to me.'

'Yes, sir.'

'Is this what you wanted, Daddy?' Lilly dodged round the butler as he left the room, nearly tripping over the long cane.

'That's it.' He took it from her and held it out to Steve. 'I hope you will soon progress to using this.'

'But I can't take that. It's a valuable cane.'

'I insist. Ah, and here are the crutches.' He

301

took them from the lad who had just arrived, and propped them against the wall, smiling. 'Nothing gets thrown away here.'

Steve was about to protest, so Bob stopped him by saying, 'Thank you, Captain. These items will be returned to you if they are no longer needed.'

'That isn't necessary, but if it makes you feel better about taking them, then I agree.'

Steve obviously approved of that arrangement and smiled. 'We are grateful for your kindness and generosity.'

'No, Steve, I am the one who is grateful to be allowed to help you. I thought you would never forgive us after what happened to your lovely daughter while she was with us.'

'That's past history now, and it wasn't any of your doing, so there's nothing to forgive.'

'Thank you, Steve; it's a great relief to hear you say that. Now, let's go downstairs and have tea with Emma. You must both be hungry.'

*　　　*　　　*

On the way home it was decided not to say anything about this hopeful sign, except to Alf and Eddie, who regularly helped with Steve. They had to be told because Bob knew that the next weeks were going to be difficult, and he would need their help.

'How are we going to sneak these in?' Steve wanted to know, pointing to the crutches and cane.

'I'll take them into my house and bring them to your room when we're on our own.'

'It was good of Benjamin to lend us these things, and let us ride his horses.'

'He's been eager to help from the beginning.'

Bob noted the use of the captain's Christian name, and was pleased. It looked as if a friendship was forming between the two men.

'I know we tried to shut him out of our lives after what happened to Ruth, but he wouldn't go away. He's very persistent.'

'He's also a good man who cares for Dad and all of you.'

'It's hard to understand why, because he's from the upper-class.'

'That doesn't bother him. I've seen a bond between men who fought in the war, no matter what their background.'

'That's true enough. That conflict did seem to level things out a bit.' Steve fell silent then, watching the passing scenery as the train puffed its way back to London.

Bob was pleased to see that he appeared more relaxed now. He had been urging caution in an effort to stop Steve from becoming too excited. He wished he could talk to Jack and Doctor Vickers, but he didn't like to phone again because that could take them away from whatever they were doing at the time. So tonight he would write to Jack explaining what had happened and asking his advice. He needed to know exactly what to do, and when he should start to see if Steve could stand.

He sighed quietly, praying that the improvement would continue. It had been good to come home and put things right with his dad. They were close now—more like friends working together to pull Steve through the bad times—but now he longed to get back to his job. There had been talk about him leaving after the New Year, but to be honest, he hadn't believed there would be much chance of that happening. Now there was a glimmer of hope, and he was so looking forward to going back and working with everyone again. His first stop would be to sit on his favourite seat and gaze at the river. It was such a restful view, no matter what the weather. He had given up his top-floor rooms, but the boys below had said he could move in with them until he found a place of his own again. The realization that he really could be going back soon made him happy. The only jarring thing about his visit home had been his relationship with Ruth, but even that was better now. Of course, it would never be like it was when they were children; they were different people now, but he still loved her and always would. He had been uneasy when she'd been going out with Dave, and quite relieved when that came to an end, by mutual agreement it seemed. When he left this time he would be coming back regularly, so there would be plenty of opportunity for them to become close again.

A slight smile touched his lips. Perhaps Sister was right and Fate had been guiding him to do the right thing at the right time. The return to London had been good, and useful, not only to Steve, but to Dave and all the others. That wouldn't have been the case, though, if he hadn't gained certain skills before coming home. Too much had happened for it to be a coincidence. Since childhood he'd had the burning ambition to do something useful with his life, and had thought teaching might be the way, but he had been led in a different direction. He had found what he'd been looking for. His life was straightened out now, and it was a comforting feeling.

*   *   *

Three days later he received a long letter from Jack, and a short note from Doctor Vickers, explaining how he was to handle Steve's changing condition. Much happier now he had their advice he began to work as they had instructed.

Improvement was steady, and Eddie could hardly contain his excitement.

'That boy's going to give the game away,' Alf remarked a few days later. 'We're never going to keep this a secret until Christmas, Steve. Perhaps we ought to tell the others now.'

Steve shook his head. 'No, I've got to be able to stand and take at least a couple of steps. When are you going to let me out of this chair, Bob?'

'Another couple of days, but remember you are going to have to learn to walk again. It isn't going to be easy.'

'I know, and I'm sorry to be so impatient, but I'll do as you say.'

'We've got three weeks to Christmas,' Bob pointed out, 'so let's make that our target.'

With Bob, Alf and Eddie working together, the days slipped by. Steve swore and cursed, but they ignored his frustration and kept praising him for every small achievement.

Two days before Christmas a van arrived with the name of the Russell Estate on the side. Jim jumped out and lifted his hand to knock on the front door, but Bob was already there, with Daisy right behind him.

Jim peered around Bob and smiled. 'Hello, Mrs Cooper, I've got something for you from the captain's farm. Give us a hand, Bob.'

305

The small van was loaded with sacks and boxes, and Bob laughed when Jim told him that it was all for them. 'What has the captain done now?'

'He doesn't want any of you to go hungry over the festive season,' Jim told him, drily. 'Come on, let's get this in the house.'

'Follow me.' Bob tossed a sack on to his shoulder and grabbed another with his free hand, and then he made for the scullery.

Daisy, with Steve beside her in the wheelchair, watched in astonishment as the room filled up with goods.

'Hope you've got a nice big larder,' Jim said as he dumped a large box on the table.

She opened a door and showed him a walk-in cupboard with a marble cool shelf in it.

'Perfect, and there's plenty of room.' He began to unpack the box. 'You've got two pork joints, two beef, sausages, chops and two fine chickens, a pudding and cakes. In the sacks you'll find all the vegetables we grow, and also apples and pears from the orchard.'

'But . . . but . . .' Daisy couldn't get the words out; she had never seen so much food in her life.

Steve and Bob were roaring with laughter at her confusion.

'You can't refuse it, Mrs Cooper,' Jim told her. 'Captain Russell said if I came back with so much as one potato he'll sack me. He also said you were to have a damned good Christmas, and thank you for the letters, Bob.' Jim gave him a sly wink.

Steve was laughing so much he had to wipe his eyes. 'I'm going to have to have a word with that man. A little help is one thing, but this is ridiculous!'

'You've got off light.' Jim was laughing along with the others. 'He wanted to load two vans.'

That was too much for Daisy and she had to sit down. 'Where are we going to put it all? We can't move in here for sacks.'

'Can we stack some of it in your old shed, Bob? It's cold out there.' Steve was shaking his head, unable to believe what was happening.

'That's a good idea. We'll put it outside the door for the moment and let Daisy sort out what she wants, then I'll move it.'

Once the scullery was cleared a cup of tea was ready. 'Tell Captain Russell we're very grateful, if somewhat overwhelmed with his gift,' Daisy said. 'And we'll do as he says and have a terrific Christmas. We'll all be writing letters to him tonight.'

'Ah, he likes receiving letters.' Jim smiled at them.

Bob nodded, knowing that Jim was referring to the regular updates he'd been sending on Steve's progress.

*   *   *

That evening they all sat around the table discussing what they could do with all the food.

'We can't possibly eat all of it.' Daisy was shaking her head. 'We must spread it around.'

A list was quickly made of all the needy families in the street, and then they began making up parcels for each one. They all contained two chops, two sausages, a variety of vegetables and fruit.

Then Alf and the children went out delivering the gifts. It was a happy task and they all returned glowing with pleasure.

*   *   *

Christmas day arrived and the house was filled with the aroma of prime meat being cooked. They had decorated the house with paper chains the children had made, and everyone was in the mood to have a lovely time.

'Ready?' When Steve nodded, Bob straightened his tie, squeezed his shoulder, and walked into the scullery where all the family were gathered preparing a sumptuous meal.

'Happy Christmas, Bob,' they said together when he walked in.

'And to you. Eddie, Dad and myself have been working hard over the last few weeks, and we now have a special present for you. Eddie, would you like to go and get our gift?'

Eddie was so excited he nearly tripped over in his haste to get out of the door.

'I wonder what it is?'

'Something you'll like, John,' Alf told him. 'Something really special.'

The door opened and Steve stood there, using only the cane for support, and he walked a few steps into the scullery.

Pandemonium broke out. Daisy sobbed, holding on to her husband. 'This is the best present we could possibly have been given. What a wonderful Christmas this is turning out to be.'

'How did you manage to keep this a secret?' Ruth had tears of joy running down her cheeks as she kissed her dad, who was now sitting in a chair.

The other kids were jumping up and down,

yelling with excitement, and Daisy shouted for them to be quiet. When she could hear herself talk, Daisy turned to Bob. 'Is Steve going to be able to walk properly again?'

'I've consulted with Doctor Vickers and he says there is no reason why Steve shouldn't now get back the full use of his legs and be able to live a normal life.'

'What a celebration this is going to be.' Daisy couldn't stop smiling through her tears.

No one disagreed with that. They had an abundance of food and best of all Steve was walking again. Not one of them could ask for a single thing more.

Thirty-Seven

New Year's Eve turned into the biggest party their street had ever seen. Dave and his dad turned up, as did Hannah Law, at Alf's invitation. The Selby family were also there, and all of the men Bob had been helping. There were so many people that the two houses were packed. Everyone wanted to congratulate Steve.

Daisy had cooked the two chickens and some of the sausages, Dave had brought along a barrel of beer, and knowing Alf and Bob didn't drink, he also brought along enough lemonade for them and the kids. Food was piled up on the large scullery table for everyone to help themselves.

The fence between the two houses was getting in the way so Alf and Bob were outside trying to remove a section.

'Can you take these, please?' Ruth was holding out two plates of sandwiches.

'Our hands are filthy.' Bob encircled Ruth's small waist with his large hands and lifted her over the fence without spilling a thing from the plates in her hands.

She was laughing when he put her down, and he thought he had never seen her so happy or lovely.

'Me too!' Sally and John were now demanding to be lifted over, shrieking with delight as he swung each one in the air.

As they disappeared into the house, Bob grinned at Alf. 'Let's get this fence down or I'll have to stand here all night.'

Choosing the weakest section the two big men pulled at the same time. There was a cracking and tearing sound as the wooden posts came out of the ground.

'That's better.' Alf pulled the section away while Bob filled in the holes and stamped the ground level. 'Now they can wander from house to house. Let's wash up and get back to the party. I'm hungry.'

At five minutes to twelve everyone crammed into the Coopers' house, glasses at the ready. When midnight struck a huge cheer went up. 'Happy 1924 and good riddance to 1923.'

'Thank goodness that one is over,' Alf said to his son. 'It's been a tough one, hasn't it?'

He nodded. 'But it's also had some good things in it. The misunderstanding I had about you has been swept away, and I feel as if I've gained a friend as well as a father. It also looks as if Steve will now make a full recovery. We've had many battles to fight, but I would say we've won more than

310

we've lost.'

'I agree.' Alf clinked his glass of lemonade against Bob's. 'I know the Coopers will have a good 1924, so I think we should toast ourselves. To understanding and friendship. Happy New Year to both of us.'

'Come on, you two, stop looking so serious.' Ruth dragged them back to the party.

Around one o'clock people began to drift off home after having a great time. When the last one had left, they sat down amongst the debris and had a quiet cup of tea to recover from all the excitement.

'Just look at the mess.' Daisy was now back to full health, and was so happy to know that the man she loved was going to recover from his terrible injuries at last.

'Close your eyes, Mum,' Ruth laughed. 'Just pile it in the sink and we'll clear it up tomorrow.'

'It's tomorrow now.'

'So it is.' She smiled, but felt a pang of sadness. This was the day Bob was leaving, and how strange it would seem without him around all the time.

*   *   *

It was ten o'clock when Ruth woke up, and one glance at the clock had her tumbling out of bed. He wouldn't have gone yet, would he? She couldn't bear it if she didn't have the chance to see him before he left.

Dressing hastily she ran downstairs, and was relieved to see him with everyone else. 'Oh, I overslept, and was so afraid you would have gone without saying goodbye.'

'I wouldn't have done that. I'd have dragged you out of bed.'

She laughed with all the others, suddenly feeling shy. He was looking smart in his best suit, and had his bag with him, ready to leave.

Standing up he slung his bag over his shoulder, his attention on Steve. 'Don't overdo things, and I'll see you in four weeks' time. I'll stay for two days so I can see you and the other men. Eddie, you know what to do.'

'Yes, Bob, I'll keep on massaging Dad's back like you taught me.'

'And see he takes it steady. You have my permission to tell him off if you think he's doing too much.' When Eddie nodded and smirked, he said, 'I'll be on my way then.'

They all followed him to the door and spilled out on the street to wave him on his way. Each one said their goodbyes, and when it came to Ruth, Bob hugged her tightly, kissed her on the lips, and said softly, 'I'll be back soon.' Then he turned and walked away.

Watching him stride up the road reminded her of the troubled boy who had left like this so long ago. That boy had been angry, lost, and had no idea where he was going. The man disappearing up the road now had fought his battles, knew who he was and where he was going.

She hoped his future would include her, but that was something only time would decide.